AUTHOR'S NOTE

This series is dark. Like, really dark. If you've read my other books and are thinking, "No big deal, I can handle this..." I assure you, this is darker than anything I've ever written before.

So, if you have any issues or triggers with dub-con, forced marriage, humiliation, or a dark ménage that will end in a MFM relationship, then turn back now.

If you just read all of this and you're not triggered, then read on and I promise you'll love what happens ahead.

THE FERAL PRINCESS - BOOK 1

[redacted]
Thank you so much for participating in the Fox Project. I hope this book makes you howl! ♡♡

defiant

ANN DENTON

LE RUE PUBLISHING

Cover by Covers by Aura

Le Rue Publishing
320 South Boston Avenue, Suite 1030
Tulsa, OK 74103
www.LeRuePublishing.com
ISBN: 978-1-951714-24-6

Dedicated to the hot alphahole who kidnapped me and swore to keep me forever.

Oh wait. That hasn't happened yet.

Dear Mr. Future Alphahole,

This one's for you.

Love,

Ann

p.s. I love handcuffs.

1

ELENA

My life is as dull as a paper cut, I think as I twist a paper clip into the shape of a dick while listening to a lecture on human evolution from a professor who sounds like a zombie.

Nothing's special about this afternoon, not the sunshine pouring through the windows or the baking heat—certainly not the smell of unwashed college students hunched over iced coffees and cookies that cost as much as they're going to make later this afternoon on their work-study shifts.

I haven't done anything unique today … I woke up after Mom had left for work and tossed my black hair up in a couple of braids, showcasing the white streaks I've put in it that my mother absolutely hates. I'd dressed in black, like always, and messed around on my acoustic guitar for a little while before I'd gathered up my laptop and backpack, tossed on some crimson lipstick, and headed off to class.

Today is just like any other day, right down to the naughty notes that Jonah and I are passing back and forth as we tune out the lecture.

Nice dick. Not as nice as mine, he writes, sliding a palm-sized little booklet my way.

Roughly the same size, I write before flicking the phallic paper clip at him with a grin. He catches it easily before grabbing the notebook back and setting it on his desk so he can scratch out my line and add a new one of his own.

I'm gonna eat you out so good tonight. He's super creative, my Jonah. Bonus: he's great with grammar. But his biceps and those light blue eyes make up for other shortcomings. Besides, with frienifits, there's no need to be nit-picky. We're mostly friends. It's not like we're dating.

I'm going to time you, I lean over and write on the notebook while it's still on his desk, scrawling in red pen. *Fifteen minutes minimum.*

Yeah? You're on. I bet I can eat you out longer than you can blow me.

I have to stifle a laugh when Jonah passes our naughty notebook back my way—partially because the professor paused in his discussion of Neanderthals and partially because the hulking Neanderthal beside me can hardly last ten minutes unless I force him to pace himself.

I can't completely smother my amusement and I glance over at Jonah in his gray sweatpants, white tank, and black beanie, his golden skin practically glowing in the afternoon sunlight. He spreads his legs and grabs his crotch as he winks at me. Cheeky fucker. Jonah's always fun to be around, upbeat.

But he's fun for another reason too, one that makes my nipples tighten as I lean over the notebook and write, *You'll come if I order you to come, so I'll win no matter what.*

He reads the notebook and grins but doesn't deny it. We both know he can't help it. Jonah's a beta through and through, despite having a physique that screams MMA fighter.

His wolf will listen to me even though mine hasn't come in yet. I still add the *yet* even though it's been two years. I know … no, I *hope* she's still coming. My mom's wolf was late. She says alpha female wolves don't submit to anyone's schedule and her own wolf was eight months late. If that's true, my wolf is the most alpha bitch of all time. I'm twenty-one and she still hasn't shown, even though Jonah's been a beta for two years.

I sigh and Jonah grabs the notebook back from me; he knows where my mind has gone. He writes to distract me, like a good friend. *Ice cream after class?*

I pull the notebook back to tell him I can't, that I have track practice ... and that's when my day does a one-eighty. It goes from normal to extraordinary in a single second.

What sets it off? I have no clue.

Is it the fly buzzing through the lecture hall that catches *her* attention? Is it the way that my back pops when I stretch from my slouch? Is it the green notification on my phone from my mom letting me know she won't be home tonight because she's going to the monthly howl? Or is it because I was just thinking about *her*?

I have absolutely zero idea what sparks *her* appearance. But, somehow—impossibly—my wolf fritzes into being like an ancient television set that just caught the station's signal. At first, I blink, unsure what's happening as the room around me sort of grows hazy and fades into the background like a camera racking focus and a wolf trots into the middle of my field of vision.

Even when she sits down in front of my eyes, it takes a second for me to process what I'm seeing.

I think back to lunch and wonder if someone spiked the ketchup on my chicken strips—because watching the vision of a wolf walking across thin air only to appear to sit down on the back of the guy two rows in front of me seems like some kind of hallucination.

I don't quite process what's happening as I stare. I admire her coat, which is a midnight shade except for her muzzle which is laced with white, or her neck and haunches, where a bronze tone appears to give her a glimmer. Her sharp little ears are alert and perked up and her fur immediately bristles when the professor clicks play on a video somewhere outside my field of vision, which has completely narrowed to focus only on her.

The wolf turns her head from side to side and it's like I'm a video game avatar. I move when she does. My own head turns and scans the room. She sniffs, and suddenly the body odor in the room doubles to a nearly unbearable fog of sweat, only one icy, mint scent cutting through the stench of humans. Jonah's.

My wolf's moon-colored eyes met mine and we both freeze in shock as we stare at one another and the implications of what's happening roll through me like a tidal wave.

Holy fuck. So I am a shifter, I think. Relief washes through me as the doubts I've suffered all these years wash away, a tide carried back out to sea. *About damn time.*

Run, she thinks back.

Her internal voice is nothing more than a whimper, but it's followed by a series of images of darting past buildings and into the trees that clearly state her intentions.

I drop the naughty notebook on the lecture hall floor, lean forward, and grip the edge of the half-desk I'm seated in, ignoring how my elbows jostle my laptop.

Next to me, Jonah leans forward, his biceps bulging as he slides out of his slouch, a look of concern in his blue eyes. He pushes up the black beanie on his forehead and the worried crease that's the trademark of all the men in his family makes its appearance. "Hey, Elena. You okay?"

I don't look over at him because I'm too busy looking inward. Staring at my wolf. Dazed.

You don't get to see other people's wolves until you shift … until you swear allegiance to the pack. I've only ever seen Jonah's wolf, and even then he only showed me after I promised him an epic blow job in exchange … and he swore me to eternal secrecy because I wasn't "pack" yet.

Pack. I'm pack now. The word sinks into my soul and anchors me. I never realized how adrift I felt until now. Now that I know where I belong, relief lifts my heart.

I'm a Lobo. The Lobo pack is the largest in the United States. It covers Colorado and a few other states. But that's about all I know. Because wolf shifters keep their information locked down more than the CIA.

I don't know much of anything about shifter life, other than my mother regularly attends fights and howls—which are meetings, based on the snippets I've overheard. Oh, and ranks. Every wolf in the Lobos has a numerical rank that can change. I don't know how many wolves there are in the pack, but I know mom's number is constantly shifting. I know Jonah's number is 1,078...so there are at least that many wolves.

I wonder what my wolf's number will be as I watch her.

She's so graceful, my wolf with her tail swishing as she stares expectantly at me and repeats her request. *Run.*

A thrilled tremor rushes down my spine and spreads out across my limbs and I stand, drawing a number of eyes, including the professor's. "Sorry. I feel sick," I lie, before darting toward the door, leaving all my worldly possessions behind—hoping that Jonah will take care of them for me.

"Elena, wait. I'll come—"

I don't listen to the rest of Jonah's sentence.

I rush outside into the blazing heat of early summer, the bright afternoon light stunning my eyes for a moment before I turn and race across the campus, past the astronomy and biology buildings toward the forest that awaits at the edge of the Cygnus grounds.

The small liberal arts college embraces its hippie vibes by enticing students with idyllic pictures of communing with nature in outdoor classes, studying forest habitats ... bullshit that doesn't matter to most humans. But to a wolf shifter or a potential wolf shifter, proximity to the forest is essential. The ability to break loose of the human grind and run free, unshackled...

I've heard about it from Jonah and my mom, from other girls in the Lobos pack, but I've never experienced it before. This desperate need just to run. Not like when I run on a track, with a goal, a time, a competition in my head. The desire to just run as its own expression of joy—as if movement is a song and I have to sing it.

I know that Mom's going to be over the moon. But I also know she's immediately going to want me to train to fight for my pack rank. She's borderline obsessive about her rank; she runs, conditions her body, even signs herself up for illegal human dog fights to be better, faster, stronger. "An alpha female never has it easy," she always tells me.

I just want to enjoy this moment.

I just want to embrace the feel of my wolf—this wild, unfettered light that's bouncing inside my chest like a dot in a sing-along video or a laser light in a concert. I'm so elated I can hardly feel my feet tap the earth as I sprint headlong past students who turn and stare.

Get to the trees, I tell myself, *to the trees.*

"Just be patient, Elena, your wolf will come," Dad's voice drifts unbidden to my mind and I wonder if he can see me right now. If he's even looking.

Before melancholy can creep in and ruin my mood, my wolf gives me a playful little yip. Her butt wiggles and her tail moves side to side before she bounds playfully around in my head. I nearly slam into a tree, I'm so distracted by her inside my head.

"Calm down," I mutter, "or I'll kill us both before I can shift."

She whines but trots out of my vision so that her presence is more of an energy, a feeling, and she's not in my line of sight. I hurry forward through the forest, crashing around bushes with absolutely no subtlety. If any wolf decides to follow, I've left an easy trail. But I don't care. As soon as I'm deep enough in the foliage that I can't be seen, I strip down to nothing, shoving my clothes under a bush so no college student wandering around off-campus gets any stupid ideas.

Then I close my eyes and call her. "Come on, little friend. Your turn."

My wolf yips with excitement and I see her bound in front of my eyes once more before she skids to a halt and backtracks. Then there's a strange tingling sensation, and my entire body grows hotter than a campfire and melts like a marshmallow in the blaze. My thoughts whirl and my senses can't keep up with the way that sensations change and mutate around me—colors dull, but scents explode, and the noise of campus (that I'd thought was distant) suddenly becomes sharp.

I hear a woman say, "Danny, you're a fucking bastard," and her voice is so clear I swear she's standing next to me.

My head turns but no one's there.

A guy's voice responds, "Genna, you have no idea, I didn't mean to—" and I realize that the couple is sitting on a bench nearly a mile away.

At least, I guess it's them because the girl throws her arms up in the air, just as I hear, "Don't! Your pants don't unzip themselves you dumb fuck. I'm done." The stomp of her feet on the pavement as she stalks away sounds like applause, like her feet are happy she's leaving the bastard.

Fucking unreal.

I feel myself shrinking and changing. I glance down and realize that my hands have turned into paws and my face is now level with a bush that used to reach just my waist. At this height, I realize that it's a wild blueberry bush, though most of the berries have been pilfered by birds.

It's the last thing I see clearly before my wolf takes over and my rational mind shrinks as sensation and freedom streak across my thoughts and we begin to run.

We run for hours, honing our muscles, giving in to our senses and experiencing scent in a way I never have before. The forest becomes as decadent as a five-star meal. I lose track of time as the need to feel the wind in my fur overtakes everything else.

Sunset paints the sky before I stop by a stream, lungs, and legs burning but a sense of contentment has settled deep inside my bones that's never been there before.

This was meant to be.

Two years of waiting and worrying after I turned nineteen and my wolf didn't show up, years where I thought I'd be relegated to the boring human world, a glimmer—one of those people who saw a bit of the supernatural world but couldn't take part in it.

That isn't me. I want to wrap my arms around my torso and hug myself in my relief, so I shift back into my human form. I plan to hug myself and laugh in joy then lay back, stretched out on the grass and dangling my feet into the shallow trickle of the stream as I embrace the new me. The sensation of shifting is still so new that everything around me whirls oddly and I fall gracelessly to my knees when it's over, shaking my head to clear my vision.

I start to recline but my wolf whines and the hair prickles on the back of my neck.

My head whips to my right and my eyes dart around. I don't see anything, but the ominous feeling doesn't go away. If anything, it increases as my skin defies the heat of the afternoon, and goose bumps rise on my arms. *Shit.*

I reach for my wolf, but fuck! She's gone.

Hey! I mentally call for her, kicking myself over the fact that I've been so caught up in running I don't even have a name for her. *Fluffy?* I try out a generic one, hoping she'll respond—knowing from my mother that your wolf is supposed to come when you call it.

But my wolf has disappeared. I don't see her in front of my eyes; I don't feel her at all. I stretch harder, squeezing my eyes shut, searching the inside of my skull, mentally begging, calling out. But she's gone. She's disappeared like smoke in the wind.

Dammit.

Fear unfurls, dark and ugly as a storm inside my stomach, as I realize that I'm stuck naked and alone in the forest—miles from campus. No one knows where I am. The shadows of the trees loom over me. The sun hides behind them and my weak human eyes imagine all sorts of terrible things.

Fuck me.

A twig cracks and I scurry to my feet, stumbling when a rock bites into my arch. Dread singes my nostrils like cigarette smoke as I glance around for a weapon only to see water-smoothed stones and grass as my two options.

Right now I hate my fucking life choices.

I curse myself and my stupid excitement. *Why didn't I just bring Jonah?* I snarl internally as I back up, telling myself that I'm probably freaked out about a rabbit or some bullshit like that. I should have brought Jonah; I shouldn't have done this alone. Or fucking brought my phone. Lots of wolves wear Apple Watches so they can keep them on during their shift and call each other after for a pickup but had I wasted money on that shit?

No. Because I didn't have a wolf yet—hadn't seen it as necessary.

I curse my past self because if I'd actually more than half-believed in my wolf's existence, then I would have been prepared. I wouldn't be having a heart attack over a stupid bunny in the woods right now ... I shake my head.

Don't be an idiot, Elena, I reassure myself. *Nothing's there.*

Nothing's there, I repeat that to myself a few times as I bring a hand to my chest and try to calm my heart.

But I'm a liar. There is something there. The shadows shift again and this time a bush definitely rustles; I see its leaves quake.

A wolf steps out from between the shadows—a huge white wolf, with glowing yellow eyes, who stares right at me.

My throat goes dry even as my limbs lock up in shock.

My brain speeds up into overtime. This wolf is alone, without a pack. Out before dark ... And he's massive. He's at least twice the size of a normal wolf. His piercing gold eyes take me in intelligently and he doesn't immediately growl. All of that can only mean one thing. He's a shifter like me.

With the pack being so secretive, I have no idea who this wolf might be, but... I look around, suddenly realizing I have absolutely no idea where I am.

OH. SHIT.

Am I even on pack land? I glance around. I paid no attention when I ran, following my every whim. And I haven't followed the pack border disputes for over a year because my wolf was so overdue—

I take a step back and the wolf's lips peel upward, revealing sharp, pointed teeth as he growls.

No. No. No. No.

Disputed territory is no-man's land. It can be a death sentence.

Wolf! Fluffy! Dammit bitch, I need you! We need to run!

Panic sears my brain but my wolf doesn't reappear and the white wolf takes a menacing step toward me, his head lowering like he's about to leap.

I turn and run, splashing across the stream, my feet slipping on the slime-coated stones, beetles made of dread skittering across my skin.

I don't even make it to the other side when I'm body-slammed face-first into the dirt. I hit with a loud thud and the air leaves my chest in a loud *oof* as a solid weight presses down on my back. A solid weight that isn't furry. That's larger than me. That is most definitely male—based on the hot and heavy hardness pressed against my thigh.

He's shifted back to human. Oh god. Tears fill my eyes as a thousand scenarios that suddenly seem worse than a wolf ripping out my throat come to mind. Humans are far worse monsters than wolves.

The arms around me move and lift his body up, caging me in as that hardness glides slowly across the back of my thigh. Each millimeter feels like a mile and anticipation crackles underneath my skin while brutally awful mental pictures assault me.

The day I meet my wolf is going to be the day I die ... if I'm lucky enough to die.

"What the fuck are you doing in my territory?" a low, raspy male voice growls as he pushes his body further up off mine, his dick finally away from my skin. I don't get a second to feel relief, however, because a huge palm is planted firmly on the middle of my back, pressing me down in the dirt. His other hand wraps in my braided ponytail and yanks my head back.

I gulp, not tasting air but sour panic on my tongue before I start to struggle. *Mom's an alpha wolf. You are too. Fight, Elena. She raised you to fight.* My legs lash out and I push up with my left arm, jerking my right elbow backward into his solar plexus. The hit rings all the way down to my bone but he doesn't even grunt.

I shove a knee up toward my chest, intending to attempt a donkey kick at his balls, but he anticipates that and smashes his bodyweight back on top of me, that thick dick right between my ass cheeks this time.

Dammit. I think I just made this ten times worse for myself. The urge to laugh and cry all at once hits me.

"Who the fuck are you and what are you doing in Lobo territory?" he growls, tightening his hold on my hair.

Wait.

Lobo territory? That's my territory! That's my pack! "I am a Lobo, dipshit," I snarl.

"The fuck you are." His body shifts and I feel his knee grind into my lower back. "I recognize all my wolves."

"All your ..." I trail off as red-hot shame colors my vision like someone just dropped a crimson scarf over my eyes. "Alpha Black?" I question hesitantly, praying I'm wrong, that this is some elaborate prank, that one of Jonah's friends spotted me and they followed me and someone's making a bad shifter TikTok right now.

"Who the fuck are you?" he demands, not answering. But I can hear the edge of command in his growl, feel it in the way my heart curls into the fetal position at his tone. This isn't a beta playing at being an alpha.

I let out a sigh as I close my eyes. "I'm Elena DeMarkus."

There's a long pause before the huge knee on my back retreats and the hand that was pulling my hair slides to my shoulder. He rolls me over until my back hits the grass, then he stands up tall as I pant, trying to catch my breath as I stare up at the naked alpha in charge of the Lobos.

Black Maddox.

Close to seven feet tall, he has a thick, muscled torso, and dark eyes that can drink in your soul with a single look.

He's in his forties and has ruled the Lobos with sharp teeth and no-nonsense rules for nearly a decade. My gaze takes him in. His brown hair meets in a widow's peak above his broad forehead then sweeps down the sides of his face, brushing past his shoulders in a way that might have been considered feminine if Black hadn't paired the hair with a full beard that makes some of my mom's pack friends swoon and whisper, "Jason Momoa" under their breath.

I don't think he looks like Jason. His eyebrows don't have enough arch. They're straight and thick and currently pulled down to match the scowl on his mouth. If it wasn't for the back-breaking intensity that surrounds Black like a forcefield, I might have thought he was hotter than Momoa. He has the same cut abs, the same kind of veins popping in his thick forearms.

I've heard rumors about the skulls he's smashed in with those thick hands, but I don't look down at those.

In fact, I try very hard not to notice the tan shade of his nipples as they protrude from pecs chiseled like stone. I most definitely do not allow my eyes to slide lower than that. I'm already humiliated enough, no need to anger my alpha further.

"Elena?" he asks, his scowl turns questioning, those dark brows lifting even as shadows hide his deep-set eyes.

"My mom's Kathryn DeMarkus," I tell him. "She's ranked alpha number one hundred forty-seven …" And fights every day to keep from slipping further down, I don't add aloud.

I stare up at Black but he doesn't respond. He just stares back at me, waiting. His nostrils flare and he leans in, giving a long sniff, like he's trying to check my scent.

I don't smell anything like mother, with her lavender and soap fragrance. I don't even know if wolves in the same family are supposed to smell alike. I never thought to even ask that sort of question in my quest to wring any information out of her or Jonah. My ignorance digs into my heels like an uncomfortable burr.

Does he want an explanation?

"I … this was my first time," I tell him. "I'm a late bloomer. My wolf showed up in class and I just couldn't help it."

Still, he doesn't move and as the sun disappears out of sight behind him and the night air plucks at my skin, I'm reminded of my nudity. My hands move to cover my nipples and my crotch. I wait again until I can't stand the silence and I ask, "Can I get up, Mr. Maddox?"

"No." His growl is soft and low and every nerve-ending in my body stands at attention.

My throat grows dry.

He doesn't move, just hovers over me and I blink up at him, not quite panicked, but nervous—on edge, unsure what he wants.

His expression flickers and something about it makes my blood run cold, though I'm not sure what.

Did I do something? Something I don't even know about?

Pack business is like fucking mob business. You don't get to know until you're in, and once you're in, you can never get out. So I'm laying here, clueless and freaked out and tears start to fill my eyes, which is fucking embarrassing, so I close them to hide my shame.

"Get up now," Black orders a second later.

I'm not sure if he's doing so out of pity, or because he has a pack howl to get to, but I comply quickly, blinking away my tears and looking back up at him.

His hands are balled into tight fists. His nostrils flare and he bites his lip. "Did you shred your clothes when you shifted?"

I shake my head. "No, I left them near campus."

He grinds his teeth together and turns away from me for a second, not quite giving me his back as he peers into the trees. "Shift so we can go back to them."

I nod and close my eyes. But my wolf is nowhere to be found. When my lashes pop open, I find Black close—close enough for me to get a hint of the woodsmoke and caramel scent of his.

His eyes flash in annoyance. "I said *shift*." There's a note of command in his voice that hits low in my belly and makes my knees ache.

I hate that my voice gets fucking breathy when I respond; I sound like a fool. "I can't. My wolf's gone."

2

ELENA

My wolf appeared and then abandoned me. Why? I can't stop the shamed tears that come to my eyes and one streaks traitorously down my cheek.

"What am I doing wrong? Why did my wolf disappear? I've never even seen her before and now…" I've never heard about anything like this.

Even though my mom's always been a tight-lipped bitch about shifting and the magic that changes us, I've learned tidbits. You should be able to call your wolf at will. Why isn't mine coming back?

A huge, rough hand lands on my shoulder, and I stare up at Black, my eyes going round as the heat from his skin soaks into mine. The wind whips up and drags his hair across his face making him look like some kind of ancient warrior as he says, "I'll fix it."

My throat tightens and I nod gratefully up at him before swiping at my cheek and erasing the evidence of my breakdown. I haven't cried in three years. Not since ... I blow out a breath and say with a shaky smile. "Guess I'll have to walk back to campus."

"I'll go with you."

"You don't have—"

"That wasn't an offer. It was an order."

There's a determined set to his jaw that I can see, even with the beard, and I realize that I won't get to just escape from this encounter and sweep it into the box of unwanted memories.

No, for some reason, Black Maddox wants to draw out this first meeting with me. Maybe he doesn't trust me. I guess that's reasonable on his part. Would I trust some college girl who just entered my territory if I was him? Probably not.

Until initiation, he doesn't meet any of the pack children. Too many become glimmers. And his job is to run a pack and keep the wolves from tearing one another apart, not cultivate hope for those who'll never belong. Or so Mom has always said.

Silence reigns as I keep my hands across my intimate areas and turn and walk back across the tiny stream. I don't particularly want Black Maddox staring at my naked ass but it's better than the alternatives.

If I had been a shifter longer, it wouldn't matter. Jonah tells me you get used to the nudity since it's just part of pack life. But my existence up to now has been very nearly human. I've only ever seen the pack from a distance, or some members when they come over for barbecues. We certainly aren't high-ranking enough for me to meet the pack alpha before now.

While Black is incredibly hot, he's also intimidating, twice my age, and annoyed as fuck with me for freaking him out and making him think I was an enemy wolf. Even now, he side-eyes me as we stomp through the trees.

This is a great way to make a first impression on the number-one wolf in a pack of thousands. *At least I'm memorable,* I tell myself sarcastically.

I sigh as I wonder just how many miles we are from campus—I have a feeling this is going to be one long walk of shame. At least it's growing darker every minute. I'm about to ask how much farther when a rock catches me off guard and I trip.

Before I can fall, two rough palms slide along my hips and catch me, fingertips digging into my hipbones and yanking me backward.

Hot breath fans across the back of my neck and my nipples tighten as I right myself, careful not to push backward against the pecs I know are just behind me.

Shit. No more falling, Elena, I scold myself. I don't need to mix the humiliation of this encounter with weird-ass fantasies about the pack alpha. Alpha wolves don't mix well together anyway. Too much struggle for dominance. And he's not even interested. He's probably rolling his eyes at me for being even more annoying than before.

"Thank you." I force myself not to sound as fluttery as my stomach feels and my words come out kind of sharp instead.

"Watch your step," he replies, his hands sliding slowly backward on my hips until they disappear.

Yup. See? Definitely thinks I'm a stupid ass little girl, I tell myself.

I feel absolutely zero disappointment when his warm fingers leave and my nipples only pucker because of the chill. The dampness between my thighs isn't something I can explain away, so I just ignore it as we continue to wind our way back to campus.

I grab onto small tree branches and trunks, determined to keep my balance as the silence builds between us like a wall and I can only speculate about the kind of judgment Black is hurling over it in my direction.

"Don't touch shit," Black growls, confirming my very thoughts. "You're scent-marking everything." I turn back to look at him as he grabs a leaf I just touched, rolls it between his palms, and then shreds it before dropping it to the ground.

My cheeks flame in embarrassment. I didn't even think about that. Fuck. *How stupid am I?* "I'm sorry." I pull my hands in close and try to step while avoiding every little branch. Mortified, I'm also irritated. He knows I'm a new wolf. I told him. So, couldn't he have said that a bit nicer instead of treating me like an idiot?

Part of me wants to reach out and grab a branch just to tick him off. But the sane, logical part of me knows that he's already at his limit. If Black was a kettle, he'd be simmering. I don't want to make him boil over.

"Anything else I should know before you yell at me again?"

"Don't get smart," he retorts.

"I'm not." I say, even though some tiny rebellious sliver inside me is being sarcastic as fuck despite knowing better. "I literally just shifted once, and I clearly know jack shit. How about you help me not piss you off?"

"Not possible."

"Not possible for you to help?"

"Not possible for you to stop pissing me off."

Okay then. On that horrifying note, I slip into silence and walk through the forest, avoiding the inky fingers of tree branches and the feathery silhouettes of the ferns.

Instead of thinking how badly I've screwed up my interactions with the pack alpha, I focus on my messed-up connection with my wolf. Did I make her angry too? Why did she leave?

What kind of shifter's wolf appears and then abandons her? Am I defective? A trickle of worry whispers that I am. Otherwise, she'd reappear. Otherwise, Black Maddox wouldn't be so angry with me.

Does he even believe that I'm who I say I am?

The wind changes direction and I shiver in the cool night air and suddenly Black's body is up against mine, his front to my back, his forearm wrapped around my waist as shock rolls over me like fog.

"Fuck," he growls. Alpha Maddox lifts me up off the ground as if I'm nothing more than a doll and runs five feet to our left. My arms have barely had a chance to grab onto his forearm, to block the bounce of my breasts against his arm, before he stops beneath a huge sycamore with branches far above my head. He boosts me up in front of him, ordering, "Climb, now."

"What?" I'm so dazed by the press of his smooth, warm skin to my chilled back that I don't process what he's saying for a second.

I feel his fingers dig into my hips as he shoves me up higher along the tree, bark biting into my skin. "We have company. And it's not the human kind."

"But, we're in Lobo—"

"Disputed territory," he contradicts me, one of his hands sliding around to my ass and gripping it without hesitation so he can push me up another few inches higher. In disputed territory, there are no rules. Pack law doesn't apply. It's the Wild West of the shifter world, where there are the quick … and the dead.

"You still don't feel your wolf, right?" Black asks.

I search for her, but she's less than a ghost. It's like she was an illusion or worse … delusion. "No. No wolf."

"Then climb the fucking tree. You have less than a minute."

Fear stings me like a bee and makes my chest swell. I turn my eyes up to the closest branch and snake my right arm up the mottled trunk but I'm still at least a foot shy of that branch. "I can't reach."

I hear a low growl from him. "Plant your feet on my chest and slide them up."

I wrap both arms around the trunk to balance myself as my feet reach back from where they're dangling in midair to find his pecs. I begin an awkward, backward walk up his chest like I'm a shitty circus performer trying to climb up onto her partner's shoulders. I try to ignore the fact that I'm giving my pack alpha a prime view of my lady bits and just thank the moon goddess I got waxed a week ago so that I can better focus on my fear instead of my utter humiliation.

Once my feet are firmly planted on Black's muscular shoulders, I reach up for the branch again. But I'm still about three inches shy. I hear a sound in the distance and instinct makes me turn.

"Don't look. Jump!" Black orders.

I leap from his shoulders, my stomach dropping even as my body flies up. My fingers wrap around the tree branch, my black nail polish chipping, nails digging in so hard I can feel little curls of bark form underneath them.

The branch sags from my weight and I dangle for a second before I quickly realize that's the quickest way for me to drop. I might run track, but my arms aren't prepared for this intensity and won't be able to hold my full body weight for very long.

I carefully bring my knees up to my chest and then kick one leg out to the side, snagging my foot on the top of the branch and slowly pulling myself up.

My chest heaves by the time that I'm balanced along the branch and trying to ignore the little shoots poking at my bare belly. But when I look down at the dim forest floor as night casts its shadows, I'm swept away by gratitude that Black tossed me up here.

Because he's surrounded by four wolves, all of them growling.

My alpha lets out a sultry chuckle that the wind catches before whipping up to trail that sound over every inch of my exposed skin. It's a dark chuckle, the dangerous kind. But it's also incredibly hot.

The wolves leap at Black as one unit and I inhale sharply, fingers digging into my perch. *Fuck.* I'm about to witness a fight and my alpha is outnumbered.

I will my wolf to come back so that I'm not stuck here, useless. I want to help, even though I have no idea how to fight. But of course, she's gone like the wind, the bitch.

I watch Black shift in less than a second. One moment he looks like a tanned Italian mobster. The next, he's a huge white wolf.

I expect him to dart away, to jump and twist in midair so their teeth can't latch onto him. I predict he's going to run and lead them on a chase away from me, but he doesn't. He stands with his feet wide and watches as four opponents land on him with snarls. I hear the chomp of teeth clamping down and my stomach churns as I realize two have locked onto his shoulders, one is on his side, and another is trying to get at his neck.

But that one gets distracted by something, glances up, and leaps into the air, snarling ... at me.

A cyclone of cold fear starts swirling inside my ribs. *Shit.* I cling to the tree's limb hard, thankful it's so fucking high, as my thighs and arms both tremble.

Black lets out one sharp bark and the sound spreads across the sky like black oil blotting out the stars—my vision literally tunnels so I can see only him after that. Somehow, I can feel Alpha Maddox's bark coat my chest and liquefy my bones. I nearly lose my grip on the branch.

Beneath me, the four wolves release him, their jaws widening, detaching from his fur—they're also clearly affected. A chorus of whimpers erupts from them and my jaw drops as I watch them bend to the ground and then roll to show their bellies one by one.

What is happening?

Alpha Black jumps onto the first wolf and there's a yelp before a ribbon of red erupts from the downed wolf's neck. Bile fills my throat as the tangy scent of blood fills the air and the other three wolves yelp and scramble to their feet, darting off into the night, disappearing into the brush of the forest so completely that I can't even hear the sounds of their footfalls as they run away.

My heart drills me like a woodpecker; I'm pretty sure it's burrowing right through my chest in its panic and will burst out my back any second. I've seen death before, but never like this. It's been a calm and cold affair. Not red and gory, steam rising from a broken neck as the life inside evaporates. I realize that I've seen death, not dying. Dying is much worse. I close my eyes and wonder, *Is this the life I hoped for all those years? Is this why no one talks about shifting?*

I always imagined the secrecy about the wolf world was something glamorous. Enchanting. But maybe it's not. Maybe shifters are tight-lipped because they've seen too much of what I just witnessed. Maybe their silence shields innocence and hope, keeps kids from understanding the darker realities of life before they have to face them.

"Get down," Alpha Black's command interrupts my revelation and my eyes pop open. He's shifted back to human and used his forearm to wipe a good deal of the blood from his mouth. Most, but not all.

I clutch my branch as ragged fear cuts into me like a serrated knife—the knowledge that he could do to me what he just did to that other wolf, the realization that he can kill without a second's pause. My understanding of Black's power, of how and why he runs the Lobos, just magnified.

"Those were just scouts. The alphas from the Dark Night pack will be headed this way," he warns. "They won't roll over."

I whimper. I can't help it.

Black extends his hands, reaching up for me. He softens his tone as he murmurs, "Come on, princess. I'll get you outta here."

I stare down at the hulking man beneath me, one whose muscles are slathered in moonlight and blood, and realize that I don't have much choice. It's him, or the other pack. And I have no illusions about what they'll do to a Lobo after they've found their packmate murdered. Even a shifter whose wolf hasn't come in yet hears whispers about the pack wars.

I swallow hard before I carefully adjust my grip and let my legs down one side. Faster than I want, due to my crappy arm strength, I'm dangling from the branch.

Alpha Black walks forward and grabs my hips, yanking them against his chest and taking on most of my weight. I release the branch and reach for his shoulders so I can balance, trying not to acknowledge the fact that my alpha's gripping my naked body against his. My hands find his shoulders and I bear down on them before I realize he still has bite marks that are healing there. I retract my hands with a soft, "Sorry."

"Don't be."

I glance at his face, expecting him to drop my hips so that I land on my feet right in front of him. But he doesn't drop me.

Black's deep brown eyes lock onto mine as he slides me slowly down his body. My breath hitches and I can't even pretend it's just from fear. As my face comes nearly level with his, I spot a fleck of blood he missed on his cheek. The instinct to wipe it away surges through me, but I resist because we're strangers, because it's presumptive, because I just shouldn't. My broken nails dig into his shoulders instead.

"I can jump down from here," I offer.

Black doesn't respond but his eyes narrow a fraction before his hands drop off my hips. I end up sliding down his torso, my stomach and breasts gliding down his pecs before I land on my feet in front of him. When I do, I look up to realize that there's a break in the trees just behind Black. The moonlight peaks through from behind his shoulders; the moon herself surrounds his head like a halo. But he doesn't look like an angel surrounded by all that white light. He looks like the epitome of darkness, villany, the devil himself come to tempt me.

I'm not sure why those thoughts roll through my head since Black literally just rescued me from another pack. I should be thinking of him as an angel, a savior. But it's impossible. Maybe it's the strength of his alpha, the predator in him so close to the surface. Whatever it is, it's intense. It makes it hard for me to maintain eye contact even though I'm an alpha wolf myself… it's clear that my dominance is nowhere near his.

I take a careful breath before my eyes lower, only to realize I never should have glanced down. Because Black is hard as a rock, and I don't mean his muscles. Fuck, does he get off on murder? Or…

I turn around before I can complete that thought. No. No way. He's nearly as old as my mother. I start walking through the forest without any plan, driven by the need to get away from the truth that was right in front of my face.

"Elena."

I freeze. Somehow his voice is a lasso that wraps around my torso and turns me against my will, but I absolutely refuse to make eye contact. Erections happen. We're both naked. It's no big deal. We don't need to talk about it.

"You're going the wrong way."

Fuck. I feel my cheeks burn and I glance up to see him pointing to our left. I give a quick nod before stomping in that direction, determined to think about death instead of the strange sparkling sensation I feel inside my chest, like I just downed a glass of champagne. I do not react that way to men saying my name. No. It's ridiculous to think that's what's going on. I'm drunk on horror.

"I've called out to the pack. They'll be here in fifteen minutes or so. But we should get into Lobo territory quickly, just to be safe."

"You called?" I can't help glancing backward to see if he's wearing an Apple Watch. I didn't recall feeling one. His wrists are clear. And far too close to that thick dick, which still hasn't gone down. I press my lips together and turn back around.

"Your mother didn't tell you much about the life, did she?" he asks.

"Everyone always says that you'll know once you're in," I mutter. "Goddamned annoying."

He chuckles behind me and I try to stay focused on the bush I'm currently wrangling instead of that honeyed sound. "Everyone says that, but follow-through isn't always the best."

I don't mention Mom's rules or the way she snarls when questioned. Besides, she wasn't the only one who told me not to worry. "Yeah well, even Jonah won't tell me, no matter how many … no matter how I bribe him."

There's a long stretch of silence after that, though it feels like lasers are burning into my back. I grind my teeth together, but the reality is I want to bite off my own tongue right now. Did I really almost mention my sex life to the alpha? Fuck. I'm an idiot.

Finally, after minutes of silent marching, Black says, "I guess they've all taken my decree seriously."

"What decree?" I ask as I climb over a downed branch. It's a small one and it doesn't give me any trouble, but Black's hand shoots out and grabs my forearm just in case.

"The decree to preserve innocence as long as we can. Until the shift happens and survival trumps innocence, the realities of wolf life shattering it." His words brush down my hair and along my neck like a caress.

"Oh." I pull my arm away from his hand like a hot potato as soon as I'm over the branch.

"Reality is an ugly beast," he adds.

I nod, thinking back to the clearing and the body that still lay there, a body that would now remain a wolf forever.

"Especially a shifter's reality."

I swallow and bring up something that's been on my mind during our walk. I'm a shifter now. But my wolf's in hiding. So does that make me a full shifter or not? Do I behave normally or not? What do I do?

I wish that I didn't have to air my shortcomings in front of the pack alpha. But he's here and the need to know what to do next presses on me with a weight greater than anything I've felt before. I lick my lips before I spit out the words. "Speaking of shifter life…is there anything I need to know? I mean, do I go to the howl tonight? Or should I avoid it since my wolf has decided to just disappear?"

Behind me, Black growls and suddenly his hand is on my shoulder, his grip digging into me in a way that's not at all friendly. I glance up at him. "No. You aren't going to the howl. You aren't going anywhere until I'm done with you."

3

BLACK

DISTRACTION, I warn myself as my eyes travel over the smooth planes of Elena's body, loving how the moon goddess makes her tanned skin glow an unearthly white. It contrasts that dark, full hair of hers nicely, even if the white streaks in it aren't my favorite.

Why young women want to streak their hair white is beyond me. But then, so are a lot of things, like fucking bike shorts. Those are just some dickwad's excuse to wear boxer briefs in public. Despite the streaks, the braided ponytail Elena's put her hair into is long and trails nicely down to the middle of her back. It's perfect for pulling.

I ignore the sounds of the forest around us, the hoot of an owl, the scurry of mice and other rodents, the crinkle of the broad green leaves in the wind—those things pale in comparison to the thump I can hear coming from Elena's chest. That rapid heartbeat is what drew my wolf toward her in the first place.

Before I caught her scent.

But then the asshole wind had blindsided me like the bastard he is.

A fucking field of wildflowers dipped in white chocolate—everything feminine and sweet rolled up into one inhale.

Dangerous, I scold, even though I can't get my eyes to rip away from her. They've been glued to that perfect, pert ass of hers this entire walk back.

This little stranger. This woman who claims she can't control her wolf.

We'll see, I tell myself. Time would tell if she was honest. A little time in my basement would ensure it.

My dick likes the idea of her in my basement, locked up, and it twitches at the thought. I've been hard as granite since the first moment I saw Elena and if it weren't for the fact that I worked damn hard to have the self-control of a goddamned Buddhist monk, I'd have already rutted her on the forest floor, letting the twigs and leaves dig into the delicate skin of her knees.

But I'm not *that alpha*. I'm not that reckless—not like Prime, the asshole who came before me. He was so distracted by pussy and the damned war between his harem of betas that he didn't even see me coming.

I remind myself that many wolves have let themselves be overcome by instinct, always to their own detriment. I refuse to be one of them.

Instead, I glare down at Elena, fighting the urge to gaze at those dusky nipples of hers, which have been hard and begging for my attention since the moment she saw me. I bite down on a smile when I see her swallow hard. Her eyes blaze back at me, but her breathing gives her away. That feathery little heartbeat tells me that this new wolf knows her place even if Elena doesn't just yet.

"You're coming home with me," I tell her.

"That is not—"

I maintain my grip on her shoulder and hold up the other hand, right in front of those plush lips of hers. The baser part of me wants to slide a finger inside those lips and see if she'd bite or suck right now. Probably bite, but for some reason, that doesn't dissuade my fantasy. But my tone doesn't reflect all the bullshit images rolling through my head. My tone is the perfect alpha gavel, banging down in a hardass declaration. "It's not up for debate."

She jerks back from me, those gray eyes of hers shooting daggers. If looks could kill, I'd be just as dead as the wolf whose blood paints my arms. "I'm not some beta b—"

I cut her off when I hear a sound in the distance. "Shut up."

Her mouth falls open in this circle that would be perfect for my cock, but we're busy right now, and I'm damned annoyed at the fact that she's proving to be such a distraction. I grab her forearm and drag her toward the car I can hear driving down the road in the distance. It's only about a mile and a half away, but since she insists on remaining human, it will be a bit of a walk until we can meet up with Pluto. I'm sure he's called back up, but I still want to hurry, because those Dark Night pussies will be crying to their daddy soon.

"What the fuck!" Her nails dig into my arm and she tries to fight me, yanking backward, digging her heels into the dirt.

I just pull harder. "If you dislocate your arm, that's on you. But my second's almost here. And unless you want to stick around to explain that body to the Dark Nights, then hurry your ass up."

She falls in line, though I hear a mutter angrily under her breath.

Ungrateful brat. I could just leave her here. I could let her take the fall for that wolf in the forest, that weak alpha bitch that couldn't do anything other than bow to me—his magic too pitiful to resist when I let my alpha strength pulse out like a sonic boom. But that would be leaving a lamb for the slaughter. Assuming she is who she claims. Assuming this was really her first shift. Assuming the Dark Nights didn't send a hot younger girl to fuck with me.

Do they know I like them in their twenties? Did that get out somehow? I mean Mila was twenty-eight—legal by all means. But a forty-two-year-old guy who likes twenty-something women ...

It is suspicious. What woman goes into the woods alone at nightfall? Wolf or not, it's not fucking safe. And who goes alone? My gut starts to churn and my eyes dart to either side, checking the shadows for hostiles just like I did back in my military days. I don't see anyone, but this entire situation doesn't feel right. It feels too damned perfect. Would fate just let me come upon a mouth-wateringly gorgeous shifter? Unlikely. Especially since Elena's long, lean legs-for-days figure is exactly my type. It has to be a setup. Has to be.

But if she's a Dark Night...would she just lay up there in that tree while I took out one of her packmates? If so, her loyalty to them is questionable.

Unless ... their little Trojan Horse had been instructed to play her role no matter what.

In which case, her sanity is questionable and I should be on the lookout.

Crap. My thoughts go in circles and make me irritated. I yank Elena's arm harder than I should and she stumbles. I catch her before she falls, not because I like the excuse to rub my hands along that trim waist, but because I don't want her fucking scent all over the place. As it is, I'm gonna have to make my guys light up that tree in the forest. That branch she'd perched on smelled like a goddamned body lotion explosion and would make us easy as fuck to track if she is innocent. Which she's probably not.

But until I know for sure … I can't treat her as guilty.

God, part of me hopes she is though, because if I can prove she's a Dark Night and that she was sent to fuck with me, then our treaty with that fucking pack will go to shit, and instead of just getting out our anger in fringe battles in disputed territory, we could attack them outright. I could gain a huge swathe of land to the southeast and eliminate the main threat to my own pack.

Visions of expansion are smudged away when the wind blows just right and Elena's scent hits me again. Briefly, I consider rubbing my skin against hers to dull it and mask our trail, but then immediately cut that thought off when it comes with a lot of salacious fantasies. I'm not driving down that road to ruin.

I let her go abruptly and turn, pointing toward the road, where I can hear the car idling. Pluto's waiting for us.

Elena narrows her eyes at me, those thick lashes of hers dramatic with her eyeliner.

"After you, princess," I tell her.

Her nostrils flare, but she doesn't argue. The girl's learning at least. But with an attitude like that, I'll be glad to get her out of my hair. There are plenty of beta women who'll bow to my every whim. I don't need her, despite my dick's protests. I'll solve this little mystery, call her out, and get rid of this sassy female wolf complication ASAP.

Elena climbs over a fallen, moss-covered log, straddling it for just a moment, her hands extended in front of her and her back arched—every thought I just had flies out the window. My wolf and I are both struck dumb by the sight—which I'm pretty certain my mind is engraving permanently on my skull right now. I'm going to forever have that image burned into my memory, a naked Elena, her back arched and nipples out just begging to be taken. What is goddamned wrong with me? Why is every second thought I have around her about fucking sex?

She did that on purpose. It is *a setup.* I snarl and her eyes widen as she glances back at me.

Elena must read the truth on my face. She must realize she's been found out. Her shoulders come up to her ears and I can see the hair rise on her arms in response to my alpha fury. She turns and scurries through the trees, her braid flying as I hop the log and kick it with my foot, dislodging the thing and causing it to roll behind me.

Elena leaps as she runs, those long legs flexing, perfectly synchronized. My eyes track her. And just like the first time she fled from me, all the blood rushes to my dick. My wolf likes when they run. He likes it a lot. Hell, *I like* when they run. Usually, it's consensual chasing. But tonight, we can make an exception.

I lick my lips. *Alright, little Dark Knight she-wolf. This is the kind of game I like to play.*

Elena looks back and her expression is nothing short of terrified. I laugh and let out a wild howl before I start to chase her through the woods.

4

ELENA

Black Maddox is crazy. There's no other explanation other than certifiable insanity for why he literally just growled at me and then started to chase me like an ax murderer. He flipped a switch.

I find myself caught in a horror movie as the shadowy trees stretch their fingers out to snatch at me and a madman laughs in low tones behind me while I streak forward until the silhouettes of the forest around me are nothing but blurs.

I try to focus on my footfalls instead of him; I strike hard with my foot and push off fast. A lot of people think that a taller person will always win a race, but I know that's not true. Having the proper footstrike is pivotal. I blow out a breath and try to imagine I'm driving a railroad spike into the ground each time my feet hit the dirt. The fact that I'm not wearing shoes quickly takes its toll on the balls of my feet and I grind my teeth together as I try not to notice.

I don't glance backward. Not when I hear Black call out, "Who's afraid of the big bad wolf?" Not when I hear him curse and the thwack through a bush behind me.

Go, I urge myself as we come upon a rise. *Just go.* The trees look like they're getting thinner, not quite so dense. The moonlight's painting a couple of the trunks silver. Maybe we're getting close to civilization again and I'll find someone who can help me.

My ankle rolls on some stupid leaf matter that slides under my foot and a twinge of pain shoots up my leg. I bite down on a cry as I crash around the edge of a bush. I force myself to keep moving. My eyes dart around in the dark and I send up a silent prayer to the moon goddess—hoping she'll send a miracle my way. I leap another scraggly bush like it's a hurdle on the track, silently thanking my hard-ass coach, Ben Trask, for kicking my ass and forcing me to enter what I'd thought was a stupid event.

But now that I'm being hunted, I wish I'd spent even more hours on the crappy willow obstacles. The forest presents one hurdle after another. A large stone. A dead branch. Another bush. I jump them all and my senses scream at me while I pant, my chest heaving as I push harder still. My concentration cracks when my foot finds a divot in the ground and my fucking ankle twists again.

"When I catch you, I'm going to eat you all up." Black's voice is way too close.

His words are cold and dark but somehow they send heat rushing through my aching limbs.

No, you idiot, I scold. My body took that comment sexually, but I'm pretty fucking sure he meant literally. He wants to rip my throat out just like he did that other wolf. But why? Why would he save me from them only to go mad himself?

Wrong question, Elena. Why'd you trust him in the first place?

I berate myself yet again, disgusted. I should have learned after everything Dad went through ... you can't trust an alpha to take care of you. Yet, what had I done? Bowed to stupid Black and listened to him when I should have run in the opposite direction.

I'd thought as pack alpha he'd protect me. I'd thought maybe some of the rumors were true, that the compliments Jonah paid him might be real and maybe I'd only ever been around assholes, not true alphas. I'm a fucking fool. Of course, if I'd tried to bolt earlier, it would have just put me exactly where I am now ... running through the forest—but at least self-disgust wouldn't be fizzing inside my stomach like nasty champagne threatening to come back up.

I can't believe I did this, but I don't try to delude myself —*I* did it. I went off on my own. I trusted Black. Fuck me for trying.

Despair starts to shutter my eyes, make my vision tunnel, and I hear Black's tromps getting closer. Fear coats my spine in sweat and I realize I've slowed down. I have to make a choice. I can either focus on the mistakes I've made or focus on getting away.

I inhale sharply through my nose and then double my speed, using everything I've got.

Black's exclamation of surprise behind me sends a jolt of satisfaction through my stomach and I grab a low-hanging branch for leverage as I change directions. If he wants a chase, then he's going to get a damned good one before he catches me. I'm not going to just roll over and show my belly like those other fools.

There's a steep rise ahead, with boulders that I can't just jump, and I have to lunge up using my hands to grab a branch on one of the hardy bushes that dot the hill. I yank on it as I try and pull myself on top of one of the worn granite stones. Something slides across my heel, and at first, I dismiss it as another branch, but then a hand clamps down on my arch and my heart sinks.

"Got you," Black's whisper is as dark as his name.

Panic explodes like bright red fireworks behind my eyelids as I feel Black's huge hand slide slowly up over my aching calf muscle. His hands are like hot coals rubbing across my skin. The pads of his fingers and his palms are rough with callouses and his skin is blazing compared to the frigid cold that's taken over my body. Fear makes my stomach lurch. I kick out, hard, and my foot connects with his thigh, pushing him back but not getting him off of me.

"Oh, no little devil," he taunts.

I shove my foot out again. Money shot. This time I get him square in the jewels.

The hand holding my leg drops away and I don't look back as I yank on the branch I'm still clutching and scurry up the boulder and then the rest of the hill, my fingernails ripping as I claw the rocks in my haste. When I reach the top, I feel like I've run a half-marathon—every part of me is on fire and my ears thrum with each breath.

I spot a yellow gleam in the distance which makes my heart slam frantically. There's someone there! It looks like someone's pulled a car over on the side of the road up the hill.

I beg my muscles to hold out just a little longer as I force myself to sprint that way.

God, I hope it's some nice human. A woman, preferably, who has a car and a gun ... *Moon Goddess, let me run into a random badass bounty hunter woman in the middle of these woods. Please let her save me.* It's probably not the strangest prayer she's ever heard.

I'm on fire as I run up along the grass and my thighs quake, lactic acid burning me from the inside out. It's not until I've crested the hill and the wind is whistling past that I realize my cheeks are coated in teardrops. My chest heaves as I hurry forward, skirting a broken bottle some asshole tossed off the side of the road.

"Help!" I try to yell but my breath has been soaked up by the chase and what comes out is barely a drop of sound.

I swallow hard and try again as I burst from the grass onto the rough, tarry texture of the asphalt. My feet cry in protest but I ignore them as I stumble forward toward what looks like a luxury town car. Confusion mars my thoughts for a second because nice cars like that typically don't go for forest drives. Rich people generally pull out their fancy gas-guzzling SUVs when they want to commune with nature.

Does it really matter? I scoff at myself.

I bring a chilled hand up to massage my throat as I scurry toward the car, searching for the driver. I see someone in a coat reclining against the hood, facing away. "Please, help, there's a crazy guy chasing me—"

The guy on the hood turns. He's got a clean crew-cut look and a jaw that could rival Orlando Bloom's—just a hint of cheekbones. Hope zings through my stomach as he shoves off the hood and comes toward me, concern etched on his face.

"Miss, are you alright?"

I shake my head while tears flood my vision. I swipe at them with the back of my hand as the stranger moves closer. "There's a man chasing me. Please—" I cut myself off when he gets close. Because on the lapel of the stranger's black pea coat is a golden pin. A wolf-head lifted in a howl. It's the symbol of the Lobos.

I skitter backward right into a wall. A wall made of muscles. A wall with arms that reach out and latch onto my forearms like shackles.

I stare down at Black's blood-splattered fingers where they grip me and hope shrivels, dies, and decays inside my chest. I don't even shiver when his warm breath fans across my ear as he says, "Gotcha."

The stranger straightens and glances curiously between us but doesn't ask. He just stares up at Black, awaiting orders like a puppet.

"Call for backup, then grab some lighter fluid and a lighter. Follow my scent. Light it up down there. Torch the tree. You'll know which one. And watch out for the Dark Nights,"—Black's hand tightens around my arm as he says it—"they're running around like vermin tonight."

"You got it." The other man's blue eyes flick over me curiously, but when Black growls, the guy just presses his lips into a firm line and pops the trunk. It's filled with weapons and camping gear and I watch him extract a pack before he slams it shut. He pulls the pack open and hands Black a zip tie.

"Too bad that trunk's full, princess," Black murmurs as he shoves my hands together in front of me and zip-ties them with ruthless efficiency, the sharp plastic nipping my skin.

Fuck. Shit. Would he really throw me in there? He is crazy, and clearly, this other guy won't stand up to him.

Despair traps me in its net and my thoughts flail wildly. What did I do to deserve this fate? "I don't understand. I'm pack." I hate the thin whine of my own voice but I can't help it. It's that or begging and I'd rather cut out my own tongue. But I'm broken right now, body defeated, and I just want to fucking know why.

"Sure you are," Black replies as he escorts me roughly to the back of the car, yanking open the door and shoving me roughly inside so that I fall over.

As soon as my feet are in, the door slams shut. I watch the men through the window dully, like I'm watching everything play out on a T.V. screen. Black talks. The other guy opens his mouth for the first time since he asked if I was okay. Black shakes his head and grabs the keys from his friend. A second later, Black's in the driver's seat, still naked as the day he was born. After our "run" that caramel and woodsmoke scent of his is so strong that it's overpowering.

In complete and total silence, Black drives me out of the woods and into the unknown.

5

BLACK

THE VIEW in the rearview mirror nearly makes me crash Pluto's car at least a dozen times on the drive home. Elena's curled up in a fetal position on the black leather seats, those slight breasts of hers pressed together to make a delectable crease, the tops of her rosebud-colored nipples peeking out just the tiniest bit above her arms as she clasps her zip-tied hands in a prayer-like fashion.

If she is a Dark Night, no amount of praying is going to save her.

If not…

The chances of her story being true are so remote that it's almost laughable. She was clearly picked out to torture me on every level—that sassy mouth, that tight body, that chase ... *mmmm*. I've been into primal play before but this just elevated it to another level.

Every other she-wolf I've been with has half-assed running away from me, not wanting to muss her hair or get sweaty before the main event. But Elena had actually been afraid of me. Which she should be.

But what kind of fucked up sicko am I for liking it? For loving the way she'd been so determined to get away? The way she'd full-on sprinted, jumping bushes, making it hard? Making me hard.

I clench my jaw and focus as I pull into the driveway. I have to stop for the wrought iron and silver gate that blocks both humans and shifters from entering, but as soon as the guard sees my face on the security screen, he opens up without a word.

The hinges creak slightly as it swings open, exposing a sprawling lawn dotted with huge trees and a winding drive. My house is a tall, two-story shadow a quarter mile down the drive. I note the moon's hiding behind some clouds. Normally, she paints my roof a soft gray at night, but it figures that she'd be hidden right now. Wouldn't be right for the Dark Night fucks to pull shit on a moonlit evening, it's much more fitting for the sky to be black as pitch.

I don't bother to park Pluto's car in the garage, I just pull to a stop in front of the main door.

I sit in the car for a second, drumming my fingers on my thigh. For reasons I can't explain, I feel a need to carry this girl into my house. I want to put my hands on her skin.

Claim, my wolf whispers in my ear, showing me mental images of wolves rutting. He liked the run just as much as I did.

But there's no damn way I'm going to claim a Dark Night. The very thought of sinking my teeth into that soft skin where her neck meets her shoulder is far more tempting than it should be.

I check my wounds from the fight quickly, wondering if I've bled all over Pluto's seat, but shifter healing has already sorted out the punctures from the teeth of those other wolves. I let three of them get away, sending a message to Stone ... but part of me wishes I hadn't for the most illogical reason in the world. They saw her.

I shove open my car door and slam it shut harder than necessary, making the car rock slightly. I'm pissed that I want her so much. I shouldn't. All I should feel toward her is fury but the moon goddess and my own wolf fuck with me. The moon peeks out from behind the clouds just then and shines right through the back window, outlining Elena's soft curves—those ripe hips and that narrow neck—and my wolf growls at the sight of the skin he wants to mark. My anger dissolves into another kind of burning.

I yank open the back door near her feet, annoyed at myself, so I decide to annoy the shit out of her, just because I can.

"Princess," I coo in a smooth saccharine tone as though she's precious and not my prisoner. I bite down on a grin as I watch her eyes grow dark and her lips thin as she glares at me but doesn't move. Damn, she looks hot like that. I've never fucked an angry woman, they're always simpering and shit, eager for this alpha cock, but somehow, she resists. I felt her attraction earlier but now I think I could get behind a hate fuck with her.

"Don't call me that," Elena snaps. She still has yet to learn her place—at my feet. But she will. As will the rest of her under-handed pack.

I stride over to her and yank on her top arm, roughly pulling her up and out of the car. She resists for half a second until I yank so hard her pretty face is in danger of smacking the open car door because her hands are still zip-tied and can't catch her. After that, she uses her legs to help me along until she stands in front of me, bound and seething.

Wanting to press those buttons more, to make her as angry as the black cloud billowing inside my chest, I bend down and scoop her up bridal-style.

Her little *oof* of surprise puffs against my ear as I kick the car door shut and I grin down as she realizes what's happened and struggles to escape my arms.

"Cooperate, or this will go worse for you," I tell her as I stride across the stone drive and up the steps to my Georgian-style brick house. It's a bit old-fashioned for my tastes, with its tall flat brick facade, pitched roof with a fireplace on each corner, and classically symmetrical windows. But it has plenty of space and enough grounds for a wolf living in the city to feel like he can breathe. Plus, it's got a stupid ballroom that's big enough for meetings when I need to call in my alphas to discuss important matters—like territory disputes or little Trojan wolves sent out as bait.

For a second, I wonder if I'm being just as stupid as the Greeks, carrying this girl into my home. "There's not an army hiding in that pussy is there?" I mockingly ask.

Her gray eyes widen and I can't help squeezing her a little tighter, letting my fingernails dig into that soft skin as I whisper, "Should I check?"

"You're fucking insane," she spits, bucking in my arms just as my butler opens the tall white front door.

Standing there in his formal penguin suit, there isn't much shifter shit that Matthew hasn't seen at fifty-two. But tonight, his eyes widen when he spots the struggling girl in my arms. It's a first for us. "Dark

Night spy," I tell him. "Get the basement storage room ready."

He nods briskly and turns on his heel.

Meanwhile, Elena's frozen and is staring up at me in shock, those eyes of hers so round that her lashes brush the ridge of skin below her brows. "I am *not* a spy. I'm a fucking Lobo!"

I clamp down on her arms as I walk across the grand marble foyer, skirting the wolf statue set in the middle. "We'll see."

"Call my mother dammit!" Elena's cheeks grow flushed with fury and her brows crease.

I ignore her as I stroll across to the stairwell. Matthew's thoughtfully left the door open so I can descend with my prey in my arms. As I carry her down into the dimly lit basement, the dark, baser part of me, that monster I normally keep chained, raises his head. His eyes gleam when Elena's mouth drops open. His head tilts in interest when one of her stiff nipples drags across my chest after she tries to escape and I clamp her to me.

"Careful. Don't want to drop you on the stairs," I tell her. And actually, I don't. I don't want her bruised from an accident. If she deserves it, I want to be the one hurting her.

She stops struggling at the look on my face, which I know is a step beyond sane right now.

Sick, twisted fuck, I scold myself. But that doesn't stop my blood from racing at the thought. Alphas always have a little evil in them. The stronger the alpha, the greater the evil, or so I've always thought. But monsters make the best protectors because we can recognize the darkness in others ... we can keep more dangerous demons at bay. Like the fucking alpha of the Dark Nights, Cooper Stone. This is his fourth attempt at sabotaging our pack in the last few years.

First, that fucker bribed the CFO of my stores to create fake vendors and pay fake invoices. The asshole drained nearly three-hundred-fifty grand before I ripped his throat out and had his severed head baked into a cake and then hand-delivered to Stone just as I'd had three of my wolves break into Stone's local bank and rob it and him blind. Another time, Stone had his wolves come across and not only piss in our territory but set out traps in our forest. One of our new wolves broke a damn leg—the girl still had a limp.

I'd gone after several of his alphas, his inner circle ... and now quite a few of them walked with a limp. Eye for an eye? No. Bullshit. I live by the code: an eye for a fucking head. Everything he did, I'd do back to him ten times over. There was an airplane incident, which I didn't like to think about. And now this.

Elena.

I wonder what her real name is.

I briefly try to contemplate what might be a suitable punishment for Stone in retaliation for sending someone like her—the perfect fucking temptation. I can't think of one off the top of my head but I've got no doubt a solution will come. Evil's never been hard for me to channel.

Elena stiffens under my gaze but stops struggling as we descend.

I stop at the foot of the stairs and watch her as she surveys the room—taking in the tan walls and plush carpet, the bar counter at the back, and the few recliners scattered randomly about. I had the basement redone a few years ago … so it's not quite got a dungeon vibe, what with the ping-pong table and dart board off to the right.

There's a bedroom and an ensuite bathroom down here too … but I head past those doors, past the rec area, to the storage room, where there are empty wooden shelves in a room lit by only two fluorescent lights, their tubes suspended on little chains hanging from the ceiling. It's some Pinterest housewife's wet dream, a huge space to store decorations for every holiday or event imaginable.

But Matthew's currently carrying my one solitary box of childhood memorabilia out of the room. He doesn't even glance at Elena when she pleads, "Call the cops. Maddox is kidnapping me."

Kidnapping.

As if human laws apply to shifters.

I refrain from rolling my eyes as I set her down and resist the urge to flick one of those nipples as she scurries back from me into the shadows.

"You wanna hide? Fine. Enjoy." I head to the door and grab the handle, scanning the room one last time for anything she might take or break. But it's empty shelves as far as the eye can see. There is only one tiny window letting light enter this room, a small rectangle near the ceiling, and the air conditioner has made the space cold.

Satisfied, I pull the door shut and hold a hand out for the key, which Matthew hands over promptly before striding off, as if watching me lock a young woman up in my basement is a bit too much for him, though his place doesn't allow him to say so.

As long as he's discreet, which I know he will be, I don't much care.

I slide the key into the lock just as I feel the round handle start to turn. I grip the knob, holding it tightly in place against Elena's attempts to tug it.

"You bastard!" she yells and pounds on the door.

But her fury provides me the opportunity I need. I turn the key and lock the little vixen inside.

What I'll do with her ... well that remains a question.

I guess it's time to get some answers so I can decide.

I've showered, wrapped myself in a towel, and am leaning over the steamed-up mirror shaving my neck and cleaning up the edges of my beard when my cell rings on the counter and I nick myself. "Fuck." I stomp over to the toilet paper and grab a square, ripping off a tiny corner and stuffing it roughly onto the cut as I simultaneously swipe to answer my phone and then press the button to put it on speaker. "Yeah?" I ask gruffly, raising my razor so I can finish the last swipe and clean off this shaving cream, which has a shit chemical undertone to its scent—I have yet to find one that doesn't.

I'm expecting Pluto's voice, so when I hear a southern twang, I'm surprised.

"Mr. Maddox, so good to speak with ya'," Stone's tone is deceptively pleasant, which is how I know he's furious. He always gets a creepy grin on his face and his southern sensibilities double when he's mad, which tends to happen a lot when we speak. Maybe if he weren't such an underhanded shit…

I blow out a breath through my nostrils and glance down at the phone, wishing I'd looked before I'd answered. I'm still a little too angry to want to deal with Stone right now—I'm more of a let-the-dust-settle and then serve my revenge cold with a side of icy logic kind of guy. But if he's called me, there's no way I'm hanging up like a pussy. I take a deep breath and force myself to relax and lean back over the mirror, finishing off my shave as though Pluto was on the phone, reporting in about the newest pups to shift and telling me about their god awful progress.

I let the silence draw out as I drag a razor blade across my throat. The reality that Stone would love to do that to me hits me and I nearly chuckle and nick myself again. I focus and finish the last line up before swiping the faucet on and rinsing off the blade under the cold rush of water.

"What are you doin'?" Stone can't help himself.

"Taking a shit," I respond, knowing it will rile him up. I grab a towel and wet one end and begin wiping down my neck, once again waiting for Stone to get to the point.

I killed his wolf. He knows it. I know it.

He just needs to pull his balls out of the drawer he keeps them in, attach them to his dick, and come right out and say what he wants to say because I've got other shit to do, like look up Elena DeMarkus. Her gray eyes flash through my mind.

"You think a fire would put me off the scent? *That* scent?" Stone finally asks.

There he goes again, batting around the topic. Yes, I did ask Pluto to set a fire to get rid of Elena's scent, mostly because I don't want Stone to know how turned on she was, smell that arousal that wafted off her like perfume ... I didn't want him to know how close to success he'd been when he'd sent her to seduce me.

But it sounds like he smelled it anyway and is calling to gloat.

My wolf growls and paces inside my head, riled up by our rival, the pack leader that's in his fifties but still top of his game, so long as the game is murder and mayhem. I take a deep breath and try to calm myself down.

If Stone's calling to brag then I need to check in on my second and make sure he's okay.

I grab my phone and send a text to Pluto while Stone waits for my reply. Well, the fucker can wait a minute longer.

Everything go smoothly? I hit send and second guess myself. What if Pluto set a fire to get rid of that Dark Night's body? I didn't necessarily mean for that to happen, but fire was an efficient way to clean up. Two birds, one match, and all of that. Get rid of Elena's scent and the evidence all at once. Maybe that's the scent Stone's referring to. Maybe he's really pissed about that little alpha wolf I ripped apart.

I lick my lips as I debate what Stone means. But I can't delay answering any longer. "You caught a scent? Didn't know you could still smell old man."

I grab a q-tip and start cleaning out my ears, scrubbing a little harder than usual with the cotton tips as I check my screen to see if Pluto's responded to my text, feigning a calmness I don't quite feel. My wolf is restless, pacing like he senses a threat.

Well, there's always a threat where Stone's concerned. If he was sure he could beat me in a one-on-one battle, I've got no doubt he'd challenge me. But—as much as I hate to admit it—that fucker and I are pretty evenly matched. Any fight between the two of us is going to be brutal, dark, and dirty because two huge fucking territories would be at stake.

"You think you're so clever." I can practically see the smile on Stone's face based on the smug tone.

"Don't think it. I know it," I taunt as I toss my q-tips in the trashcan and debate whether or not I should brush my teeth with Stone on the phone.

"You know, I could attack based on that wolf of mine you killed out in the forest. I'd be justified, already checked with the other pack leaders and they all agree."

The hairs on the back of my neck rise up and I set the toothbrush I just grabbed back down. "He attacked first."

"Mmm. Gotta couple witnesses on my side. Seems you've lost your edge. You left three survivors," Stone retorts smugly.

I grind my teeth together and tell myself that letting them live wasn't weakness. I hadn't wanted to start a war. Not over something that stupid. Stone operates differently than I do though. He's probably killed more shifters than he can count. *You don't want to be him,* I remind myself, though right now, my blood's pumping hot and I wish I'd sunk my teeth into their necks.

"Could put you in a bit of a tight spot, boy."

It's the use of "boy" that nearly sets me off. Based on Stone's chuckle, he knows it and said it deliberately. I force my eyes closed and make myself take a few more breaths. Stone could shove me into a corner if he wanted to … the Lobos aren't on the best terms with Timber or the Dead Rabbits. They might turn a blind eye if Stone decided to turn this fight into something more. The Lobos are bigger than either of them but combined… My heart grows tighter and my wolf presses hard against my skin. But I swallow my growl because that's what Stone wants to hear.

"What is it you want?" I run my tongue across the front of my pearly whites, tense, while Stone lets the silence draw out painfully. Then I hear a clink from Stone's end of the line. "Driving you to drink am I?" I ask, forcing a grin as I hear a second ice cube hit a glass. I'll be damned if I let him hear anything other than smug amusement from me.

"Nah, this is a victory drink. I'm celebrating."

"Special occasion?"

"Just found my mate."

That news startles me. Stone's been married for nearly fifteen years. As far as I know, his wife hasn't kicked the bucket. But I speak smoothly, not missing a beat. "Congratulations."

"Well, thank you twice."

"Twice?" Is he going senile? New mates, thanking me? He was literally just threatening me. I feel like a kite yanked in every damned direction, someone else pulling my string.

“Thank you once for the congratulations. The other time for finding her.”

Finding her? What the hell is he talking about? I stay silent, waiting.

“I’ll send a car around to pick up that delectable little wolf from the forest tomorrow. But don’t fuck with me, Black.”

Click.

Stone hangs up on me.

It takes a second for me to register what he means but my wolf snarls when I do.

Is he talking about *Elena*?

6

BLACK

What is it about this girl? I toss on boxers and a pair of sweatpants and hurry downstairs in bare feet to my office, hardly noticing the change from carpet to hardwood when I cross the threshold. I lean down and press the button to power up my desktop and my hair sweeps down in front of my shoulders. I brush it back, annoyed. I didn't even comb it after Stone hung up on me. His declaration made me tense. He knows something about Elena that I don't.

There's nothing more uncomfortable than that—someone having one up on you.

As an alpha, there's nothing more dangerous.

I drum my fingers on the wood of my carved desk, eyes scanning the white, floor-to-ceiling bookshelves to my left that is filled with expensive first editions I never touch anymore. Those books are full of pack knowledge and hold the wisdom of centuries. But now it's all been transcribed and put into searchable databases. Those books are just a decoration, a remnant of what was—a link to our past.

My phone vibrates in my pocket and I pick it up, this time checking to ensure I'm not surprised by the caller.

"Pluto," I greet him gruffly as I log into my computer, the screen saver blinking on to display a pack of wolves racing across a frozen tundra.

"Just got to the hospital. Cody got hurt. We had a tussle with the Dark Nights." Pluto's voice is tired, I can hear the strain in it.

"Fuck. He okay?" I ask, even though the word "hospital" implies he's not.

"Broken arm and a couple broken ribs. Concussion."

"Bring him here after," I tell my second. If Cody's that out of commission, he needs to recuperate somewhere safe. And I've reinforced this place to the nines.

"Will do. Maddox—Stone came with them." Pluto's voice turns questioning, though he doesn't pry outright.

"He called me. Arrogant prick. Said he's sending a car tomorrow for the girl."

Pluto immediately growls through the phone. "Like hell."

This gets my curiosity going, as I use my mouse to click the icon and open up our pack database. With nearly five hundred alphas and nearly two thousand betas spread out over fifteen thousand square miles—a territory nearly half the size of the state of Maine—I didn't know a lot of members of the pack personally. Locals in the Durango area, I might recognize by face. But not Elena. Curiosity and a dangerous burning need fill my chest. Who is she? Why does Stone want her? Why is Pluto getting aggressive in response to this threat? I don't ask, I simply wait. My second's smart enough to know I'm waiting for him to explain himself.

"Look, Maddox, I know … this isn't a challenge alright?"

My hackles rise, I can feel the hair on the back of my neck stand up, and I slide my tongue along teeth that have suddenly become quite dangerously sharp. Wolf-like. Even though Pluto literally just prefaced his statement with acquiescence, something has me shooting to my feet, gripping the phone tightly—I barely contain a growl.

I can hear Pluto swallow, and I know he's picturing my reaction right now. "Let me just get to a better spot, okay? Let me go outside."

I pace, dragging my feet across the hardwood planks toward a large square window on one side of my office. I stare up at the moon, wondering what the hell she's put into her beams tonight. Has every damn wolf gone mad?

I know I feel like I have.

I don't react this way to women. I select them online, have them researched to ensure they'll meet my needs —younger, good ass, beta but not quite vanilla—then carefully construct our meetings via friends. I control everything. I *don't* meet women when I'm out on shifted runs in the forest through disputed territory.

My nostrils flare at the memory of catching Elena's scent. The way my paws had turned automatically in that direction, sprinting full out, my wolf not even cautious about potential danger, just desperate to find the source of that scent. And then I'd seen her. Naked and laying in the moonlight like some dark goddess, some Greek myth sprung to life.

Pluto's voice breaks me out of the reverie. "Maddox … she just … that smell. It's so intense that I nearly couldn't see straight."

I acknowledged that understatement with a grunt.

"You can't let Stone—"

"Stone's not touching her," I snarl as I hang up the phone before I snap at him for trying to tell me what to do.

No one's going to touch Elena—no one but me.

I turn back to my computer and take a few deep breaths before tossing my phone carelessly to the side of my wireless keyboard. I sit down in my leather chair and try to gather my composure as I click to open the database for the Lobos and search her first name. Twenty-five Elenas pop up, but I dismiss them quickly when their photos load. No. No. No. I stop dead when I see Elena's face staring back at me, defiant, her black hair loose in the photograph, a white tank top showing just a hint of her cleavage. A look of defiance that I'm already familiar with appears on her face.

She was telling the truth. That first thought hits me like a right hook across the jaw, a burst of painful reality that I didn't quite see coming. *I'm an asshole.* But that second thought isn't new—it's something I've known about myself for a long time. You don't get to be in charge by being a nice guy.

I've got one of my own shifters locked up in my basement.

My eyes dart toward the door just in time to see Matthew enter with a tray of food. He's got a Philly cheese steak sandwich and some sliced green apples for me and my office fills with the scent of sauteed mushrooms and onions topping the sandwich, making my stomach suddenly remember that it's empty. I nod in thanks and gesture vaguely for him to put the food on the desk before I turn back to my screen, eager to read all the details I can about Elena DeMarkus.

Her major is biology and I briefly wonder why, wonder what she's drawn to, what makes her tick. She's on the track team with a partial scholarship, running the sprints and one hundred meter hurdles—that explains how fast the little vixen was. I put a hand to my chin and scratch my beard as I lean forward, closer to the screen, hiding the contents with my bulk like some girl might hide a naughty book. I don't want Matthew to know what I'm reading.

But, ever the proper butler, Matthew sets down the tray without glancing up at my screen. Then he walks over to my bar on the right side of the room, grabbing a glass and a water bottle. He returns, and sets them both down with a soft plonk-clink, but doesn't leave.

I glance over at him, trying to hide my annoyance. Matthew's typically comfortable being invisible, so when he has something to say, I stop and listen.

"Should I make anything for your … guest?" Matthew hesitates on that last word.

I sigh. Fuck me. I should have thought of that. I nod briefly and lift my hand from the mouse to gesture at my own plate. "Same. But bring it here. I'll feed her." I meant that I'd bring food to Elena because she's probably shifted into a wolf right now and I don't want her attacking Matthew, who's only human. But, as soon as the words leave my lips they take on a whole new meaning, complete with a naughty fantasy where I picture a naked Elena kneeling at my feet and accepting bites from my bare hands.

I slide my chair forward a bit so that Matthew doesn't see the hard-on forming in my lap at the thought of her lapping at my fingers.

The older man nods and slips out, closing the doors to my office behind him.

I grab an apple slice and bite into it, letting the sharp sweet taste distract me as I glance back at the screen, willing myself to look only at the facts that surround Elena's profile and not her picture. I need to go back down there in full control. I need to figure out what the hell I'm going to say. I need to figure out who Elena is and just why the hell she smells so good. Good enough that another alpha wants her based on scent alone.

Oh fuck.

That thought propels me back to my feet. I shove the rest of the apple into my mouth and stomp over to the books that line my shelves, the library of wolf history that's all but wasted. I could pull up the computer database to get the same information, but in this case, I know exactly which book I'm looking for. Hell, I even know which chapter. This particular book holds a fantasy I used to beat off to when I was a teenager, back when adulthood still seemed like this awesome mystical thing, instead of the shithole reality it is. Adulthood is a pendulum swinging between monotony and bloodshed.

I snag the book, a green hardback that's got golden scrollwork on the spine. *The Mating Ceremonies of Wolves Throughout the Centuries.* It doesn't have a great porn title, and it's filled with so many facts and figures that accidentally flipping to the wrong page can be a total boner killer. But Chapter Seven used to fascinate me because it told about a wolf shifter that was literally one in ten million, a type that hadn't been born for at least three generations. No one I'd ever known had met one.

I lick my finger as I flip through the pages hurriedly and find the illustration that used to make me wild. It's an etching of a woman, her head thrown back in carnal pleasure as her mate ruts her from behind, her breasts and nipples in his hands, her stomach on display as she arches back on her knees and takes an alpha's knot inside her.

My dick pulses at the image as if it's been trained to do so.

I force myself to look over at the paragraphs that introduce this section and actually read for once.

This chapter will cover what to do upon the rare occasion that an omega wolf is born into a pack, beginning with ways to identify the omega. Omega wolves are unique, and not only because of the anatomy that will allow them to fully satisfy their alpha mate. While there is nothing that will identify an omega for certain before the appearance of their wolf, one of the most telling factors in identifying an omega is their wolf's late appearance in life (omegas have been known to show up as late as the twenty-fifth year), but also for their sweet scent, which carries a much more floral tone than other wolves and responds to an alpha's purr—

I drop the book on my fucking toe and hardly notice the throbbing hiss it sends up my spine because my mind is otherwise occupied.

Oh god.

This is bad.

This is worse than bad.

Frustration and rage swell up inside me and swirl around like dirt devils, biting and stinging. I want to punch something. No, not satisfying enough. I want to punch someone. I've got a damned omega in my basement… I found the pot of gold at the end of the goddamned rainbow. And my worst fucking enemy knows. Wants her.

I want her.

Fuck!

Rage colors the edges of my vision a hazy red as I grab the reading chair that's nearest to me. It's a leather wingback chair and I heave it up over my shoulders before launching it with a yell across the room. I watch it smash into my computer screen and destroy my tray of food as it slides across my desk before landing with a dead thump on the wooden floor. Even though my chest heaves from the effort, it isn't enough to vent the fury I feel building inside me, the hot coals hissing and heating me up, the pressure growing stronger.

When Matthew walks back in with a second tray, he stops short at the sight of the chaos I've created. One look at me and he knows better than to speak.

I stomp toward him and grab the new tray. "Shield all the windows. Call in the alpha elite and tell them to wait for me in the ballroom," I bark, giving him not further explanation.

Matthew's graying eyebrows shoot up, but I don't explain because how the hell am I supposed to tell him that the little shifter in my basement is about to cause a fucking pack war?

7

ELENA

That evil fucking asshole. My blood pumps and rages and I feel like an ancient gladiator, trapped underneath the arena about to face a death match as I tromp back and forth down the dark, narrow hallways of Black Maddox's basement storage room. He's been gone for nearly ten minutes and I've been wearing down my feet pacing, clutching at the air, and pretending that it's his throat. But, seeing as my hands are still zip-tied together I doubt that I could get them around that asshole's thick neck.

He kidnapped me! My own fucking alpha didn't believe me. He tied me up and shoved me in here—I glance around at my cage for the eightieth time; this fucking storage room is lined with wooden shelves big enough for huge tubs of crap. Surprisingly, it's empty, though I would have expected Black Maddox to keep his collection of sticks in here … the ones he shoves up his ass—pompous fuck. I search for something, anything that might remove my zip tie.

I don't give a damn that he found me in disputed territory. As soon as we made it to his friend's car he could have borrowed a phone, called my mom or someone, and cleared this shit right up. He didn't—because he's a psychopath.

A huge, hulking, brawny-as-the-Hulk, alpha mental case…and he'll be back down here at some point.

What am I going to do when he comes back?

I've asked myself this question at least a dozen times and I still don't know the answer. No lightbulb clicks on inside my head…

I shuffle a few steps forward and reach up for the first of the pull chains on the fluorescent lights and turn it off. Then I make my way around the middle aisle of empty shelves, turning the corner and walking until I come to the second dangling light. I reach up and pull until I hear a click and darkness surrounds me.

It's not much, but at least it will give me a small advantage, I tell myself as I wait for my eyes to adjust. I glance over at the small window that's now the only source of light, letting in a dull gray strip that paints a stripe through the air and a rectangle on the floor. Walking toward the window, which perches in the wall above a set of shelves, I tell myself that I can't count on Black coming back down and being reasonable. That shit's just the foolish hope of victims. He's already proven he's a lock-girls-up-first-and-ask-questions-later kind of fucker.

I need to prepare for the worst, not the best.

Why do the hot guys always have to be crazy?

Make no mistake, Black is "make you wet with a look" hot. I've always liked muscles and guys with a bit of a brutish glare, but he's got this savage Highlander look down pat. He just needs a kilt. He's already got a sword…

Nope. Erase thought, Elena. You are not thinking about his sword. It's probably cursed anyway. Maybe it's the source of his madness.

Fuck. I'm going insane down here, I realize when I see how ludicrous my thoughts have become. I don't want to picture Black in a kilt with his hair blowing in the wind. I want to picture his eyes closed, those long lashes brushing his cheeks for the final time. Dead.

For some reason, my head rejects that image, probably because I'm not a madwoman who thinks death is just another tantalizing thrill. Unlike a certain alpha.

I stop pacing for a second, leaning against an unfinished two-by-four post that runs up to the ceiling. I take a deep breath and Jonah comes to mind. His bright blue eyes, his blond hair, his easy smile.

My heart gives a longing pang, the kind I didn't think I'd ever have for him. We've always kept things casual. Loose. I mean, I don't see other people because I'm too damned busy with track and all the applications for nursing school.

But I've never asked him if he sees other people. I've always assumed he's seeing multiple girls. He's just that kind of sweet flirt—who could resist? I certainly wouldn't begrudge other girls. He's the only hot guy I've ever found who doesn't have all these dominance hang-ups.

A lot of beta guys still like to be the dominant ones in bed but my fuck buddy is the softest, sweetest teddy bear I know. He offered to help me earlier when he thought I was sick and now I longingly wish I'd taken him up on that offer.

I'm an arrogant fool.

Part of me hopes he's raised an alarm but another, more jaded part of me doesn't want Black to associate him with me at all. That wouldn't be good for Jonah because there's a gleam in Black's eyes even when he glares at me, a sort of pulsing want that I recognize, because despite myself I feel it too. There's a bolt of intensity between us that sizzles—a feeling that I don't want to identify because I shouldn't feel anything but hatred and caution where he's concerned.

I tussle with the self-disgust that wants to rear its ugly head and tell me how stupid I am. I don't have time for it. Self-pity has to take a back seat because I need to figure out my next steps. What I need to do is *maim* Alpha Maddox. I need to escape.

My eyes scan my surroundings. I want to disassemble one of these shelves and take a screw to his fucking balls. But I've got nothing but my hands to work with and they're fucking strapped together. The window has some glass ... if I can't escape, can I bust it and use a shard to free myself and stab him?

If I do stab him and don't slash deep enough or fast enough, it's a death sentence ... but the hair tingling on the back of my neck makes me think that I'm facing the reaper either way. Alphas don't lock up wolves in their basements without the plan to hurt them badly.

I should know.

No. Not going there. Focus, Elena. Climb.

I blow out a slow breath through my nostrils and then wrap my hands around either side of a support post before stepping up onto the bottom shelf and testing whether it will hold my weight.

It's just plywood and I brace myself as I lift my other foot off the ground, tensed and prepared to jump back. The shelf bows under my weight but doesn't break, so I breathe a sigh of relief. I lean over far, so far that a good chunk of my upper body weight rests on the top shelf.

My gaze searches for cracks in the glass I can use. "Please, Moon Goddess, let there be a crack," I whisper as I lean forward, stretching, and the edge of the wood bites at my stomach, the splinters as sharp as shifter teeth.

But my prayers go unanswered. The stupid window is double-paned perfection. Shit.

I slam both fists into the glass anyway, because my nerves squeeze me tight and the need to do something —anything—overcomes me. He's going to come back and when he does, there will be hell to pay. That's how these things work. Alphas, bad ones, take everything out on their betas. Frustration, disappointment, fury.

And while I'm not a beta wolf, I know for a fact that there's no way my wolf is as strong as Black's. I've only met her once but even so ... I just know. I have two choices. Sit here and take it. Or fight. End it on my terms.

Gah, the thought clogs my throat but I don't let it overtake me. I pound the window harder, making the glass shake in its sill, rocking my entire body back and forth to get better leverage so I can hit harder. When my fists simply skid along the smooth glass, I get angry. I lean forward onto my stomach and raise my feet to the second shelf, trying to give myself the ability to lean up and get a better angle. But with a creak and quake, the shelf under my feet collapses followed by the shelf I'm leaning on and I plummet backward to the hard cement ground.

By some miracle, I land on my feet but stumble back and scrape my back on the row of shelves behind me, the blow sharp enough to make me gasp in pain and heat lick up my spine. *Fuck!* Anger is the first emotion that pulses through me when I can breathe again.

The sight of the window sends a surge of broken fury through me because my only hope now gleams like a blue sapphire but it's surrounded by jagged chunks of wood that dangle uselessly. There's zero chance that I'll be able to reach that window again.

The need to cry overwhelms me but when I glance at the ground, it's quickly tackled by delight. One broken bit of shelf looks like a gorgeous, beautifully haggard wooden dagger. I lick my lips as I lean down to pick it up and golden triumph makes me giggle madly. Here it is. My unexpected advantage. Now, I just have to wait. I rise stiffly, my back starting to feel the effect of my fall and make my way over to stand behind the door.

I don't wait long.

It's only a few minutes before I hear the key kiss the lock.

This is it. My moment. "This is your one chance," I whisper under my breath. But I'm disgusted to look down and notice my right hand, the one gripping my weapon, trembles. I tighten my grip, fighting panic that threatens to surge through me like a tidal wave. Flashes of memory flicker like a slide show before I quickly press the off button and absolutely refuse to think about the past.

Black's deep, grumbling voice comes through the door in a muffled fashion as the knob turns and I watch it—every fiber of my being so focused on that door that I hardly hear him say, "Elena, you didn't tell me the whole truth—" The door swings open and I leap forward, my heart screeching along with my mouth as I aim for Black's stomach.

"I'm going to gut you!" I scream out my intentions as I thrust my arm forward and jab at him, but my makeshift weapon skips across his shirt, and I see an angry red streak appear instead of a deep puncture. *Motherfucking dammit!* I wrench back slightly and try again, pressing harder, frantic. But other than an *oof,* he's a wall, he's made of stone, impenetrable.

My resolve starts to crumble and familiar panic creeps around me like vines, tendrils spiraling up my legs, tossing off shoots and leaves and choking me as the vines grow thicker together until it's hard for me to see. Hard to breathe. I start to pant.

A second later, Black's hands form manacles around my wrists and he lifts me up until my feet dangle and my eyes are level with his own. His gaze is darker than his name. Between those lashes of his are twin orbs that are the gateway to my own personal hell.

I clutch my now-useless weapon in my hand as Black turns and exits the storage room in silence, me hanging in front of him, suspended like a marionette.

The bright light of the living space in the basement makes me squint, though blindness is the least of my problems. Cold sweat forms at the base of my spine.

"You tried to hurt me," Alpha Black growls as he stomps across the room.

"No. I tried to kill you," I snarl, kicking out, hoping I can land a hit to his balls and make him furious. Furious is better than calculating. It hurts more at first, but less in the long run.

But Black Maddox doesn't become enraged. He just flips me around and clutches me back against his stomach for a second, my arms still lifted high above me, before he shoves me face-first onto a table with a dark chuckle.

Pain murmurs in my ear and I know things are just beginning. They're going to get worse. Worse. Worse.

Bile coats the back of my throat.

Black wrenches my arms up painfully overhead and stuffs both wrists into one of his hands, still not bothering to disarm me.

I don't know what makes me more furious—the fact that I'm impotent against him or the fact that he knows it.

I clench my teeth to avoid letting a sob rip through me and I try to stare straight ahead.

Go somewhere else, I tell myself. *Go somewhere else and stay there.* I close my eyes and try to picture this lake we went to once when I was a kid. Our only family vacation. There were a bunch of aspen trees, their leaves golden—

"Oh no, Elena. Eyes open. I want you fully here for your punishment. I want you to feel everything," Black's breath swirls over my ear before he licks my earlobe and then nips it, sending a shiver down my spine.

I don't want to think about the things he has planned, but the command in his voice is too strong. As soon as his words washed over me, the press of the table grew twice as cold. My awareness of his heat grew twice as strong. I can only guess what that means for what's to come.

Fuck. How do I make this better? I've tried resisting, I've tried making him mad. Maybe he's the kind of alpha that will go easier if I just submit. I peel them grudgingly open, knowing that right now I'm completely at his mercy. Does he even have any?

"You have guts, little wolf. But we need to redirect that beautiful rage in a better direction. I have a couple ideas about how we might do that." Black leans against me and I feel his cock press against my ass through his pants. Unlike in the forest, where the touch might have been incidental, now it's very clearly intentional. I can feel how thick and long it is as he rubs it gently up and down.

My throat goes dry and tears form in my eyes even as I feel a low-level pulse between my thighs. Is that what this is going to be then? I steel myself. If he's going to force himself on me then I'm—

"I can see those pretty wheels turning. I can smell your interest, princess. But only good girls get this cock. And you've been naughty."

He pulls away, his weight and warmth suddenly gone from my back, and I blink as a tear slides sideways down my cheek as I grind my teeth in frustrated confusion. What? He's not gonna fuck me? Relief, disappointment, anger swirl inside my head, each emotion a different color. They swirl together until my feelings are a murky gray.

"Get on with it then," I hiss. He's fucking toying with me.

He chuckles and slides a single finger slowly down my spine. "You're a Lobo. I looked you up. Or at least you will be once you register. Which makes you *mine*."

The way Black says that last word makes my breath catch. His words temporarily stun me. He makes me feel like an innocent fly who stumbled into the spider's web. I'm trapped in his house and he's wrapping me slowly up with words that cling to my ears and slide along my skin.

I smack talk, trying to knock some sense back into myself because there's no way a psychopath's possessiveness should be enticing. "So what, I'm a part of your pack. For now. Don't worry. I'll find a new one soon."

Black's finger turns into an entire hand on my back and the air bursts from my lungs as he compresses them, pushing me into the table hard. "You. Will. Not." His hand lets up a moment later and I have to gulp to restore my breath.

"Why would you care?" I grit out, frustrated even as my nipples tighten at the alpha tone in Black's voice, a phenomenon that has never happened before. I don't get aroused by alphaholes. I don't. I refuse.

Alpha Maddox leans back down and I can feel his hardness again, though he only lets his dick slide across the outer edge of my hip, far from where I want it. Don't want it, I snarl at the base part of my brain that's lit up my senses. That idiot part of me in charge of procreation wants to roll out construction signs with all kinds of arrows to redirect Black's dick. Turn here. Go over the hill. Lane splits into two. Drive Straight.

Fuck my brain.

Do not think about Black and sex together, I order myself, which immediately has the opposite effect. An image of Black reclining on a king-sized bed and moaning as I slowly slide down his shaft trickles into my brain. If I could scratch out the brain cells that think about sex right now, I would, even if it meant I'd never think about sex again. "You don't give a shit about me, Black," I whisper, as much for myself as for him.

"I do. I care because you're going to be mine." He lets out a hum that almost sounds like the purr of a kitten, a rumble in his chest.

Immediately, my vision tunnels, and heat gathers in my belly. The sensations I've been fighting against snowball, doubling in size in a matter of seconds as if his purr really did melt all my mental faculties. I try to cling to reason but when he purrs again I find myself wet and aching. I have to transform a moan into a growl mid-sound. What the fuck?

"Oh, you like that," Black's arrogant tone makes me verbally snap.

"You sound like a lawn mower," I lie. He sounds like a fucking dream, like a vibrator ... and the effect his purr has on me is pretty much the same.

He just purrs louder and my thighs start to rub together of their own accord.

No. Distraction. Escape.

"When I get out of here—"

Black's purr stops abruptly and he pulls back, alpha anger fired back up as if he hadn't just sounded like a fucking house cat. "You're not leaving. Ever."

I bite my tongue because I'm so damned relieved that I pissed him off enough to make the purring stop. My pussy is soaked and my thighs were about to be and I would have died if that had happened.

My eyes focus on what's in front of them because I sure as hell am not going to focus on my traitor body. There's a short green net and realize with a start that Black shoved me down onto the ping pong table. I have that realization exactly one second before the first *thwack*. My ass burns, stings, and I realize he just hit my ass with a ping pong paddle. But it's nothing like the beating I expected.

Still, I try to wriggle out of his grip, yanking down my arms, trying to get away.

"Stay still!" Black orders.

My traitorous body immediately complies. *Dammit.*

Black chuckles, like he knows how pissed I am about the fact that I just listened to his order, my limbs falling like dominoes, self-preservation taking a backseat to his command. "Did you feel that, Princess? That's spanking number one. Count them."

Another smack makes my left ass cheek burn, driving my self-loathing away as pain becomes a more pressing concern. But though the strike was hard enough to push my hips into the table, I realize with a start that it's nowhere near a quarter of Black's strength. He could easily break me. One hit at full force could make me black out. So why's he taking it easy? Or … is he toying with me?

Whack! "You didn't count, Princess. If you don't count, you get extra."

"One," I say on an exhale, still trying to puzzle this out. But the spankings start coming more rapidly and the strikes set a wildfire ablaze on my ass. Then Black starts to purr while he spanks me. My vision blurs as the purr slides in through my ears and turns my thoughts into floating sparkles. I can't think straight about his motives, about his intentions, about anything after that.

I become a mindless mess of sensation as Black spanks me and my mouth automatically spits out the count, though my brain doesn't even register it.

Black shoves my legs apart and keeps spanking me, each strike of the paddle edging a little closer to my pussy. His purring intensifies and I hear the keen erupting from my mouth. My mindless wail ends on a desperately broken, "Black, please."

I'm not sure if I'm begging for mercy or an orgasm. Perhaps both.

But it must be the signal he's waiting for. Black steps back and I hear the clatter of a paddle on the table next to me as he tosses it aside.

I straighten slowly, stiff, and still unable to use my bound hands. When I'm upright I look for Black, who appears in front of me with a knife in his hands.

Fear kicks me, but Black simply takes my hands, pulling them toward himself. Then he slices through the zip tie that was restraining them. He pulls away my wooden stake. He tosses the tie and my makeshift weapon on the carpet.

I meet his gaze and am startled by the intensity I find in his eyes. The air rumbles between us and the earth quakes, and though neither of us says a word, I know without a doubt that something monumental has just shifted between Black Maddox and me. What I don't know is if I like it.

8

BLACK

I CAN SEE how fast Elena's breath is coming, how hooded her eyes have gotten, and that scent … there's no denying she's as affected by me as I am by her. An omega. The most fucking rare of the shifters and I've stumbled right over one who's perfect. She's delectable. Delicious. So goddamned gorgeous that she takes my breath away. Pile that scent on top. The fact that her little body will take my knot once I get her into a heat. Or even how she'll beg once I get her into a heat. Fuck. She'll make me the envy of every damned alpha out there. Including Stone. Because I'm keeping her.

But I want to do this right with her. Elena's going to be my mate and we're going to have to live with the memory of our first time forever. I want it to be seared into her mind as the most erotic moment of her life. So

I back off, even though all the blood in my body has fled my head and I'm almost dizzy with lust.

"Go shower," I order, pointing across the room to the white paneled door that leads to the basement bedroom and en suite bath.

Elena stares at me with those moonlit eyes for a second before she dashes away like she's afraid I'll chase her.

Part of me wants to. But if I do, I know what will happen and she's not ready for it.

Besides, I've already caught her.

She's on the hook. Now I just have to reel her in.

I hear the water start and I can't help walking closer. I head through the doorway of the bedroom and torture myself with the sight of that closed en suite bathroom door, knowing that my fantasy lies behind it.

I wonder if she'll finish what I started while she showers? I glance down at my dick, which strains against my pants, and decide that *I* need to finish what I started. I shove my sweats down my thighs and spit on my hand before I grip the top half of my dick in my right hand. I start to stroke, picturing the red marks on Elena's ass after I spanked her, how she'd unconsciously bucked once or twice to meet my paddle. She fucking liked it. I know she won't admit it now, but one day I'll get her to

—one day I'll have her begging me to spank her. My eyelids flutter closed and I use my thumb to swipe across the sensitive head of my dick, my balls tightening.

And then I smell it. My head jerks up, toward the bathroom door, which she closed firmly behind her—locked no doubt.

I walk forward, pants falling farther down my legs and puddling around my ankles as I do. I take a deep inhale.

Yup.

There's no doubt about it. Elena's in there touching herself. That soft, sweet white chocolate and floral scent is so strong that it drifts underneath the door and makes my dick harder than a rock. Inside my head, my wolf howls his delight as I picture Elena leaning against the tan tiles that line the shower. Her black hair is soaked and sticks to her skin, the sides of her breasts, hanging down her back. Water droplets trail over her nipples. Her hand slides down that firm, smooth stomach to her pussy, spreading those lips so that her thin fingers can dip inside herself. But it won't be enough.

She'll lean there against the wall and imagine it's my dick plunging into her, spreading her apart. She'll reach her other hand down to play with that little clit of hers at the same time, circling around and around until she spirals into oblivion and her thighs buck.

I hear a *smack* like she just hit the wall of the shower, and I imagine she's coming. I imagine her sweet pink pussy is pulsing around her fingers, milking them in that wet heat. *Fuck.* I stroke faster and harder, intensity searing my spine until I feel my balls tightening and I come. My load shoots all over her bathroom door as my chest heaves. I slide my hand up and down my shaft a little longer, softly now, dragging out the sensation.

Oh god.

My tongue rims my lips and I let out a heavy breath. If coming while just thinking about her is this good I can only imagine how amazing the real thing will be. I've never been this drawn to a woman before. My wolf arches a brow smugly, as if he's known all this time that we were just waiting for an omega. For the type of wolf who could actually serve our needs. For the type of girl who could bring out our fire and take the heat.

I hear the water shut off in the shower and I hurriedly come down from my high and bend to snag the waistband of my pants, yanking them back up. I don't bother wiping the cum off the door. Hopefully, she'll smell it and know that I know what she was doing. Maybe that will embarrass her and make those pale cheeks turn a soft pink.

Mmmm ... I like that idea more than I should.

I stride quickly out of the room before I can dwell on why Elena's taken all my fantasies down a dark, twisted path. I nearly run headlong into Matthew, who's in the main rec room of the basement, folded clothes in one hand, the scent of onions trailing from him. No, not him. I look over to the bar and there are two fresh trays with sandwiches, apples, and trail mix.

"I thought you'd want fresh ... everything. And your guest,"—this time he uses the word with a bit less hesitance than last time—"will probably want to be dressed before the elite team arrives."

Fuck.

I'd nearly forgotten I'd ordered them to come over, that was how completely captivating and distracting my little she-wolf was.

I toss Matthew a nod of thanks and he puts the clothing down on one of the brown leather recliners before turning to head back up the stairs.

I call out to stop him. "Matthew! One last thing." I reach down into the pocket of my pants for the key to the storage room. I fish it out and hold it out. "You can have this back."

He comes forward and plucks it out of my hand. "Excellent." I can hear the relief in his tone.

Unfortunately, my next words quell it. “I need the key to the door at the top of the stairs instead. Ms. DeMarkus will be staying down here.”

Matthew swallows hard but, just like everyone who works for me, he knows to keep his mouth shut. He fiddles with his key ring, flipping through the keys with a *plink* and a *plonk* until he finds the right one, extracts it, and hands it to me. “Will she be staying awhile sir?” he asks.

“Oh, she’ll be staying forever.” I give my butler a smirk as he nods—stoic as usual—and retreats and a tingle works its way up my spine.

I turn to see Elena standing in the doorway of the basement bedroom, her glare the cause of the sensation along my back. While I’m certain she wishes that laser gaze of hers could carve holes into me, all it does is make me want to shove her back into that bedroom and close the door behind us. She looks amazing, those fit muscular legs of hers on display.

I don’t ravish her, though the sight of her in that towel is porn worthy. My self-control practically makes me a fucking saint.

Instead, I grab a set of my more casual things from the stack that Matthew brought down and hold them out like a peace offering. “Why don’t you get dressed and then we’ll eat?”

"Oh, you're feeding me now? Not locking me back up inside that torture chamber?" Her eyes glint furiously and her hands roughly and quickly snatch away the pile of clothes so she can clutch them to her chest.

I don't bother to answer her because she's being a pouty brat. I'm an alpha. I'll do what I need to do to protect myself and my pack and I won't apologize for it —not even to my mate. I turn my back on her and drop my sweats so that I can change into the casual slacks and gray button-up.

I hear a loud gasp behind me and then the tromp of feet as Elena rushes back into her room, pretending she's offended and she doesn't like what she sees. We both know that's a lie. I work out two hours a day. Plus, her little bathroom performance lets me know all I need to know about our chemistry. It's there—whether she wants to admit it or not. Our chemistry's as strong as lightning—when I finally do strike, she's going to get the shock of her life.

I get dressed and walk over to the bar to make myself a drink. I pour a double whiskey on the rocks and top it off with a bit of water, then grab a spoon to stir it.

Like a nice guy, I pour Elena a glass of wine before I realize I don't know if she likes red or white. So, I pour another glass in another color—bases covered.

When Elena steps out of the bedroom, she looks adorably hilarious. She's swimming in my clothes and though I'd guess she's five foot five or so, she looks tiny in my things.

I'm not even sure how she got my pants to stay up on her waist because they're at least four times too wide for her slender form. They cover her bare feet except for the tips of her toes, which peek out under the hem as she walks. My worn black San Francisco t-shirt, a remnant of my youth, is so baggy that I can't see her figure. But her scent now mingles with mine, which sends an entirely different, entirely new sort of rush to my head—this sort of visceral pride, this pleasure, a sense of satisfaction.

I'm rubbing all of her clothes across my body before I give them to her from now on. Maybe I'll even use her underthings to jerk off before I let her wear them. She'll be conditioned to my scent ... fucking hell, I'm getting worked up again. I need to eat. I'm light-headed. That's what this is. That's why I can't focus. I had a fight, had to heal, and I haven't eaten. Low blood sugar is driving me crazy.

I snag a sandwich from one of the plates. It's still warm. Moon Goddess bless Matthew. He knows I hate cold sandwiches. Normally, I don't make this much work for him. But nothing's normal tonight, I realize as

Elena stands near the bar and I stare at her delicate wrists as she traces a finger along her tray.

I realize what I'm doing—who the fuck looks at wrists? —and quickly set down my sandwich and wipe my hands on a cloth napkin from my tray before pushing both wine glasses toward her.

"Wine?" I ask.

Her gaze flickers over both glasses and then at my own whiskey. "We're a little past the get the girl drunk and take her home phase."

"I'm not trying to get you drunk, I just didn't know what you liked."

"You don't give a shit what I like."

"Shut down the sarcasm, little wolf. You're on thin ice right now."

"You fucking locked me up!"

"Yeah. And you attacked me. You're lucky you just got spanked. If you had any other kind of pussy, Matthew would be changing the carpet right now because little bits of your damn skull would be in it."

Her eyes widen and she takes a step back. But it's time she learns the fucking score. I'm the alpha. Elena's the lowest ranking wolf in my pack. Without me, without the protection I'll offer, she has nothing.

She needs to learn right here and now, that gratitude is the only attitude.

Her eyes flash with anger and tell me that she's clearly not gonna become a sweet little flower.

I grab my whiskey and down a gulp. This is not how women act around me. Granted, I don't lock most of them in my basement. But ... still. I let her shower, alone. I gave her clothes. And considering how fucking hot she is, the fact that I let her get dressed is a huge sacrifice on my part ... one that she clearly doesn't recognize.

As I lower my cup, a raisin hits me square in the forehead and falls into my drink with a *plop*.

I narrow my eyes and turn to glare at Elena, who gives me a fake innocent look before grabbing her tray and stalking across the room. She picks the recliner farthest from me and sits down in it, putting her tray on her lap and picking up her sandwich, taking a big bite.

I watch her chew as I shake my head. She's pissed at me and I get it. I'd be furious if I was in her shoes—and if there's one thing I've learned through the years it's that if you can't stand in the heat of someone else's fire, you aren't meant to be a leader. Another thing I've learned ... anger is one thing but disrespect is another. I don't want her thinking she can get away with throwing things at me, even harmless little things like raisins.

She needs to learn a lesson. My eyes automatically travel over to the ping pong table and think about that lesson and I get half hard. But the punishment has to fit the crime and flicking a raisin isn't nearly as bad as trying to attack me.

I reach into the glass bowl that Matthew filled with trail mix and grab an orange M&M. Elena's about to learn who's boss all over agai—

Another fucking raisin beans me in the forehead and my eyes snap up. Elena quickly lowers her head to look at her plate as if she's never seen anything more fascinating than her sandwich in her entire life.

Fury and disbelief blast through me. Did she really just throw that from across the room? And hit her target? I shove down the grudging admiration that starts up in the pit of my belly. No.

I clutch my M&M and gauge the distance between us. It has to be thirty feet. When Elena reaches for her napkin, pretending she's completely unaware of me, I let the M&M fly. It arcs up and smacks the ceiling, tumbling harmlessly down onto the carpet.

Motherfucker.

Elena's eyes shine with disdainful amusement as she peers out from behind her napkin and I glare at her, turning back to my sandwich to regroup. I take a huge bite, wondering how the hell she got that raisin all the way across the room. I pretend not to look at her, practically daring her to try again—only so I can figure out her technique. Then I'm going to pelt her with so much dried fruit she could make a fruitcake.

Her thin hands travel across her tray and I feign interest in the dartboard. Out of the corner of my eye, I watch her fingers move and she balances a raisin between the tray and her fingertip, like a paper football. With her other hand, she flicks the raisin. I watch it sail in a straight line, heading right for me. At the last second, I duck to my left, but I can tell—beyond a doubt—that if I hadn't moved, she would have hit me dead center again.

This time, I can't quash that smidge of admiration. My girl has skills.

"Where the hell did you learn a useless trick like that?" I ask, attempting conversation to cover up the fact that I'm grabbing a huge handful of trail mix.

"My dad, not that you care," she responds before returning to her sandwich, opening it up and pulling out a thin slice of steak, and eating it before licking her fingers.

"I care now that I know you aren't a Dark Night," I respond with a casual shrug before grabbing a slice of apple and eating it. "I just had to make sure first."

She rolls her eyes. "Don't believe you."

That annoys me. In the future, there will be consequences for her rolling her eyes at me, but I force myself to inhale slowly and remember that it's our first night together and this is new for her. I'll let her have that one.

The raisin thing though—that's just fucking unacceptable. When Elena digs through her sandwich, shoving aside onions to find more steak, I distract her with more conversation as I reach down and position a raisin.

"Why would your dad teach you something so useless?"

Her lips purse and she debates telling me but ultimately she relents and responds, "We used to go to baseball games a lot. I'd get bored. He taught me so I'd have something to do while he watched the games..." she trails off, a wistful look on her face that makes me want to cup her cheek. Why the hell do I want to do that?

"That's kind of sweet," I say, because that look on her face prompts me to say something.

But then her glare slides back into place as she turns toward me. "That was a food-induced confession. Don't fucking act like we're friends now."

"Oh, we're not, princess. Never gonna be friends with you." I have plans to be so much more than friends.

I flick my raisin at her.

It doesn't even make it past the first armchair near me before it falls to the ground.

I hear Elena snort.

I stomp out from behind the bar, quickly crossing the distance between us. With the tray on her lap, she's slow to react and I get to her before she's fully standing. I take the tray from her hands, setting it down on the floor as my face gets close to hers. Then I push her back into her seat, loving how her shoulder fits snugly into the palm of my hand. I wait, holding her in place, watching as her eyes burn and nostrils flare—my little vixen's pissed but she doesn't say anything. Because she knows who's in charge.

"I have to go prepare for a meeting. When I come back, we're going to have a little competition with these raisins."

A smirk comes over her face and it's so adorably diabolical. "If I win?"

I lean in close and inhale her scent one last time, letting that white chocolate sweetness fill my mind until my wolf lets out a plaintive whine inside my head. He wants her. I stare at Elena to find her eyes wide, breath caught—she's just as enraptured by this connection as I am. I reach a hand up to stroke her hair, thrilled when she doesn't pull away, when she inhales sharply. "Don't worry about winning. You won't."

Her eyes narrow instantly and she shoves my hand away with both of hers. I straighten, chuckling. Then I walk up the basement stairs without a word. At the top, I turn and look down at her. She's still in her seat, though she's turned sideways to stare up at me. The expression on her face is a mixture of lust and confusion.

Or maybe I'm projecting.

I always wanted to find an omega wolf—always dreamed about it, though I never thought it would happen—the elusive, special wolf who'd satisfy my every need. But as I lock little spitfire Elena in my basement, I can't deny that the fact that I've caught an omega has my chest dancing in a way that confuses the shit out of me.

Despite my confusion though, I'm certain of one thing: If I have to, I'll make a deal with the fucking devil and sell my twisted, stained soul in order to keep her.

Elena's mine.

9

JONAH

MY STOMACH CRINGES. I've got that nervous-sick feeling I get when I have to present in front of a class, which I hate. It doesn't help that my wolf is restless—he has been since Elena ran out of class hours ago. He paces inside my head, his gray fur bristled. He wants me to shift, even though I know that's a bad idea. I might be able to sniff her out and find her quicker, but I've got a better chance of helping her if I stay human. My wolf's too fucking docile to fight. Me—not so much.

I can't believe she just left like that, clutching her stomach but full-on sprinting. I hope she's okay. *God. Nothing better have happened to her.*

I pull her cell out of my pocket and stare at the black screen. I wish I wouldn't have locked myself out of her phone trying to look for her mom's number. Now, I'm not sure what the hell to do but keep searching campus for her. I've never been to her house. I could call someone in the pack and get her address but she's told me point-blank at least a dozen times that no male beta is allowed to step foot inside her mother's house. I keep pulling her phone and then my own out, swapping between them, hoping she'll call one. Even just a text.

I exchange her phone for my own and pull up my texts. There's nothing new from her but I stare at our texts from last night.

My finger's in my pussy right now. She always texts when she's horny.

Bet you wish it was my dick.

Bet YOU wish it was your dick.

You know it. Pump that finger for me. I'd been in the living room of my cheap-ass apartment with my roommate watching Sports Center when she originally texted, but I'd quickly abandoned him and hurried to my room, a stiffie building, just like it always did whenever she was involved. I'd slammed my door a little too hard and Steve had yelled at me.

I'm fucking myself with my fingers. It feels good. Now what? She'd handed me the reins last night, which was rare. Elena typically liked to be the bossy one. She liked to shove me down and take it from me, which was fucking hot—how can a guy complain about the sight of a fine woman riding him? But every so often she got in a mood and she needed me to top her. She turned soft and compliant beneath me and I always ended up fucking her rough and hard, holding her down by her throat as I stared into her eyes—fascinated she'd trust me that much.

How wet are you? I'd typed those words as I'd tried to undo my jeans one-handed.

Pretty wet.

Smear some of that cream on your clit for me baby. I'd fallen back on my bed and fished my dick out of my boxers so I could stroke it. *I wish I was there to eat you out.*

As I walk down a set of stairs to a lower level of campus, I scroll, hoping a new text has popped up, but it hasn't. Last night, our texts had devolved into pictures. She always makes me delete them after, and I killed last night's too. But once I've seen something, my brain has picture-perfect recall. I remember the sight of her pale thighs spread apart, that soft pink pussy stuffed with three of her fingers, which still didn't come close to the width of my dick. That sight had made me spurt all over my stomach yesterday.

How fucking different tonight is. Last night I was a horny wreck. Tonight I'm a nervous wreck, wondering where the hell my girl has gone and if she's okay. I don't know if it's paranoia or instinct, but something tells me she's not. And it just fucking kills me.

I glance up at the moon goddess. She's standing on a building in the distance, her bottom edge touching the roof. I stare at her but she just stares blankly back at me like she always does. I don't ever get that sense of connection other wolves have to her.

Elena always jokes I'm a shifter atheist.

My throat tightens as I picture Elena's smirk, the way her full red lips quirk, and that expression she gets when she makes fun of me. I let out a huff of frustration and tell myself I haven't done enough yet to start checking hospitals to see if they've admitted an Elena DeMarkus, though that thought has crossed my mind. I mean, I've searched the whole fucking campus. And Elena's not here. She never came back.

I waited after class. I missed my lecture for Composition 201 after I realized that she forgot her phone. But she never showed.

I wandered the campus all afternoon. I know her schedule, I memorized it when we started hooking up last semester. Sometimes she lets me fill those gaps between classes by filling *her* gap. God, she's so fucking … just so … everything. Hot. Wild in bed. But then level-headed. Low drama.

Sometimes I can't believe she's picked me.

Like, what did I do to get so lucky? Part of me wants to question it and ask her but the other part knows I should just shut the fuck up and take the lotto win. That's what it feels like, having her want me—like I became a billionaire overnight and the world is at my fingertips. Sometimes just thinking about it makes me feel high, like I smoked some good ass shit. I'd make it official if she gave me half a chance but she's skittish about that shit. Won't let me buy her food but will let me buy her vibrators.

One day, though. One day.

Another student walks by as I pass underneath a tall tree that lines one of the major paths on campus. The guy gives me a nod and calls out, "Hey, Jonah! Going to that Phi Kap party tonight?"

"Nah. Got plans."

"You're missing out."

I smile back to be polite and give an open-armed shrug as if to say "what can you do." I've got zero clue who that dude is even though the campus is relatively small. I do my thing here and then between the gym, my job at the mechanic's shop, pack shit, and Elena ... there's barely time for a social life. Sometimes I go out with the pack betas bar hopping. But if Elena's free, I always choose to hang with her.

I walk quickly back to our Anthro lecture hall, running a palm up and down my black beanie, pushing it backward on my head before pulling it down again. I wonder for the zillionth time if she's back there—pissed at me for wandering off.

I worry a lot that she's gonna get pissed at me. Or that her alpha wolf will show up and dismiss me.

That right there is my biggest fear.

And part of me wonders if it's hers.

Her wolf hasn't come in yet, so how can she take any relationship seriously? No matter how well we click. A wolf can appear and change it all.

I've seen it happen. A good relationship is going and then someone's wolf shows and bam—done. Over.

My uncle and aunt were like that. High school sweethearts. Married young. Posey was pregnant with his kid and then his wolf came in—an elite who wanted someone farther down the beta chain. He left her while she was still pregnant and she came to live with us. I had to share my room with Posey. I was five. I fell asleep to the sound of her crying into her pillow for months. I fucking hate Michael and his goddamned wolf. He's never even seen my cousin Jimmy.

Part of me wishes Elena's wolf would come in and this constant worry would just end. The other part of me hopes she's a glimmer, someone who's born into the supernatural world and knows about it but doesn't have magic. Because then I could keep her forever.

Mine, my wolf whines.

Yeah. I want her to be mine. And so does he. Those fierce gray eyes of hers. The way I can erase her badass strut sometimes and win a soft smile from her. I know that tickle spot on her right side, one she refuses to acknowledge exists ... but if I get her just right under her ribs she'll be kicking and screaming in mirth. Once, she even snorted—a fact I like to remind her about when she's feeling playful.

I glance up at the moon skeptically. She's moved up from the buildings and is wearing a couple of clouds now.

Moon Goddess, if you're real ... please ... make Elena mine.

Of course, the moon just sits there in the sky and I feel like an idiot for thinking that. *So dumb.*

I reach the anthropology building and focus my attention back on my search. My eyes scan the dark windows of the two-story hall. There's nothing but a light wind shaking the trees behind the building.

Goose bumps start up on my skin when I hear a howl come from the forest.

I turn my eyes toward it. My throat grows dry and I wonder...

Nah.

She wouldn't go in there. The campus isn't too far from disputed territory. Elena might be a bit of a risk-taker but that's more about sexy stuff. She fucking loves it when we almost get caught. Once, she pulled down her panties but left her skirt on and had me do her right behind the astronomy building while a class went on inside. We were literally just below the fucking windows. The high from the anxiety combined with the slick feel of her pussy clamping down on my dick—it had been a short round. I'd made up for it with my mouth later though. Twice.

I lick my lips and then bite the lower one at the memory. Yeah, Elena's a little scandalous sometimes, but never full-on reckless.

She wouldn't head off into the woods.

I wonder if something's up with her mom.

But, no, that can't be right. Elena just stood up in the middle of class and ran out without even looking at her phone.

My heart thumps faster and I know. I just know.

Her wolf's here.

I can't think of any other reason she'd disappear this long.

Her wolf is here and she didn't come back.

Because she doesn't want me.

I try to ignore the way my throat goes dry or how my wolf tilts his nose up and howls inside my head. Something dark spreads inside my chest that feels like rot, as if my insides have suddenly gone bad.

Fuck.

I blow out a breath and tell myself not to have a fucking breakdown on campus. I hoof it over to the parking lot, and as I get close my phone rings. My heart jumps. *Elena!*

But it's not her number I see. It's Damon's. One of the other betas from school who is also in the Lobos. I swipe to answer as I walk across the semi-abandoned lot, eyes still scanning in case I recognize Elena's silhouette.

"Hey," I say.

"Dude, where are you?"

"What do you mean?" I ask, furrowing my brow.

"Pack howl. Duh." He laughs at me.

Aw, shit. I completely forgot. "Has it started?" I pick up my pace and cross underneath a streetlight to my beat-up old Camaro, my fixer-upper, a girl named Dolly.

"Official start time was delayed ten minutes or so. Some kind of Elite's meeting going on or something." Damon replies evenly. "If you floor it, you might make it in time."

I press my key and unlock the chipped, scratched cherry red doors, carefully bending and setting my bag and Elena's on the passenger seat before climbing in myself. "Anybody new there tonight?" I ask, trying to keep my voice casual as I start the car and pull down my seatbelt.

"Not that I've seen."

"Can you ask around for me? Someone I know was due for the change."

"Do you mean Elena?" Damon replies, a hint of teasing in his voice.

I might have drunkenly confessed how into her I am one night during beer pong.

"Dude—" That's all the warning I give him. My wolf might not kick his ass, but I definitely will.

"I haven't seen her. Calm your tits. Just get here so you don't end up on Alpha Maddox's shit list." With that, Damon hangs up.

I floor it, the sound of my baby's purr bringing a small smile to my face even if my arms are still tense. Dolly jets out of the parking lot and I take the curved ramp that leads to the highway way too fast—chasing an adrenaline high to stave off the fear that's eating at me.

If Elena has shifted, then she'll be at the pack howl. If she's not there, then maybe something bad has happened. Maybe she puked her guts out in a bathroom on campus and passed out. Goddammit! Why didn't I think of that before? I should have checked every bathroom stall or something. Or maybe something else happened. Something worse.

Maybe what I need is Alpha Maddox's help.

I've never actually spoken to our pack alpha beyond initiation day when I first shifted and swore allegiance to the pack. The memory of the cliff side in the moonlight comes back to me.

I'd changed right at nineteen, along with two other guys in our pack. We were all betas. We'd gone to our first pack howl slightly drunk to dull our nerves. The entire group attending that night had followed us from the meeting house—a bigass cabin—out to the Drop. That was what they called the cliff. Though most of our land was forest, there was this epic canyon not too far from the pack house. A small river, maybe more of a stream—I don't really know—wound through the center of it. It wasn't Grand Canyon level, but it was still impressive. The sheer sides of stone, the scent of mud and fresh water … the smell of pine around you as you stared down into an abyss that could kill even a shifter. No way any of us could live if we jumped. Quick healing wouldn't be enough to save you.

The smells that night are always the first thing I remember, because of how intense they'd suddenly become. Beyond the scents of nature, I'd smelled the hot dogs and burgers that someone had grilled at the meeting house for after the ceremony and our first run with the pack.

The crowd had been huge. All shifters were required to attend at least one monthly pack howl. Locals often went every week, though. I'd guessed at least five hundred were there that night since it wasn't just a howl, but an initiation as well.

And all of them had watched as Alpha Maddox made us climb up onto a rock near the edge of the Drop, strip naked, and repeat after him as he stood on the ground below us, wearing a full suit and an intimidating expression.

I'd tried not to shiver as I'd cupped my junk and recited, "I call upon the moon goddess tonight to witness my vow. I vow to follow the law of the Lobos, to honor our head alpha, and swear my soul to the protection of the wolves of my pack so long as I live."

Alpha Maddox had then sworn back to us. "I accept you as wolves into my pack and under my protection. I vow to do everything to protect you, guide you, and keep you safe so long as I live."

I swear a shiver ran down my spine that night. I blame it on the breeze whenever I think about it, or nerves. But my wolf flashes his eyes at me whenever I do that. He disagrees. He's adamant the vow means something. It satisfies his need for order, place, instruction—eases that anxiety that sometimes comes when I take him out for a run on my own. He's not big on that. It makes him uneasy not to have a lead wolf to follow, to not have pack members watching his back at all times.

I call him a damned mouse whenever that happens and he fucking hates that. His ears go back and he'll deliberately run at a tree and then shift at the last second so I smash my head.

My wolf fucking chuckles at my current thoughts as I pull into the pack house parking lot, just a second shy of the howl's start time. "Yeah, yeah," I say aloud to him as I check my pocket for Elena's phone and climb out. I pull it out for a second and sniff. Her scent is faint, definitely mingled with mine. But I hope it will still have enough of her scent on it for Alpha Maddox and his elites to help find her. If not, I leave her bag in the car as a backup, so that the scents of several hundred other wolves don't overpower whatever's left of hers.

My wolf feels confident, certain, almost eager—to get Alpha Maddox's help. Of course, he sometimes likes to hand over his problems instead of solving them himself.

I hurry across the asphalt toward the glowing yellow windows, which light up tons of shifters mingling around. They're still in human form right now, thank fuck. Otherwise, it would be far harder for me to get to Alpha Maddox and explain what I need.

I hurtle into the check-in station, where one of the elites narrows his eyes at me. He's a big tall dude. He goes by Pluto for douchebag reasons that always make me roll my eyes. Asshole thinks he's "lord of the underworld."

"You're late," Pluto says in a clipped tone.

"Barely," I say, ducking my head and dipping my eyes down to the electronic tablet he's using for check-in.

"You can help clean up after." Pluto's tone brooks no argument.

Not that I'd argue. I'm about to ask for a favor after all.

"Yes sir."

"Name?" he asks.

He doesn't remember me. None of the high-ranking alpha pricks ever bother to remember the name of betas. I give my pack nickname, one I don't fucking love, but—unless you're an alpha—you don't get to choose. "Murky," I sigh.

My fucking friends thought it would be funny to name me after Rainbow Brite's stupid villain. Dicks.

Pluto smirks as he marks me present. "Go to the changing room. Good luck finding sweats in your size."

I make a face. He's right. Being late means only the small sizes will be left. Dammit. I scrunch my nose. "Guess I'm ruining these pants." No way I'm trying to squeeze my ass into pack-issue sweats, which are rip-aways for when we shift.

"Up to you. Enjoy streaking back to your car afterward. Personal effects?" he asks. We always have to give up keys, wallets, phones, anything of value so that nobody loses stuff during a shift. Pack members don't steal from one another—a fight to the death makes the penalty way too fucking stiff—but apparently, a lot of arguments used to break out when people lost their keys.

I hand over my keys, wallet, and my phone—though I keep Elena's. He hangs the keys on a board full of numbered hooks behind him, taking the key tag, and pulling a sticker off of it to mark a Ziplock with the same number. In go my wallet and phone. Those get stacked inside an open safe while I watch. Then Pluto puts the key tag onto a black leather dog collar with silver buckles before handing it to me.

I toss it around my neck and latch it with a sigh. My wolf loves the collar. I … tolerate it.

Pluto turns to someone who came in even later than I did and I escape the entry hall and go to the main meeting room, which is filled with more chairs than most churches. People hang out near the coffee machines at the back, snacking on sliders and veggie trays, getting a last caffeine buzz for the night before we sit down to hear any pack updates.

"I hear construction of the new swimming pool is going well. It'll be so nice to have a place just for shifters—"

I push through a group of shifter women chattering, my blue eyes on high alert as I scan the crowd for Alpha Maddox. Normally, he does what he calls "mingling." But that usually only involves the richer shifters. He's never once talked to me since my initiation.

But I'm not going to hold that against him tonight. Not when my chest is still spinning like a police light. I feel like there's a big flashing alarm going off inside my body and it's driving me insane.

I finally spot Alpha Maddox toward the back of the crush. He's got notes in his hand like he always does for his addresses at these things. He's also wearing a suit, like always. He's so damn tall that he dwarfs the guy next to him. I'm six feet tall myself and he towers over me. And while I've built muscle, the dude is just... massive. Not to mention that intimidating glare he likes to give. He's got that exact look on his face now as he whispers to an elite whose pack name is Knife.

Shit. I don't remember Alpha Maddox's real name. Is that going to matter? His pack name is Black—the irony of his name is that his wolf is pure white—but I don't recall his first name. Whatever. Stick to formal.

I stride closer and hear Black say the word "reinforcements."

"There aren't enough alphas for the numbers you want," Knife grumbles, scratching at a pockmark on his cheek. He's a balding guy, not attractive, but sharp-witted as fuck. Huh. I wonder if that's how he got his name.

"Use betas then. Just tell them they aren't allowed to shift."

Knife gives a brief nod and turns away, opening the door to one of the back offices that adjoins the main room.

I step forward to ask Alpha Maddox for his help but he turns and the airflow from that back office passes over him. Alpha Maddox's scent drags across my nose. And there, underneath his caramel and smoke smell … I can smell her.

Elena.

Alpha Maddox raises a brow at me in question.

I avert my eyes and mutter, “I was just … looking for someone. Sorry.”

I move away, my stomach now tumbling end over end. My palms grow slick with sweat.

Elena’s missing. But Alpha Maddox has her scent on him.

And not just any scent. I smelled her arousal, that sugar-sweet, mouthwatering scent I’ve become addicted to over the last several months.

The room grows a bit hazy and I have to blink hard to clear my vision.

It feels like someone’s taken an ax to my ribs. I’m pretty certain they’ve shattered inside my chest and little shards of them are stabbing every part of me.

My worst fear’s confirmed.

Elena’s shifted.

She’s left me.

10

ELENA

If a genie appeared right now ... I'd wish for him to cut off Black's balls and boil them while the man watched. No. I'd wish that my wolf was more alpha than Black's wolf and that he'd cower in front of me. But then I'd have to run the pack, which I'm pretty sure consists of a lot of day-to-day bullshit.

I scrunch my upper lip toward my nose in an expression that my mother abhors as I try to think of a wish that's bad enough for Black while I simultaneously search the basement for a way out. The only window near the ping pong table has bars over it so I don't even bother heading in that direction. Instead, I make my way to the bar, studying the wood wainscoting behind it.

I tap the wood with my knuckles and bend to listen to the sound of my own knocking. *Is that hollow? Would I even know what hollow sounds like? No. But, don't old houses always have secret passageways?* I slide my finger along the grooves but don't find any secret latches. *Damn you, Nancy Drew for giving me false hope!*

I sigh as I round the bar after unsuccessfully tapping the wall behind it. I sullenly grab one of the wine glasses Black poured for me and take a big, unladylike gulp. Immediately, the red wine explodes across the roof of my mouth with the warmth that always comes with good wine—that signal you're going to get a buzz really soon.

Getting tipsy sounds good right now, after the bullshit of this day and everything in it. It went from normal, then zoomed up to awesome before plunging into nearly the worst damn moment of my existence before doing a loop-de-loop causing a headrush of confusion. This day has been a roller coaster and frankly, I want off the ride.

I want out of here before Alpha Maddox comes back.

I call for my wolf inside my head, begging with her, pleading with her to show up. Maybe her teeth could mangle the door lock and get us out of here. But I hear nothing, not even the echo of a howl inside my head. I have no idea where she's hiding and no idea why. I wish I could hide too, rather than face Black again.

I don't want to show him how much I can kick his ass at raisin flicking. I don't want to see his dark brown eyes light up in annoyed amusement like before. In fact, I don't give a damn what that alpha thinks of me. He can rot in hell for the way he's treated me. My eyes drift to the ping pong table and land on the red paddle lying innocently on top. My throat tightens and so does my lower belly, but not in fear like they should.

I curse my body. The memory of his punishment shouldn't make me hot, it should make me furious. Normally it would, so what the hell's wrong with me? Why am I breathing hard just staring at a stupid paddle?

I briefly wonder if my wolf coming in has anything to do with my messed up reactions … pheromones are a big thing among wolves … but alpha wolves are supposed to hate submission. I close my eyes and search for my new gray-haired friend, wanting to puzzle it out with her, wanting her to explain it with mental pictures … mostly, I just want her to come back. I see a tiny flicker of something, but it's gone in less than a second. She's hiding or something … probably because Black scared the shit out of her, the bastard.

That's another reason I should hate him—my belly twists at the use of that word though. Hate is something I generally only reserve for one person. Should I really add him to that list?

"Fuck this," I say aloud, sick of my own internal ramblings, annoyed by how part of me wants to go grab that paddle and relive the memory while I touch myself. Black would definitely be able to scent if I did that so no fucking way. Plus, I'm not turning something humiliating into something hot. Not happening.

I try to swallow that lie as I stomp into the bedroom to see if there's another window in there, in case I might escape out of it. It's the one room I haven't really checked.

I flick on the light and glance over the beige walls, ignoring the neutral, clearly designer dark wood bedroom set. There is a window! A small but beautiful rectangle on the far side of the room. It's currently so dark outside that I can't tell if bars are blocking it off, but it's definitely bigger than the one in the storage room. I might be able to squeeze out.

I hurry toward it but stop short when I pass the en suite door. The scent nearly makes my knees buckle; the smell of Black, but not just him … there's sea salt tingeing the caramel and woodsmoke flavor that's swirling through my head making me dizzy, settling on my tongue so strongly I can almost taste it. I bring my hand to the bathroom door, which I'd just left open when I exited. I slowly close it, staring, wondering why the hell his scent is so strong in here as my eyes lock onto the white smears that coat the lower part of the door.

Fuck.

Instantly, I know he heard me in the shower. Black stood outside the door and touched himself while I … exorcised the demons he made possess my body. I clutch the doorknob so tightly that my palm hurts as heat flickers up my spine and my eyes zero in on the evidence of his crime. When my mouth waters, I freak the fuck out, because that is not a normal reaction to dried cum.

I drop the bathroom door handle and bolt from the bedroom like it's on fire. The problem is that the room isn't burning … I am. There's an intense set of flames crackling between my thighs and I'm desperate to put it out. I head for the only liquid in the room: The other glass of wine.

I down that sucker quickly and force my thoughts away from what Black must have looked like stroking himself, his huge hand around a cock that I'd tried very hard not to look at, but was so massive that my peripheral vision hadn't been able to completely deny its existence.

Shit! Shit! I don't want to be here thinking about the alpha's dick. Tears form in the corners of my eyes because everything has gone to shit since my wolf came in and right now I'm not sure I really want her.

A twinge of guilt hits me hard for thinking that—I've waited years for her. And she'd finally shown up. She didn't disappear until Black showed up. It was his fault.

I slam down my wine glass, doubly determined and slightly tipsy now because I definitely only ate half of that damned sandwich.

I am gonna run away from him and—for some reason my brain doesn't imagine running home to the house I grew up in. I've only stayed there because Mom required it until my wolf came in to protect me. Or so she says. Sometimes I think she just wants the live-in house cleaner because she's a slob. I blow out a bitter breath and stomp toward the stairs. I don't want to think about her. And I definitely don't want to analyze why I just pictured running straight to Jonah, his arms open wide and those bright blue eyes shining at me brighter than the moon.

Both of those are fucking pits I don't want to fall down.

Focus, Elena. Maybe we can find a blowtorch and burn down those bars. It's a pathetically unlikely hope but I find myself drawn closer to a small closet door near the stairs, wondering if there's something inside I can use. It's probably just got extra ping pong balls and sheets and stuff but who knows. Maybe another Harry Potter lives in there. *Oh, I am definitely buzzed.*

I wander toward the closet and stop near the air conditioning vent, craning my neck up to stare at it. Why, oh why do Black's vents have to be normal size? Why aren't they the industrial size that appears in every goddamned movie so that people can slither along in them like snakes?

I pull open the closet door and blow a full-on raspberry at the shelves when I see board games in there like Black is some normal guy and not a psychopath. I spit all over his games before slamming the door shut.

"I should have eaten more." I should have but I wasn't planning on drinking because I almost never drink. I take a deep breath and shake out my hands like I do before a race. I concentrate on my breathing … telling myself that this is a strategic run, a long race, one where I need to pace myself. I need to make the right moves, pull ahead at the right time, not just blast out immediately and burn off all my power at once.

My eyes drift to the stairs that lead upward. I haven't considered them because I heard Black lock a door at the top … but I can break through wood more easily than iron bars. Or try that hinge pin thing … again *Pirates of the Caribbean* is probably steering me wrong and this door won't pop open like Jack Sparrow's jail cell. But there's a shot. I'll probably be spotted, but I literally think that might be the only way out of here. "Stupid anti-fire code old house," I grumble to myself as I grab the handrail and start to make my way up the carpeted steps. I get to the top and turn the knob. As I expected, it's locked.

Motherfucker.

I hear the jangle of keys and the click of footsteps. I scramble back down the steps and hurry toward the bar, not wanting Black to catch me in the act. He might smell me, but I can always say I just sat on the stairs for a second or something.

But Black doesn't descend into my giant underground prison cell. His butler does.

Wearing a formal penguin suit, his gray hair slicked back and his back straight as a ruler, the man gives me a tight smile with his thin lips. He's carrying a picnic basket on his left arm that looks like something out of a spa magazine. It has a loofah, what looks like body wash, some towels, and a variety of other unidentifiable objects. He walks past me and I can't help but glance toward the stairs. Did he leave it unlocked? Could I make a run for it?

But the door is closed. Knowing Black, he gave orders to this guy to lock it.

"Hello. I'm Matthew."

I turn to see the butler smiling at me, his basket set down on one of the many recliners facing the huge flat screen to my left. The old man smiles at me expectantly and there's something about him that makes my edgy anger wane a bit. I don't typically think "welcoming" when I think about butlers, but this guy radiates warmth. His crow's feet crinkle as he says, "This would normally be where you introduce yourself."

I clear my throat and shift on my feet. Black didn't tell him my name? Why not? What does that mean? I try to shrug off the little voice second-guessing things inside my head as I extend my hand. "I'm Elena."

Matthew's shake is firm and strong despite the fact that he's got a few age spots on the back of his hand. I'd guess he's around seventy or so.

"So, you brought staples for the prisoner?" I gesture at the basket.

"I brought supplies for Alpha Maddox's lady," he replies evenly.

I want to laugh because Black definitely doesn't see me as his lady. But I don't laugh, I decide to use the moment to try to win Matthew over a little. Maybe … if I ask nicely, he'll hand over the key.

"How long have you been working here?" I ask casually, as I move closer to the basket, peering at what Matthew's tucked inside. There's a toothbrush and toothpaste—thank fuck—even a hairbrush with a new package of ties. I'm slightly impressed for a second before I realize that Black might wear ties in his own dark hair sometimes. But, hey, Matthew still gets credit for not being an utter ass. Unlike his boss.

"I've worked for Alpha Maddox for nearly five years." Matthew pulls at his cuff, straightening it.

I suck in a breath through my teeth in sympathy. "You've survived that long? You must be made of steel."

"No. You know, he comes off a bit gruff—"

"A bit?" I interject, tipsy me unable to help myself.

Matthew chuckles. "He's got a lot on his shoulders. But I've never once seen him shirk his duty. I've never seen him turn away someone in need. He even took me in after my wife passed."

"I'm sorry." I see grief crease Matthew's face for a moment before he gives me a wistful, regret-filled smile.

"You always think you'll have more time. We had thirty long years together, me and my Melva. But somehow, that still doesn't feel like enough. I still feel cheated. Robbed." He swallows hard and waves a hand as if to dismiss his emotions. "You got me off-topic. I was supposed to come down here and take your measurements."

I furrow my brow until I see him bring out a soft tape measure and a pen with a small square of paper. Then I take a step back.

"Whoa. What?"

"Mr. Maddox has asked me to get your measurements so that I can order some clothes," he repeats patiently as if I'm hard of hearing.

I heard what he said perfectly, I just don't understand it. "Why would I need clothes?"

Oh god. He's not going to let me go.

Ribbons of fear and lust lace up my neck and tie themselves together into a knot at the base of my throat.

Black Maddox is going to hold me prisoner. Panic blurs my vision for a second and heat floods my cheeks as I stare at the ballpoint pen in this man's hand. I could stab him in the neck … steal his keys … escape.

What the fuck is wrong with me? I turn my eyes down, disgusted with myself for even thinking something like that. It's something my mother would think. And I swore a long time ago that I'd never fucking end up like her. "Why the hell would I need to *order clothes*?" I ask again thinking about Black's dark eyes. Before he'd left, he'd been almost playful and I'd been so shocked by that side of him that I hadn't even thought to question why he'd still locked me down here. Maybe the clothes are a bribe? Maybe it's not because I'm a prisoner but for some other reason. Now that we're past the whole "Dark Night Pack" fiasco, he'll want to have me sign some papers or something—make a promise not to sue him for defending pack territory or whatever, right?

But cash would be just fine.

Cash would be great, actually.

Clothes ... are weird.

I don't understand.

"I don't need clothes."

"I don't need a lot of things, but I do need this job, Miss Elena," Matthew parries. "Part of keeping this job involves following orders, be it the fact that Alpha Maddox likes me to put two tablespoons of disgusting raspberry flavoring into his coffee or—"

"He likes raspberry? What guy likes raspberry?" I ask, curiosity getting the best of me. That little tidbit derails my train of thought.

Matthew just raises an eyebrow at me. "Oh, the things I could tell you."

That ... definitely sounds like a bribe. I grind my back teeth together as I stare into Matthew's twinkling eyes and he waits patiently, knowing he's hooked me.

Dammit.

"Fine. I don't want you to lose your job," I sigh, giving a fake roll of my eyes as if I'm put out.

"Glad to hear it." He comes forward and quickly puts the tape up on my left shoulder, measuring down to my elbow before making a mark on his little square of paper.

I try to be patient, wait for him to bring up some new topic, so I can segue it into knowledge that might help me figure out Black's motives. But he doesn't say a word, just measures to my fingertips, and then wraps the tape around my wrist. He's smart. He's not going to give me anything I don't explicitly ask for. Dammit though. I hardly know where to start. It needs to seem innocuous.

"So, if Black likes raspberry coffee, does that mean he has a sweet tooth?"

"Alpha Maddox is very disciplined. But, if I had to say, I think white chocolate-covered pretzels are his favorite."

"Sweet and salty," I say aloud, though internally, I'm telling my brain to come up with something more clever. Something useful. I very much doubt I can buy Black's goodwill with some damn pretzels. But Matthew mentioned discipline. That is similar to my mother. Discipline and structure ... control. Alphas love that shit.

"Does he ever do anything to relax?" Maybe if I can get him relaxed.

Matthew raises a brow and gives me a look that makes me blush fire engine red. "Besides *that*."

The old man clucks his tongue, thinking as he slides the tape gently around my waist. "Well, he does like leatherworking."

"That's a thing?"

Matthew chuckles. "Yes."

"But..." I trail off trying to picture it.

"He creates images and imprints them into wallets or belts or journals."

"Who still uses wallets?" I ask, mostly aiming for a chuckle from Matthew—whom I've decided is a bit of a sweetheart—but simultaneously filing that information away. I don't think it can possibly be useful ever, but who the hell knows? I tuck a strand of still-damp hair behind my ear as the old man struggles to bend to one knee and measure from my waist to my ankle. "Can I do that for you?"

He waves me off. "I'm spry. I do yoga."

My jaw drops when I see the old man move to sit criss-cross applesauce so that he can measure my lower half. Unlike most men, whose knees end up around their ears when they try to sit that way, Matthew's knees are nearly parallel to the carpet.

"Yoga?" I question, intrigued.

"I'd say I go for my health but … the views are pretty damn good. Friend Charlie got me into it. Every couple of classes, one of us gets a muscle spasm." He gives me a naughty grin. "Those are the best days."

I full-on belly laugh, probably ruining a few of his measurements as I picture the pair of them pretending to tweak their back so that all the women in the class will fawn over them. Suddenly, Matthew morphs from a butler into the kind of grandfather I always imagined, never having met my own. Sweet. Fun. Pushing the envelope a little. "If you ever need a yoga buddy, like Charlie can't make it or something…"

Matthew pushes off the floor to his knees and then stands. He gives me a wink. "The day that Charlie misses a class is the day he's dead. You can join us sometime, if…" he trails off and his eyes dart to the side.

"I would love to see you in action," I tell him.

But he's moving around me before I finish the sentence.

I turn, only to see someone new on the stairs, a man with tawny brown hair and narrowed eyes, wearing jeans and a light blue t-shirt.

He's a wolf—I know instantly by his smell, a sharp grapefruit and vodka bite to his scent—and an alpha at that. Underneath his normal scent is an iron tang. Blood.

I rush around Matthew toward the other man, asking, "Are you okay?" I realize there's a bandage wrapped tightly around his chest; I can make out the bulge underneath his shirt.

Instantly, the guy on the stairs flares his nostrils to scent me. His eyes dilate and he doesn't blink as he steps off the final step, heading toward me. His breathing grows ragged and I see his teeth turn to fangs.

Something is very, very wrong with him.

I backpedal toward Matthew, turning my head to make sure the old butler is out of this guy's path.

But the stranger doesn't focus on the butler. His eyes never leave me. I see a flash of gold and realize that his wolf is close to the surface.

Shit.

What do I do? I try to think back to things my dad told me. Palms out, head tilted to the side for submission. Avoid eye contact.

"Fuck." Matthew yanks a cell phone out of his pants and lifts it to his ear. "Cody came downstairs. No!" Matthew smashes a button on the phone and I hear Black's voice roar through the speaker.

"Cody, get upstairs now. Get in bed and do not leave until morning." The alpha tone of his command is undeniable—even my back hunches and my ears come to my shoulders, though I'm not the one getting yelled at.

Cody shakes in his spot, clearly torn, his thick hands clenching and unclenching. He takes a shuffling step closer to me, his nose twitching as he inhales again.

Matthew speaks into the phone. "Again. He needs more."

Black yells into the phone. "Cody, turn around. Now. If you take one more step, I'm going to consider that a direct challenge."

Cody's eyes clench shut and I watch him grit his fangs until slowly they retract. He turns and bounds up the stairs, a groan ripping from his lips as he clutches at his chest. But he doesn't stop running.

"Is he gone?" Black asks, his own breathing heavy, like he's running.

"Yes, he went upstairs."

"Lock her in the bathroom. Tell her to get in the tub and use all that damned bodywash. Lock the bedroom. The basement. His room. I'll be back in ten."

Shock rolls through me.

"What the fuck is going on?" My hands fly to my hair. I always knew that becoming a wolf came with strange side effects. My dad always warned me that once my wolf came, life would never be the same. But I'm surrounded by chaos and no one is explaining a damn thing.

Matthew just hangs up the phone and shoves the basket in my hands, his eyes wide. "Please, Elena."

I swallow hard and hurry into the bathroom with the basket clutched to my chest. The tiles feel cold on my feet and when I look into the mirror, my cheeks have grown pale. I glance back at Matthew.

"I'm sorry, but it's for your safety. Cody's not himself right now. Well, neither is..." Matthew cuts himself off before shutting and locking the door and I'm ninety percent certain he was going to say that Black Maddox isn't himself either. I sink down on the tiles, wishing I'd brought one of the bottles of wine in here with me.

Is every male shifter insane?

No. Jonah isn't, I remind myself. But right now, Jonah seems a million miles away. I'm locked in the alpha's basement with no idea when he'll release me. If he'll release me.

My hand tightens around the basket handle. No. Bull-shit. I'm not going to wait for Black's go ahead—he's obviously just as unstable as that other shifter who wandered into the basement. Black might have the upper hand right now, but he's got weaknesses. And I just made a friend who might be able to help me exploit them.

11

BLACK

I'M NOT sure which emotion wrecks me more—fear or rage. Alphas can lose their shit around omegas, the pheromones can drive our wild side to darkness, depravity. Unmated omegas are fucking dangerous things—temptation and ruination rolled into one. I should know. I'm about to break all the damn rules to make her mine.

Elena's face filters through my head, the soft curve of her cheeks, her sharp chin, the spark in those gray eyes.

Fuck. I never should have left her nor assumed that the sedatives from the hospital would keep Cody knocked out until I got back from the howl. I just should have skipped the fucking howl.

Arrogance is the only explanation for my stupidity—that or ignorance—and I'm furious with myself for letting either of them get the best of me. I pride myself on thinking straight, thinking things through … but I hadn't been able to spend another minute in that house with my elites trying to subtly adjust themselves as they caught her scent through the vents, watching their eyes dilate even as they pretended to listen to me and agree with my plan to defend her from Stone, my plan to keep her instead of handing her over.

I'd seen the truth in their eyes, smelled it in the aggressive eagerness that wafted off them as they heard that we had a damned omega in our ranks … if I would have stayed, it wouldn't have ended well either. I would have had to fight one or even all of them. My wolf would have demanded it.

As it is, I'm not sure how everything is going to go down for Cody.

My fingers flex and I grab the neck of the gray Lobos sweatsuit I'm wearing, yanking on the cotton piece of shit because the damn things shrink in the wash and my neck swells when I'm irritated.

Pluto drives, flooring the gas, while I sit in the passenger seat of his Audi, fists clenched as I try to tell my wolf a damned car is gonna get him there faster than his own four feet.

"Mate," he growls at me, pissed. His snow-white fur bristles and I can see him pacing, teeth clenched, head low—like he's ready for a fight.

"Yeah, I know. But we have to make it official," I retort out loud.

Pluto side-eyes me but doesn't ask. Among alphas, it's not uncommon to have your wolf instincts go to war against your human ones. It's why the Lobos host weekly fights for the alpha wolves and why rank is doled out numerically, constantly changing based on the outcomes of those matches. Some wolves hate it, others love it ... but the hints of blood and victory keep the feral side satisfied. That makes our pack more stable than most, our alphas less prone to violence—keeps our betas safer.

I glance outside as everything but the stars streak by in a blur. Only the sky is constant. The moon goddess stares down at me and I feel her reprimand for leaving Elena in danger as sharp as my own mother's tongue would have been. An old memory resurfaces, of her face, hands cupping my cheeks, wiping away a drop of blood from a fight I'd gotten in at school, a fight I hadn't won, because back then I hadn't had my wolf for backup.

"That girl isn't your mate, Tommy. She's trash for even looking at another guy. You shouldn't have fought over her." She'd pulled me in for a hug, and I recall how her hands were slightly rough because they were covered in flour. Even now I associate the scent of flour with her—she was always baking. She'd whispered in my ear, "Someday, you'll find your mate. And you'll just know. Your wolf will just know. It will be like magic. Until that day, no girl is worth fighting for." She'd pulled back from me but kept a grip on my shoulders as her eyes had flickered between my own. "You hear me?"

Thinking of mothers makes me remember Elena's. Her pack profile had said that my mate's father was gone, but Kathryn DeMarkus is still very much alive. And I'd planned to speak with her, do the whole antiquated 'ask her permission' routine. It's what Mom would have wanted.

"Fuck. I didn't get to speak with her mother." My hand slams onto the dash and I hear Pluto suck in a breath because this car is his baby.

"You can do it tomorrow," Pluto suggests as he floors it and takes a corner and I have to use my feet to brace myself so I don't grab onto the bitch handle as my stomach slides into my ribs.

"Stone wants to get her tomorrow," I retort, fury filling me at the thought of his grimy old paws touching Elena's soft skin. My wolf snarls and my vision changes for a millisecond, sharpening, before I wrangle him back into a corner of my mind. Stone will never touch her so long as I'm still breathing. No way.

She's ours, I tell my wolf.

His lips still peel back and reveal a deadly set of teeth, his white fur still expands.

"Well, those fucking rules about trading omegas are outdated. I already told you that during our elite meeting. There hasn't been one for generations ... not since the fucking purge. We can't just give her—"

"We?" I turn to glare at him, feeling my wolf so close to the surface that I'm surprised fur doesn't erupt on my arms. I turn in my seat so that my shoulder is pressed against the back and stare at the man I've thought of as a best friend for nearly a decade as dark thoughts swoop through my heads like black crows.

One of Pluto's pale hands lifts off the wheel and he holds it up, palm out, trying to placate me. "Calm, man. I meant the pack. Not we as in me. Trust me, I smelled you when you came out of that forest. You'll fight to the death for this girl, which means I'm not interested."

"You'd better not be," I growl, unable to let it drop. He hasn't shown me his neck or dropped his eyes to the ground. The logical side of me knows that he can't—he's driving right now, but the feral side of me wants to smash his nose in and make sure his wolf matches his words—submissive, compliant, backing the fuck away.

"I'm not. She's gorgeous, so don't rip my dick off if you scent shit. But you know I've got a lockdown on my wolf better than that. Better than yours." He couldn't help the jab, an ongoing thing.

My wolf growls but I tell him to shut the hell up because we're home. I see my house through the trees, and while my eyes normally roam to the upper windows and my room whenever I return, tonight they're drawn to the base at of the front stairs as if I can peer beneath the stone steps and see her. The porch light is on, waiting for me, a little tradition Matthew has always kept, that I've never appreciated until this moment.

"Look up options." I bark at Pluto before hopping out of the car that's still moving, ignoring Pluto's curse, and hurrying inside. Matthew meets me in the foyer, his brow wrinkled in consternation.

"I want a raise—"

"Done," I reply, even as my eyes stray to the basement door, which is locked again, now with a chair shoved up against it. A book sits on the floor beside the chair and I have no doubt that my human butler placed himself in harm's way to protect my girl from Cody. That lights my heart up in a way it hasn't for years, not since my mother passed away.

"Well done, Matthew. Double your salary. And take a couple hours on the jet. Go somewhere nice with one of those flexible ladies you like."

Matthew snorts but I shake my head, marveling both at the set of balls Matthew's got and the fact that the issue with Elena is so damned precarious. I'm pissed that I let it come to this, my butler protecting my mate. He's human and as such has nothing to fear from my shifters; a Lobo who attacks a human forfeits not only their own life but their entire family's. Cody knows that. The strong aren't meant to exploit the weak—that's been the motto for generations here.

I can't help but feel a twinge of sour guilt thinking of that because I definitely want to exploit every weakness Elena has to get her to bow to my will, turn that ferocity burning in her eyes into a different kind of fire, the kind stoked by my fingers, my lips, my dick.

I need to mate her, marry her, and mark her soon. My wolf howls in approval at all those thoughts, an image of Elena's little wolf racing beside mine underneath the moonlight appears in my head. She needs to become mine in every damned way. Or else I won't just be worried about Stone—one of my own alphas might challenge me for her. Tonight proves it. If Cody came down here with sedatives still in his system, then the call of her scent is more dangerous than I realized.

My teeth grow slightly sharper, nicking my tongue, and my wolf threatens to come out at the thought of anything jeopardizing our claim on our Elena. I want to shove him aside, but that will only end up in a battle for dominance over this body—a fight I've lost before. So instead, I soothe him.

I tell my wolf, "You can smell her right? She's safe down there, slathered in bubble bath crap." I speak in front of Matthew but not to him, walking just a few steps away from him and closer to the basement door, letting his senses eclipse my own for a second so that the smells become sharper. Cody's scent hits my nostrils first and a tiny growl escapes my throat at the blatant musk of interest he emitted.

After that, Matthew's scent—some awful combination of fresh soap and anise from his cologne, which I always tell him smells like he mixed together Brussel sprouts and black licorice. Does he care? Of course not, the man just grins, knowing he cooks well enough that I'll keep his stinky old ass around no matter what. He probably buys that nasty shit on purpose.

I sniff again and finally detect Elena's scent, that smell that hits my sweet tooth just right. But there's a salty note of fear to her scent and, for some reason, my dick hardens at that—probably because that was how she smelled during our chase in the woods earlier—though I absolutely hate the thought of anyone else scaring her.

She's so damned young. And innocent. Part of my mind wants to add corruptible to that statement but another part chimes in first with precious. God, this omega is twisting me up ... I need to fuck her and erase this angsty bullshit from my system.

My wolf gives a pant of agreement before retreating and letting me bolt up the stairs two at a time as Pluto enters the foyer from the side, having parked his precious car in the garage. I hear the soft thud of his footsteps behind mine on the carpet runner as he follows me. He's always got my back.

I walk through the hall confidently without flicking on the light but realize perhaps I should have when I hear a thud and Pluto curses, having stubbed a toe on a vase.

“Motherfucking dammit! Why the hell are we being stealthy in your own goddamned house?" he curses, never one to hold back when he gets hurt, a tendency that makes him easy to tease, but a habit he just can't seem to break no matter how much I jab him.

"Well, we aren't stealthy anymore," I mock as I try the knob on the third bedroom down the hall. I'd tried to have Cody put farther back so that Elena's scent wouldn't be as prevalent, but I should have known better. Maybe I shouldn't even have brought him here at all, but I always have my wolves recover here—always give them the best care, especially if they're hurt in service to the pack. It would have been wrong to deny him. A new lock system might be in order though.

I push open the door to the gold room—the damned decorator themed all the guest bedrooms by color or some such ridiculousness. There's a dark four-poster bed dominating a massive shag rug. I spot Cody laying in bed shirtless, the white-and-gold striped covers shoved carelessly down to his waist, the bandages on his ribs in full view. He's shoved aside the curtain so that the moonlight shines down on his face, which is relaxed and peaceful, a little smile edging the corners of his mouth. I realize that Matthew has strung up some thin silver wire around all four posts—not a ton, but enough to force a wolf to think twice, enough to make them try to jump over the wire, a feat that would be difficult with broken ribs. Something Cody doesn't even know about yet because he's dead asleep, a snore escaping from his lips.

Dammit.

I realize that part of me had been hoping he was still awake so I could rip him a new one, lay into him for trespassing, for scaring my fucking mate—now all the tension buzzing around inside me like a swarm of hornets has nowhere to go. My fists clench as I glance over at Pluto.

"Not it," he declares, raising his hands in the air. "Not gonna let you kick my ass when you look like that."

I grind my teeth together in annoyance and jerk my head toward the doorway before stomping down the hall and all the way back downstairs.

I shove open the door to my office roughly and head first for the bourbon, which is on a sideboard on the opposite side of the room from my bookshelf.

A portrait of my parents smiles down on me as I pour myself a double shot and down it quickly, reveling in the burn as the liquid feels like someone tossed a match down my throat.

Hoping it will help take effect quickly and dull a bit of my agitation, I move toward my desk, flick on my computer, and pull up a copy of our treaty with the Dark Nights … a treaty my predecessor created but I'd agreed to because I hadn't fucking had any omegas in my possession at the time. It hadn't meant anything. I grind my teeth together as I read for a few minutes, looking for loopholes, hoping that one will just pop out at me.

Pluto slides into the guest chair across from my desk, crossing his legs casually and leaning on one arm as he swipes at a tablet he's grabbed, doing the same thing I am. A few minutes of silence stretch between us before he weighs in. "Treaty terms are pretty solid. I mean, Dark Nights are going to be furious if you do this."

He's stating the obvious and I debate throwing my paperweight at him. But it's a pewter wolf from my father, so I don't.

"There's no *if* we are doing this. She's mine." I lean back from my computer screen and my vision brightens for a second as the feral side of my mind takes over. A lightning storm erupts inside my head, jagged fury followed by a loud crack of wild don't-give-a-fuck.

Pluto holds up a hand. "I know. I'm just saying. Unless she's pregnant or something..."

A wide grin spreads across my face and Pluto freezes. His eyes go round as his mouth gapes for a second before he gives a little shake of his head. "Omegas have to go into heat in order to get pregnant."

I crack my knuckles and roll my shoulders, calm confidence sliding over me like a cloak. I'm almost giddy at this solution. The idea of rutting pretty Elena again and again, of watching her pussy gape as my cum runs down her thighs, makes me feel drunk. This is probably the best possible news I've ever heard in my life, including when it was announced I won the fight to become alpha. My tongue runs over my lips unbidden. "Pregnancy will really do the trick?"

"I...think so?"

I snag my phone from my pocket and shoot off a text to Stone. *She has a fever. Doctor here. Might need a few days before hand-off. Nothing major.*

Instantly, I get a reply. *You'd better not be fucking with me, otherwise our little clashes in disputed territory will seem like a picnic. By treaty, the omega is mine.*

I'll send you a doctor's note, just like in elementary school.

No. I'll send a doctor. Or better yet, come myself to get her.

Sounds good. Hopefully she's contagious. If you die, it will be easy to take over your pack.

With all the sons this little omega is going to give me, I'd be more worried about your own.

Oops. Didn't I mention it? She's already pregnant?

I toss the phone on the desk and it skitters across the surface before settling with a clunk. Let Stone blow it up with text messages wondering if I'm fucking with him or not. I don't give a shit. By the time I'm done with Elena, she's going to be so sore she will need bed rest. I'll also fill her belly with so much of my cum that I make both my lies a reality.

Then I lean down toward Pluto, expression as deadly as a knife. "Make sure you know so."

I turn and stride to the office door.

"Where are you going? I thought we were researching this shit!" he exclaims, turning in his seat to watch me.

I glance back as I grab the door frame and I give him a wolfish grin. "I'm going to go send my little omega into her first heat."

12

ELENA

MY ENTIRE BODY aches as if I've run a marathon … I've decided that I hate tile floors. When I have my own house, I'm ripping out all the tile. I don't give a shit how practical it is to clean, being trapped in the bathroom for hours has made me hate it. Piling the bath rugs together and the towels on top didn't do a damned thing to make any of it softer. My hips are sore, my ass is sore...though I don't know if that's entirely from the tiles. A little red paddle might be slightly responsible for that.

I roll onto my back, close my eyes, and raise my hips off the ground, trying to ease the ache in my spine. Sleeping naked in the bathroom is going on my list of "never again." I lift my hips a little further until I feel a delicious pop in my back.

That's when the door flies open and Black appears, a loud purr echoing through the room immediately and dazing me for a second.

"Now, this is how I want to be greeted whenever I walk into a room," he grins, his eyes not even bothering to travel up to my face, just feasting on my pussy. Gold flickers through his irises for a second, as if his wolf is close to the surface.

The shock of seeing him there wears off, quickly replaced by embarrassment as I scramble to my feet. "Your house is worse than a fucking jail cell. Seriously? A bathroom?" Irritation helps hide my embarrassment when I bend to grab a towel to hide my nudity, though he's seen it all already anyway. I wrap it quickly around myself and clench it tight, part of me wishing I was clenching Black's neck instead. How I'd like to throttle him.

"Seems like you were having a good time in here," he shrugs one of his massive shoulders as he steps into the room, instantly making it feel small and crowded as his scent drifts over to me and causes a very unwanted shiver down my spine. He gives another purr and the sound vibrates through me as if I just straddled a running motorcycle. I can feel it in my thighs.

"I was stretching," I defend myself. "Because I've been forced to sleep on a tile floor! By you!"

Black's eyes dance. "Is that what you call it these days? Stretching? I'll help you stretch, Elena."

I want to spit in his face but he's grabbed my wrist and pulled me in front of him before I can even blink.

We stand at the counter in front of the sinks and I stare into the mirror as he holds me with one arm pinned behind my back, my other hand clutching the towel. The contrast is intense. He's massive compared to me, his skin a rich, ruddy brown against my pale skin. His biceps are three or four times as big as mine, even our eyes are polar opposites ... his, a dark chocolate so deep that they almost look black, mine a soft dove gray. We look like we come from different worlds, except for our hair. We both have dark hair. And we're both stubborn as fuck. That's where all our common traits end, however, because I will never let myself be an alpha like him. Not ever. I won't allow myself to be so smugly certain or fucking lock-up total strangers like a psychopath.

“Do I get to leave now?” I bite out gruffly, making Black's eyes rise to meet mine. His smile spreads slowly and makes me swallow hard because, while it doesn't look evil, it does look intent—purposeful—and that makes goose bumps pop out along my arms.

“You don't get to leave. But you do get to come.”

I watch, frozen, when his hand comes up to the top of the white towel I'm clamping against my body. *Did he really just say that?*

"That's the worse fucking line I've ever heard. Did that actually work *back in your day*?" I enjoy the way Black's brow descends at that jab but I quickly change to another more pressing topic. "What happened to psycho shifter?"

"He's tucked away in bed."

Rage blinds me for a millisecond. "*He* gets a bed?" I try to turn in anger, but Black's grip is too strong.

"He was attacked by Dark Nights defending you and I had Matthew put you in here for your own protection—"

"I'd be safer anywhere but this house full of insane alphas." It takes a second before I register the previous part of Black's statement. "Wait. Defending me? From fucking what?"

Black doesn't answer and when I look up at his reflection, his eyes have strayed from my face down to the swells of my breasts. His thick fingers close over mine on the towel and he leans down, his neck curving until his lips hover near my ear.

"Elena," he whispers my name and all the fury and annoyance that just filled me seems to evaporate.

Maybe they turned to steam because the space between our bodies suddenly feels as hot as a fire.

I step sideways to get away, but he fills the gap quickly and I find myself trapped between the countertop and his body, pressed tighter, the rough planes of muscle press against my back and I can feel them even through the layers of clothing, and well, towel in my case, that separate us. His dick presses firmly against my spine and I inhale sharply, unable to speak, when his hand drifts down to my towel and slowly plucks it out of my fingers.

I ... what? What's happening?

I want to run but I can't. I'm captive ... captivated by the way his massive hand slides across my nipple, the rough callouses teasing my sensitive skin, making it harden. His grip moves down and I watch his reflection as he cups my breast, feeling the weight of it, eliciting tiny shivers from me as he drags his thumb over the softness there.

"Get your hands off me," I try to snarl, but he tweaks my nipple and I gasp, erasing any of the harshness in my tone. I call for my wolf, but she's gone. Long gone. She's smarter than me. She's hiding from this alpha predator, while I'm caught up, dazed by hormones or maybe the alpha command in his voice.

"I'll take my hands off," Black replies, dropping my breast roughly so that I feel the full weight of it bouncing, see how hard he's made my nipple. "But then I'm going to have to use my tongue." Immediately, his mouth dives down toward my neck and I watch his teeth sink roughly into the junction of my neck and shoulder.

All thoughts are erased from my mind like it's a whiteboard as his bite turns on some primal portion of my mind that I didn't know existed. My toes curl into the tiles and my head automatically arches to give him more access. Black's tongue dances across my skin and I slowly realize he's spelling his name on me.

I try to rile up the fury to call him a caveman but his teeth skim down my spine and liquefy my protests. They come out as soft moans.

I'm not certain what's happening to me, why I'm *letting* this happen. I shouldn't be. I should be shoving him away. *He's an alpha, the worst of all alphas. He threw me down here, locked me in...*

He purrs as his tongue slides down the curve of my ass, tracing the underside and I shock myself when I find my legs suddenly spread. Some dim part of my mind shouts as if from across the house, *I don't like alphas. I don't sleep with alphas.* But that voice is muted. Though I fell asleep declaring my eternal hatred for— "Black," I whimper his name when his tongue glides over the back half of my pussy and he gently starts to lap at me.

The sensation is soft and sweet, unlike everything else about him, except for his scent, the scent that swirls around me and settles on my tongue like the most expensive liquor … is that why I'm letting him touch me? Am I drunk on his heady combination of caramel and woodsmoke? Or is it sound? I wonder when he purrs once more and it makes his tongue vibrate gently against my opening.

I blink, dazed, and slide forward until I see my breasts dangling, arching my back so Black can get a better angle. In the mirror, my eyes are heavy-lidded and I look the picture of feminine sensuality. "I still hate you." I finally manage to breathe out some of my vitriol and feel smug for a second before his tongue stops lapping at me and I want to curse myself for hurling the insult before I got an orgasm. Double stupid.

Black chuckles darkly. "You won't after I melt your mind, princess."

He so certain, so arrogant, that I can't help but grind my teeth. "Doubtful, old man. Alphas are too full of themselves to be good lovers."

I should have expected the smack to my ass, but I didn't. I'm surprised by the sting and even more surprised by how turned on I am when I see Black stand, mouth glistening from where he licked me, eyes narrowed in fury on my reflection, anger just as piercing as if I faced him head-on.

"I'm going to enjoy proving you wrong."

"I'm sorry ... did you stop so that you could grab a little blue pill? I don't understand why we're talking. Someone half your age wouldn't—"

Black gives a low growl as he picks me up and stomps from the bathroom. He throws me onto the bed hard and I laugh as I bounce. "Need to go get a ping pong paddle again and spank me? Come on, *Alpha*, don't you like a little challenge?" It's as if there were a dam inside of me that's suddenly broken loose and angry words are gushing past my lips unrestrained now. And they have absolutely nothing to do with wanting to get out of here. Because suddenly, I don't necessarily want to run. At least not this second. I want to bring Black Maddox to his knees, get him right on the cusp of an orgasm, and then rip it away. I want to dominate him and make him feel as small as he's made me feel.

If sex is going to be my weapon, so be it. He's clearly desperate for it. And I ... I lie to myself saying I can maintain a clear head ... because the second his body dives on top of mine and his forearms cage in either side of my head I become breathy and light-headed. Black leans down and sucks a nipple into his mouth, drawing out a spark of pleasure that's so bright I'm nearly blinded by the burst of red behind my eyelids. He suckles as one of his giant hands slowly caresses down the front of my body, pressing me deeply into the mattress, holding me down, and worshiping me with soft touches at the very same moment.

It's far too easy for him to control me with touch, I realize, as his thick fingers drag over my sensitive opening. So I retaliate the only way I can, determined to get the most out of this one-night-stand before I leave him high and dry. I yank on Black's long hair until his mouth pops off of my breast and I lean up, biting his lower lip with all my strength.

His counterattack is vicious. He uses his broad fingers to separate my pussy, stroking gently along the lips until my legs splay open and I can't resist gasping, releasing my furious bite, though I can taste the tiny metallic tang of blood. Black doesn't even seem pissed about it, he just grins down at me and his stare grows intense; it burns into me as his fingers continue to trail over my most sensitive spot. Fuck. It feels like sparklers. Tiny sparks, hints of deliciousness. But I want the full goddamned fireworks show.

I try to raise my hips to increases the sensation. but Black's other hand comes and pins my pelvis in place.

"I'm playing."

"I don't want to play."

"Too bad, little wolf."

My eyelashes flutter and falling stars flash past my eyes when his finger drags up over my clit. But he doesn't linger. With a growl, I run one of my hands down my body, ready to finish what he started so that my freakin' mind will return to normal and I can get the hell out of Dodge.

"NO!" His command is deep and dark as he uses his leg to block my access to my own pussy.

"I was going to stroke your cock," I lie smoothly.

He chuckles. "Liar."

"Well, I don't really think I owe you the truth, *kidnapper,*" I retort.

"Protector," he counters. "Do you know what would have happened if those Dark Night scouts would have found you instead?" His smile fades and his look grows somber, his eyes glancing between mine with something indefinable, something akin to regret. We stare, connected by his glance and that unnameable emotion for a second before he breaks the moment and his lips dive for my throat. I expect another bite, another name spelling, something dominant. But his lips trace feather-soft kisses over my pulse and the fingers at my pussy stop their teasing and begin slow figure-eights over my clit.

Oh, this. This is what I needed.

"More," I tell him. "I like circles better—"

"Elena—" he warns. "This pussy is mine. And I'm going to touch it however I want to touch it. That means if I want to do this—" He spreads my pussy lips apart and gently strokes a slow circle over the entire circumference that makes my blood boil. "Or if I want to do this…" Black trails off as his fingers close slowly over my clit and gently pinches it, then tugs it rhythmically, pulling it over and over again until the ceiling light overhead blurs and my breathing becomes as shallow as the lacy fringe of the sea.

I float away on a cloud of sensation. Bliss takes me to another plane as Black works my body higher and higher into oblivion—into a space where his wrongs don't seem to matter as much, just for a minute.

When I'm on the edge, my thighs trembling, mouth opening and closing in soft musical moans, he shoves two fingers into me. I erupt with a scream that Black devours when his lips travel back to mine. The white ceiling of the room becomes streaked with black as my vision flickers. I fist the comforter in my hands, distorting the cotton into clouds as fuzzy as my thoughts. The room fills with the scent of me and I grind against Black's palm, trying to drag out the sensation. He helps me, thrusting in gently but regularly, dragging the pads of his fingers in ways that make me shudder.

When I collapse down against the mattress, I lean my head back against the pillow to catch my breath. Black leans on his side, still fully clothed, slowly removing his fingers from inside me and then bringing them to his lips. He licks them clean as he gives me a very smug alpha look, reminding me exactly why I should have hit him instead of letting him touch me in the first place.

I debate it—the idea of letting my fist fly and catching him off guard is immensely satisfying. But as the alpha who reigns over all the Lobos, he can make my life a living hell … fuck. "I'm going to have to find a new pack," I say, sitting up in bed, the realization sudden and harsh.

"Whoa. What the fuck?" Black sits up next to me immediately, but I don't look at him as I stand.

"Thanks for the orgasm, for ruining my life as I know it, and basically being an all-around asshole," I give him a little nod as I walk, nude, toward the bedroom door. "Here's to never seeing each other again." I reach for the handle, counting on the fact that all the clothes that Matthew had brought down in that basket are still in the basement's rec room and that crazy shifter from earlier is gone.

Black's hand slams into the door just above my head. I yank on the door anyway, though his full body weight presses into it and the wood doesn't give an inch, as if it's as beholden to him as the pack is. When his other hand grabs me and drags me back against him, it isn't gentle.

"You aren't fucking going anywhere, Elena. Not now. Not ever. You're my mate."

His words rip across me like someone yanking duct tape from my mouth and a harsh laugh spills from my lips. Disbelief, shock, and a resounding hell no reverberate through my bones. "Your mate? Bullshit. Nice try." I wriggle, trying to escape the prod of his erection. "There is no such fucking thing as a fated mate. Wolves choose their mates. And I sure as hell am not accepting you."

This time, it's Black's laugh that's dark as it pours into my ear like poison. "Accepting me? No, little princess. You don't get to accept me. You're a fucking omega. I'm an alpha. I'm claiming you. And there's nothing you can do about it."

13

BLACK

My dick is hard as granite, the knot at the base aching as I stare down at Elena, whose breath catches, making those dusky nipples of hers rise slightly and her ass move a tiny bit against my swollen cock. The shifter side of me wants to do nothing more than hold her in place and rut her from behind, fucking up into that soft heat I just felt clamp around my fingers. But the man in me knows that if I do that, she'll hate me. And while I'm interested in a hate fuck from her … I'm not interested in pure hatred. So instead of grabbing onto her hips, I put my palm on her shoulder and slowly turn her to face me, biting back a need that's more intense than any I've ever felt before.

She looks so small there in front of the door, her shoulder thin enough to fit easily into my palm. Small and delicate. "I told you that a shifter's reality is ugly.

This is yours." My voice comes out rough and husky instead of understanding like I meant it to ... I sound like an asshole instead of someone who sympathizes. Shit. I try again. "When I found out I was an alpha, and not just any alpha but a strong one, my life became a blur of fights. Sometimes ... life throws things at you that you don't expect. Or want. But they are what they are and you have to face them head-on."

Her eyes flash at me and her hand comes to my chest—she tries to shove me away. I take a step back, letting her have this space ... for now.

"I'm not a fucking omega, you dickhead!" Elena's features contort until she looks feral, wild, almost unhinged, even more so than she did earlier.

I chuckle. "We both know that's not true."

She uses both hands to push me again, this time taking me off guard, forcing me back a step in the plush carpet toward the bed. "Fuck you! My mom's an alpha wolf and so am I!"

"You're the farthest thing from an alpha wolf there is," I tell her. Disbelief and confusion color outside the lines of reality, turning my mind into a mess of scribbles. How can she not know? The second my wolf came in, I knew.

"Your parents don't determine what kind of wolf you become," I try to speak gently, holding up my hands to calm her when she starts to pace, grabbing at her white-streaked hair, clearly agitated. Goddammit, this is not the reaction I expected. Most girls would kill to be an omega, to be valued and treasured above all others…to be capable of starting a war between men who beat at their chests and beg to give them multiple orgasms a day.

Elena gives a laugh that's as bitter and broken as a shattered beer bottle … and just as dangerous. "Oh, I know that. Just like I know parents don't determine the person you become." She stops pacing and stares at me, jaw tight, and I wonder what the hell she's thinking.

"You're a liar." Her feet are planted and her hands fisted at her sides, and she looks like a statue of some defiant goddess with all that smooth silky skin. An angry goddess.

"I haven't lied to you."

"You lie to yourself to justify what you're doing. I told you I was pack. You could have checked easily. But you didn't want to. You're lying now."

I can see she believes what she's saying, that her words ring true inside that skull of hers. I've dealt with a lot of people who insisted they were right in my time, a lot of people who can't bend, can't see the other side of the coin. I'll be damned if my mate becomes one of those. I'll be damned if she makes me into the villain in all of this. I stalk toward her, well aware of how she slinks backward, how I intimidate her, how underneath her bravado, she's scared of me.

I don't want her scared, but I'll settle for that for now … until she sees the truth.

"I found a naked girl in the woods in disputed territory splayed out on the grass like an offering from the moon goddess herself. A girl who ticks every single one of my boxes."

She hits the beige wall near the television and can't back up any further. I take the opportunity to pin her in with my arms, reaching out and planting my hands on the wall on either side of her shoulders and dragging my gaze over every inch of her perfect body. "That girl has legs for days and creamy skin. She's got the most piercing light eyes I've ever seen. And she *claims* she can't get her wolf to show. As an alpha, I'm bound to protect her." I let my eyes find Elena's once more, locking our gazes together as I continue. "Less than ten minutes later, I'm attacked by Dark Nights. Tell me, princess, what would you have assumed if you were in my shoes?"

I see her plush lips part but she doesn't argue, which means this girl has a decent head on her shoulders. Thank fuck, because a stupid mate would have been more than I could bear. I watch the play of emotions on her features as she reconciles the fact that I couldn't quite trust her.

"You didn't have to leave me naked," she finally settles on a retort.

I bark out a laugh. "I like you naked. Pretty sure I just proved that." I lean closer so that I can inhale her deliciousness again. I love the salty musky mix of her sex mingling with the lighter notes of her everyday sweetness. I think I could drive myself mad just scenting her all damned day.

She crosses her arms and I watch her become smaller as her voice grows tight and taut. "I'm not an omega," she repeats.

"You are, sweet thing."

Elena glares before ducking out from underneath my arms and striding toward the door. "Omegas are pathetic. They're weak. I'm not a *goddamned* omega. If I was, I'd fucking reject my wolf and live as a human!"

She might as well have shot me. Reject her wolf? That's unheard of. No one does that. Your wolf is part of you. It's integral. Annoying at times—my own wolf nips at me internally for that thought, but I dismiss him, too filled with pity for Elena's creature. No wonder the poor thing doesn't want to come out. I wonder if Elena had thoughts like that while she was running. My own wolf's hackles rise and his gums peel back from his teeth, showing true anger toward our mate for the first time as she continues to rant about how having a wolf isn't worth it if her life is stripped away. He wants to bite her for her insolence, for her potential denial of her sweet wolf. But rather than punish her, I want her to see the truth. I don't think she realizes what being an omega means.

"Elena," I call out, yanking my shirt off my head, balling it up, and tossing it toward her. "Put that on. And then wait here."

"I'm done waiting. I'm done being here."

I ignore her as I stride past. If she wants to leave my house, there's no way she's going to do it without going for the pants and shoes that Matthew brought down. I take the stairs up to the top of the basement two at a time, reaching into my pants pocket as I do. I retrieve the key I got from my butler and unlock the door, bellowing into the front hall, "Pluto, get down here!"

Pluto's in front of me, eyes curious and brow raised before Elena even reaches the bottom step.

"What?"

Her scent makes his eyes dilate. I hold up the hand I had inside of her so that the smell of her sweet pussy can reach his nose. Though he's been a rock-solid best friend for years and has amazing self-control, it's too much. With a flash of gold, his eyes change from human to wolf and he darts past me. I let him.

I stride down the steps just as Elena screams. When I reach the bottom, I turn to see Pluto pinning her to the carpet on her front, one hand holding down her neck, the other pawing at the pants she's donned. My brows shoot up—the craze has taken over faster and more intensely than I expected. I run forward and yank him off her with a roar, pinning him to the wall. "Mine!" I snarl.

"Omega!" He thrashes against my hold and I watch as his upper body transforms into the half-human half-wolf monsters we typically reserve only for the most intense of shifter battles. His torso elongates and shaggy gray fur erupts from his skin. His fingers stretch and widen into long, dangerous claws. He stays on two feet, but his pants stretch to nearly bursting as he grows and his legs thicken to giant proportions. His head turns into that of a snarling wolf, ears tilted forward aggressively.

My body responds instantly, my own fiend erupting, white hair covering every part of my upper body. My pants were designed with extra elastic in the seam, so they strain but don't rip as my body expands until I'm a third bigger than Pluto, my head nearly brushing the ceiling.

I hear Elena's tight gasp behind me and my fury at Pluto doubles. As does my anger at myself. I keep doing everything associated with my little wolf wrong. I wanted to show her that she's an omega who will drive alphas wild—I wanted to teach her once and for all that she's irrevocably mine. But I didn't expect my best friend to lose control this badly. I thought he'd tackle her, I'd yank him off, have him scare her a little, underscore the point that she can't fucking defend herself in our world. Instead, Pluto's swinging a clawed hand at my face, revealing the beasts we don't usually even let shifters see until they're a year in.

I block Pluto's swipe and growl when he smashes a fist into my torso and knocks half the wind out of me.

Shit.

This was a fucking horrible idea.

His eyes don't hold an ounce of humanity in them when he comes at me and the full weight of what I've just unleashed becomes apparent as he bowls me over and body slams me into the carpet. My head cracks and pain lashes me with a whip.

I tuck up my legs and wrap them, flipping us so that I'm on top, but before I can get him in a chokehold, he's got a foot underneath me and flips me over his head. We both scramble to our feet at the same moment. My adrenaline whispers, *Kill him.*

We circle for a moment and I catch a glimpse of Elena by the far wall, as far from us and as close to the stairs as she can get. Another two steps and Pluto lunges for me, giving me an opening. My arm shoots forward to grip him by the neck. I shove him hard against the wall, cracking his skull and possibly the wallboard—the television rattles on its mount—but right now I don't give a damn about the house. Even about him. All I care about is getting him to submit. My wolf senses have taken over, and the need to dominate Pluto, to see him yield, drop those yellow eyes that are locked tight on mine, overwhelms any other thought. Fury runs through my veins and they swell like river rapids, turgid and wild as I lift Pluto an inch off the ground and watch him gasp under my monstrous hand.

I show my teeth.

Come on, Paul. Back the fuck down, my human brain urges somewhere in the recesses of my mind, even using Pluto's real name, a name I haven't even thought in more than a decade.

But an omega's scent proves too much.

Pluto kicks me hard in the stomach and the pain bursts all the way to my spine.

I drop his neck and he immediately lunges for Elena. I turn to see she's already halfway up the stairs. *Fuck. I didn't lock the door.*

I shove Pluto hard to the ground before leaping across the room and up the bottom steps, stretching and grabbing her ankle as she's halfway up the stairs. If she goes up … and any of my other elites have arrived … they might rip her apart in their lust.

I yank on her until her ass falls to the stairs. She twists and tries to kick me but I pull harder on her leg, only releasing when she goes limp. I point a warning claw at her. My choice to save her backfires when Pluto's claws rip into my side and agony slices me to ribbons. I duck low and reach back, grabbing Pluto's leg, yanking it forward between my own. He falls backward, but his claws are stuck in my flesh like a fork—so I end up falling right on top of him. Quickly, before he can get an arm around my neck, I roll away, even though that means his claws get a longer stretch of skin to stain red.

My chest heaves and my vision fritzes for a second. But when Pluto gets up and lunges for the stairs I force myself up. I lumber forward and grab him by the shoulders. I slide one claw down to his hip and then I pick him up and twist, heaving him into the air until he falls onto the ping pong table. It collapses underneath his weight, the legs on one side buckling, the tabletop smashing into the ground underneath him in a tumult of thunder and howling.

Now I'm angry at him for another reason. I was going to save that fucking table forever. Suddenly, the burning in my side fades to nothing as my nostrils flare and I stomp over to Pluto, who holds up an arm to block me. I can scent exhaustion on him … this kind of shift wears us out quickly … and neither of us is in our twenties anymore.

Pluto stretches his head upward toward the green net that's now nothing more than a shredded bit of dangling plastic. He drops his eyes with a sigh. He shows me his neck and drops his gaze.

My wolf gives a growl of approval, but he's still not completely satisfied. I lift Pluto up, yanking his arm gruffly before I drag his limping ass over to the very storage room I locked Elena in. He goes in without a protest. He knows the deal. There'll be an extra layer to his punishment tonight because the storage room still smells like her—it'll give himself a chance to desensitize himself, to reprogram, to clarify to his fucking wolf that Elena is *mine*.

I shut the door and realize that my hands can't handle the fucking keys when they're like this. But my wolf won't give up control enough to let me shift back, his grip on my body is as tight as Elena's pussy will b… I don't finish that depraved thought. It won't end well when my wolf is already half-hard and ready to celebrate after winning submission from Pluto.

I tell myself to take deep breaths and walk slowly toward Elena, but the sight of her splayed and scared on the stairs, my clothes on her body, our scents commingling; it's all too much and I end up sprinting to her and startling her. She tries to scoot backward, up a step, her fear as crystal clear as glass, but I lean down and let my hips rest on hers for just a second, mulling over how well our bodies fit together even when I'm pure monster. *Some day,* my wolf licks his chops. *Some day.*

My wolf wants to do more, but I finally get control when I remind him that she's human right now, not in a heat, and he'll hurt her.

That makes him retreat enough not to automatically just grind into her, not to take what he wants. Instead, he lets me gently use our clawed hand to grab Elena's softer, smaller, oh-so-delicate fingers.

I push her hand toward my pocket so she can grab my keys. Her fingers accidentally swipe over my cock through the fabric and it swells even more in response to her soft touch. Her eyes widen and she tries to pull back but I close my claws around her wrist and gently glide her hand in my pocket toward the keyring settled deep at the bottom. When her fingers close on it, I turn my head in clear expectation toward the storage room, and then back to her.

Her breathing gets short, and her teeth dig into her lower lip. "Are you sure it's safe?" Her tone is softer and more compliant than it's been since I met her—I succeeded in scaring her. More than I intended, that's true, but hopefully enough for the message to sink in. I lean forward and reassure her the only way I can until my adrenaline dies off and my wolf feels certain she's safe—until I'm able to shift back and talk. I drag my muzzle up and down along her cheek, mussing the soft fur of my nose, delighting in the feel of her skin. And then I give a quick playful lick to the bottom of her chin that makes her gasp—first in fear, then in outrage, before I pull back with my chest shaking in amusement.

"Gross," she swipes at her chin and glares at me. "Well. Get off me so I can go lock up someone who deserves it more than I did because your crazy ass apparently can't—"

I flip her over on the stairs and smack her ass, careful not to let my claws scratch her. Then I flip her around and point at the door to the storage room, which Pluto hasn't touched. He knows better. Challenge me once and I'll defeat you. Twice and I'll kill you.

My mate narrows her eyes but keeps that plush mouth of hers shut as she stomps down the stairs and over to the door. I follow half a step behind, just in case. When the lock is secured, I also make a fist and pound on a panel in the wall, which opens to showcase a hidden green button. I use the side of my fist to press it and a thin sheet of silver slides out of the ceiling and covers the door, making it essentially shifter resistant.

Elena's lips drop open at that and her nose scrunches. "Dammit. Nancy Drew was right."

She doesn't explain and I don't ask—because I can't—but also because now that she's safe, the adrenaline drains away quickly and the pain in my side becomes twice as prominent. I tell my wolf that we need to shift to take care of the wound. He's reluctant, and I'm worried he'll start a struggle for control over my shape. But when I shove the image of a scared Elena at him, he allows me to take the reins. I shove through the shift quickly, even though the transformation makes the pain stretch and grow and gape into a more hideous wound.

I don't check it as I make eye contact with my little omega, carefully tracing her features with my gaze. I need to make sure she understands the rules before I can deal with anything else. It's too damned important to ensure she's aware of her situation. "Do you see now? You try to walk away from me and dozens of wolves will pile on top of you. They'll fucking rip you apart trying to get to you, driven mad just by your scent."

I watch her eyes as the knowledge grows there, an ugly truth full of thorns.

"Pluto is loyal as fuck. He's been my second for years. Swore he'd never touch you. All it took was a single inhale, Elena. He didn't just shift, he went full monster."

Her throat clenches and I watch it as she swallows hard, lowering her eyes, accepting her new reality.

"That's right. There's no fairytale here. You're an omega. Your wolf can't save you. You depend *on me*."

A single tear tracks down her face before she wipes it roughly away, looking back up and me and nodding, jaw stiff. She's pretending to be tough, but she doesn't need to be because I'll be that for her. For now, I'm just relieved she seems to have gotten with the program. Finally. Damn.

I glance down at my wound, the ripped flesh, and feel myself get light-headed as the pain rushes up as soon as my mind lets go of the reins. That feeling only doubles when Elena steps forward and takes my hand, saying, "Let's get you in bed."

Yes. Me in bed with Elena on top of me. I know it's not what she's planning. But I make the plans and *that* sounds like the perfect prescription.

14

ELENA

I LEAD Black by the hand back to the boring beige basement bedroom, trying not to tremble. *I need to stay focused on his injury right now. I can think about everything else later.* My compartmentalization skills come into play and I filter through some of the things I've learned interning at the hospital, not thinking about myself, thinking only about wound care.

My patient eagerly follows, even laying down on the comforter at my sharp command.

"Mmm. Yes. Let's finish what we started." His eyes dance playfully up at me as he tucks his uninjured hand behind his head, like an asshole in a porno waiting to get sucked off.

All my plans and any residual pangs of fear, sadness, or regret are all washed away by Black's lascivious expression. "Are you delusional? You're bleeding out."

"It's a flesh wound."

Men. Alpha shifter or horny teenager. They're all the damned same. I roll my eyes and stroll to the door so that I can get something to deal with Black's wounds. I intend to scream for Matthew to come help, but I turn out the bedroom door only to find he's already tromping across the basement rec room, a plastic basket filled with medical supplies in his hands.

"This happen often?" I ask with a raised brow. "You're well prepared."

"More than Alpha Maddox would want me to mention," he retorts.

"Matthew!" Black's sharp disapproval rings out from the bed.

Matthew just gives me a little smirk that makes me fall a bit more in love with him before he yells to Black, "You said the wrong line by the way. The Black Knight's first line after he's hurt is, 'Tis but a scratch!'"

"What?" I look at Matthew confused, clearly missing something.

"Monty Python," they both retort simultaneously.

I just give Matthew a classic 'okay Karen' expression before taking the supplies back into the bedroom. The butler calls out behind me, "You need to educate this woman, Black. She's missing out on one of life's best comedies."

"I need to educate her about other things first," Black mutters as I set the kit down on the nightstand.

"No, you don't," I tell him, knowing exactly what he's implying. A blush rises on my cheeks, which is ironic, because I'm always trying to make Jonah blush, but this is different. Jonah's so go-with-the-flow and easy go-lucky. He's the polar opposite of Black's domineering, overtly sexual presence.

I wonder if he's worried about me. If he's called the police. I fucking hope so, though I doubt they'll be able to do a damned thing. The shifters have glimmers on the force, and Black's rich enough to have more in his pocket. I hope Jonah isn't making himself sick over me...actually, a little part of my chest pings at that thought, marking it a lie. But I don't have time to examine that. Not with Black here making dirty innuendos while a wound the length of the Grand Canyon stretches between his ribs.

I turn to check on Matthew, to see if he'll help me hold down the big alpha so we can change the subject to something cleaner ... like wound sanitation, but the old butler has abandoned me. He's disappeared from the basement entirely, leaving me alone to deal with Black.

Great. Just fucking great.

"Hope you're not a little bitch about alcohol."

Black raises a dark brow at me. "Sure you want to talk to me like that?"

"Pretty damn sure, yeah."

"Girls who mouth off get punished."

"Assholes who get their friends to attack girls apparently do too." I nod in the direction of his side, where five long slashes trace his ribs. "You totally deserve that. I was rooting for him to bite your head off."

Black grunts a laugh. "True enough. But I'll heal up just fine. Don't worry about me. Just get up here and ride my face so we can finish what we started earlier, little mate."

I glare at him for calling me that—and because those words make my pussy clench. The thought of straddling Black's face and using it, grinding down on his nose and lips, the feel of his rough beard scratching my thighs, smothering him, and not even giving a fuck as I take my pleasure ... all while his hands knead my ass. *Shit. Shit. Shit. I need to get myself under control.* I look away from him and focus on the basket of supplies, which holds everything from band-aids to thread to sew shifters back together. I grab the bottle of alcohol like it's a weapon and take great pleasure in smiling viciously at Black as I tear open a sterilized cotton pad.

I round the bed, holding his eyes the entire time, letting my gaze drink in his bare torso for the first time. I've seen him naked before, chasing me. But that didn't allow a lot of time for perusal—I was a little more focused on fleeing for my life.

And seeing his monstrous form, a form I didn't even know wolves could have... Well, I don't want to think about how that made me feel—how butterflies had filled my chest and dove down at the sight of him, fluttering lower and lower, particularly after he'd beat the shit out of his friend and then made me grab his dick ... I mean keys. I should have been horrified, should *be* horrified.

But I'm not analyzing that shit right now; I'm not going to ask myself any questions about my messed-up reaction. I'm going to blame it all on stress. Yup. That's my story and I'm sticking to it.

My eyes drag over Black's solid pecs, his dark brown nipples, and his abs that are bigger than my fists. He's got that V-cut above his hips that's always made my mouth water, not to mention broad shoulders. When my gaze darts to the hollow of his neck beneath his beard and I have the urge to lick it, I force myself to look away. I don't want to think about how hot he is or how good it would feel to take him up on his offer, because those are just distractions from a reality that's barreling down on me, tires screeching, at sixty miles per hour. I'm about to be crushed by it.

"I didn't know shifters could become—that," I say articulately as I sit down on the bed.

"This world has a lot of secrets," Black replies. "Most of them are dark and brutal. But some secrets, like you, and what you are, are beautiful."

His words surprise me, catch me off-guard, and open up the acid that's corroding my hope and turning my dreams into a graveyard. Being an omega isn't a fucking beautiful thing. It's a goddamned curse.

His hand reaches for me, but I pull away and focus on flipping open the cap of the alcohol bottle like it's complicated. "My mom hates this part," I say with a bitter twist to my lips as I douse the pad. "Maybe that's why it's my favorite."

A question slides across Black's features but he's too smart to voice it. Good. Or bad, maybe, because I want to take my own pent-up aggression out on someone. Part of me thinks—after that display with Pluto or whoever—that Black's telling me the truth. That my life is fucking over. That everything I've chosen, my career as a nurse, the little house without tile floors, the beautiful Siamese bitch of a cat I've always want to get, even my random daydreams about Jonah, the ones I always quash as ridiculous ... all those dreams are gone.

That leaves a bitter taste in a girl's mouth, a kind of charcoal smudge across her heart. It makes me want to lash out and hurt someone the way that I'm hurting. Black's the perfect candidate.

He's the messenger. Who better to shoot?

He's also my captor. The arrogant prick who thinks he can just stake his claim because his dick says so. Who thinks he doesn't even have to win me over.

Yeah. He deserves it.

I take the bottle in hand. *Fuck dabbing gently.* I turn it upside down and spray it all over his wound.

Black gasps, hissing and curling away from me when I pour a generous amount of alcohol on his side.

"Dammit, Elena! I said I'm fine." Black tries to use his hand to bat me away, but it's a technique Mom uses that I'm quite familiar with. I just sidestep and then am right back in place a second later with an even more generous gush of disinfecting alcohol from the clear bottle Matthew brought me. I don't spare the comforter either, letting it get soaked.

Unlike with my mother, with Black, I don't hold back. For some reason, my mouth is determined to defy him, even if other parts of me aren't so inclined to do so. "Shut up, you man-baby. You might heal fast but infection hits shifters just as much as humans and if his little claws were dirty—"

"They weren't. Okay? I'm good."

"You're good when I say you're good." I shove him back down on the bed and straddle him so that he can't get up without lifting me, so he'll stop fighting. Because I still want to be in control. I need control, I've wanted it ever since he stole it from me. I'm not done punishing him for my life turning to shit in a matter of milliseconds. When my thighs clamp down on the outside of his hips, Black stills and becomes compliant. I'm sure he could buck me if he wanted to right now, but I'm also pretty smugly certain that it would hurt his wound to do so.

Black's nostrils flare in annoyance. "I need to gorge on you, baby. Climb up here and let me distract myself while you torture me."

"Gorging makes people puke. You'll end up sick of me."

"Never, princess. I've been dreaming of you my entire life."

I narrow my eyes at him and jab the cotton pad in his direction. "That shit's just gross. Okay? No cotton candy lines. I'm not buying that."

"You'd rather I tell you that your pussy feels like a dream? That the stretch of those lips, the way they gaped open around my fingers made me think of how much more they'll gape when I finally get my cock in you."

Fuck. It's like Black's got a magnifying glass and a bright hot sun—he knows exactly how to aim his words to create a beam full of syllables that burn right through to my core. I'm on fire. I shove the pad down on his wound as I grind into him, turned on and pissed about it, determined to wreak revenge. "This little thing? Sorry, I thought you had a screwdriver in your pocket. A short skinny one."

Black throws back his head and laughs, and it's the most luxurious sound in the world. It feels like mink rubbing against the skin, like water on a parched throat. It's a beautifully soothing sound. My fury abates for a second and smug satisfaction replaces it as I watch the lines around his eyes crinkle and the slightly crooked tilt of his mouth as true amusement washes over him.

Black ends his howl with a groan and his hand clutches his hurt side. I can see pink edges to the wounds, but it's nowhere close to healed yet and I know he has to lay still for a bit longer. Whenever Mom's like this, I give her a bottle of wine and set up the television. She likes crime shows best. I glance back over my shoulder at the t.v. "What do you like to watch?"

"You." Black's statement is instantaneous and I roll my eyes as I move to climb off of him, but his hands clamp down on my hips and I marvel at their size. If he spread his fingers, he might be able to cover half my upper legs.

Before I can get caught up in inappropriate imaginings, I flick one of his hands with my finger. And that gives me an idea. "Hold on, one second. I'll be right back." I scoot backward out of his grip and then crawl off Black and set down my nursing equipment on the nightstand before turning toward the door.

"Don't you dare leave—" He starts to get up with a groan.

"Relax. I'm grabbing drinks. Lay down, fucktard. I do this all the time for my mom. You need to get drunk and you need a distraction while you heal." I grab the doorknob and give Black my best Mother Hen impression to get him to lay back down on the gray comforter.

He does so with a dark look that might have intimidated me an hour ago, but at this point, he's given me so many that I'm starting to feel immune.

"I'm listening for you. If you put so much as a foot on those stairs—"

"Yeah, yeah, you'll monster out. Got it," I say with a nonchalance I don't feel.

Actually, stepping outside the doorway of the bedroom, leaving Black's presence, nearly gives me a panic attack. I keep picturing another alpha shifter walking down those stairs, his eyes finding mine, body contorting…

My heart twirls a set of drumsticks and then taps out a staccato rhythm against my ribs and my face grows hot —I have to force my feet to walk across the short distance to the bar.

I grab a bottle of whiskey since that's already open and won't require any effort. I don't bother with glasses because I've got an idea to keep Black occupied while he heals, which, in my semi-professional opinion (based on the dozens of times my mother's come home with similar wounds) will take at least a few hours. I grab what I need.

My eyes do stray toward the basement stairs as I walk back, but this time, they don't symbolize freedom. When I look at them and think of what's beyond them, I worry that it's a whole lot more violent and unpredictable than the man in that bedroom I'm returning to.

He might be a monster himself … but better the monster you know, right? *No, that doesn't even make sense,* I argue with myself. *I don't know him. I only met him this afternoon. God, that feels like light years ago.* And still, despite the fact that I don't really know Black, despite the fact that he's manhandled and manipulated me and I should be running in the opposite direction, I find my feet turning toward his bedroom.

I might possibly be just as stupid as my father.

15

BLACK

I FEEL a strange twinge inside my chest when Elena steps back into the bedroom, like something inside of it tightens. I brush the feeling aside; I probably twisted and hit a nerve aggravated by my injury when I'd leaned up to watch her go.

I had flipped onto my side when she left, eyes glued to the tiny sliver of the stairs I could see from the bedroom door, certain that she'd try to run. I'd skimmed my foot off the side of the mattress and let it dangle halfway to the floor so that I could sprint after her fleeing form and save her from herself—and any other monsters that roamed tonight. Because the only monster I'd ever let Elena face was me.

My muscles had coiled, tensed, and readied to strike. But she hadn't even tried. The predator in me is equal parts fascinated, excited, and disappointed by her return. My wolf is cocky, sitting back on his haunches with a smug smile.

"Couldn't resist coming back, huh?" I ask casually, but underneath my solemn gaze, my heart beats quickly and I find myself interested in her reaction. I want to know if she's returning because she's drawn to me or if it's fear guiding her choices right now.

Her expression immediately hardens like a shell and I can't tell the true emotions lying underneath as she arches a brow and cocks a hip, making my huge sweats sway down the length of her legs and drawing my attention. "More like … thought about running and decided it'll be better to do so after you've passed out drunk." Her eyes dance when she says that last line, however—I swear this girl gets off on being a smart ass.

I'm surprised by the fact that her sass turns me on so much because typically when someone pokes and prods at me that way, I want to quash them flat and see them cower at my feet. The urge for submission is strong. With Elena, though, it feels almost—affectionate isn't the right word, and I'm not quite certain what is. But the alpha in me doesn't feel threatened, just amused. I have to force a frown, instead of the smile that wants to cross my face at how cute she looks with smug satisfaction radiating out of her. Maybe I like that expression on her because it's close to the one she wore after I made her come hard on my fingertips. Or maybe I just like it. It's hard to tell as her scent fills the room again and sends my mind into a lazy spiral like a coin dropped into one of those plastic wishing wells where it rolls on its side in a hundred circles before dropping to fulfill its destiny.

Elena saunters in and perches on the side of the bed, grabbing my hand and setting a little glass bowl of trail mix in it. "Here. You need to practice," she asserts, before unscrewing the cap of the whiskey and raising the bottle to her lips. I watch her take a long pull, her lips wrapped around the tip of the bottle. My wolf and I both imagine her mouth wrapped around something else. Damn. I need to breed her soon because my every thought is turning into a carnal obsession and I can't afford that. If I'm going to keep her, I need a clear head to deal with Stone. Thoughts of that brutal alpha are a boner killer and help me focus. Somewhat.

"I thought that whiskey was for the patient, *doctor*."

She squints as the burn of the alcohol hits her. "We are not playing dirty doctor."

"You're the one who said it aloud, *doctor.*"

"You were thinking it—"

I cut her off as I set the little bowl of trail mix on my abs and reach for the whiskey bottle. "Well, since you mention it, I do think my dick got hurt in the fight. Maybe you should check it."

"Your dick is about to hurt in half a second when I kick it."

"Climb up on the bed and prove it, princess. I dare you." I grin before I lean up carefully so I don't tip over the bowl, ignoring the whine of my ribs so that I can take a long drink of whiskey as she glares at me. But Elena refuses to rise to the challenge and climb back up on top of me. I try to tamp down on my disappointment, knowing she's right and my side could use another couple hours to heal. If she had straddled me again I would have pulled her down on top of me and then flipped us so that she couldn't get away.

I debate doing it anyway but the pain must fuck with my poker face because she takes a smooth step backward and wags her index finger at me. "No sir. We're working on raisin flicking like you promised."

"I did flick your raisin," I give her a wink. "But sure, I'll do it some more. Come back over here."

"Did that scratch turn you into a twelve-year-old boy? Not everything's about sex."

"Baby, your scent did that," I confess. "I can't be in the same room with you and not think about making you mine. It's the blessing of an omega."

“You mean curse. It’s fucking bullshit.”

I stop short, before taking another shot straight from the bottle. Well, I think that answers my earlier question about whether she’s drawn to me or just worried about her wolf right now. I take a deep breath and try to tell myself it’s not personal as the whiskey muffles the pain banging a set of cymbals in the back of my head. I’m not even sure if it’s pain from my wound right now or from the look that twists my mate’s face as she thinks over her fate. I try not to let disappointment color my tone or show on my face because as much as it feels like rejection, I need to sympathize. Empathize. Because I’ve been there.

I hand her back the whiskey bottle and take a deep breath, drawing on the memory of my father, standing in the kitchen after I came home missing a wallet and a tooth after one of my first alpha fights.

His brown eyes had crinkled at the edges and his lips had thinned but he hadn’t said a word. He’d pulled out a kitchen chair and gestured for me to sit while he went to the freezer and pulled out a steak. He’d slapped it on the side of my face and taken the seat beside me, the pair of us towering over Mom’s tiny pine kitchen table.

I remember the light flickering—I’d let a moth inside when I’d stomped home. It had made the whole thing eerie when Dad had unleashed his words of wisdom.

The same words I tell Elena now. "Wolves are something that happen to you. Like looks. Like intelligence. They aren't a choice. What you do with them once you've got them—that's where the choice is."

"Well, considering my wolf stayed all of two minutes and has proven herself to be a useless bitch who's only given me a scent that makes my worst nightmare come true, I think I'll pass. Thanks for that pep talk though. You should really go chat with Oprah. Maybe she can give you your own show." Elena takes a final drink from the bottle before setting it on the nightstand with a loud thunk.

"Bitterness doesn't suit you."

"Suddenly you're an expert on me?"

"I plan on becoming one."

She rolls her eyes and I hold up three fingers, distracting her and making her brows furrow. "Um, should I even ask? Or are you checking your eyesight after that fight? I probably should have done that but I figured at your age you'd know if you had a concussion."

I tick up another finger for the age insult, enjoying the play of emotions across her face as she slowly figures out what I'm doing. It's not lost on me that her body responds—her nipples tighten under my t-shirt and she swallows hard.

"Maybe you can make the number of spankings I owe you go down a bit by teaching me how to turn dried fruit into deadly weapons."

She fights a grin for a moment before letting amusement stretch her gorgeous face gently. "I suppose I don't have anything better to do since I'm stuck here until I figure out how to get rid of this stupid scent."

"Or embrace it," I suggest, scooting gingerly over, trying and failing to avoid the wet patch left by the alcohol she poured on me. Fuck it. I hiss as the sting drags across my cut again and Elena hurries over to check on me.

"Hold on. Let me get a towel, you big man-baby."

I lift up another finger and she rolls her eyes. "Please. Keep counting. Count to a hundred if you want. Infinity. But the day I stop insulting you is the day I'm dead."

"Good thing I like spanking you then. We'll have to make it a daily thing," I tell her retreating form. She freezes for a moment, turning back to me. She chews on her lip for a second, like she wants to retort, but she swallows down whatever words are on her tongue and I don't get to know if she was going to add another infraction to the list or try to reject me.

A dark, sullen part of me thinks it's the latter, but I shove him away because I'm going to prove him wrong. And her. If Elena thinks she has a hope of walking away from me now, she won't before the night's through. I'll make sure of it. Once I've decided something, it's always come to be. And I'll be damned if the most important decision I've ever made—to keep her—will be ruined by anyone. Including her.

Elena comes back with a set of towels folded over her arms, her dark hair spilling over her shoulders as she leans across the bed and forces me to grab the little bowl of trail mix and roll onto my uninjured side while she lays the cold towels out on top of her mess.

"You know, if you were actually a good nurse, that wouldn't have happened," I point out helpfully.

"If you were actually a nice guy, that wouldn't have happened."

"Nice is boring."

"No. Nice can be..." She trails off and I roll onto my back to look up at her, annoyed that she's broken off mid-thought a second time. What I see stops me short. There's a soft, dreamy look in her eyes—it sends a black dagger right into my chest.

Fury smacks me across the face and I yank on her hand, pulling her onto the bed, deliberately interrupting her thoughts about some other guy. I know what that look was. And I'm going to erase it. I'm going to erase anyone but myself from her mind. I pull her close, so close I can see the zebra stripes in her irises, and feel the warmth that radiates between us. If a look can generate this much heat, I can only imagine what will happen when we come together later. My eyes drop to her lips for a second before coming back up, pleased when she doesn't pull away.

"Fuck nice. I want to be a lean, mean, raisin-killing machine."

"Oh my god. You should hear the ridiculous things that come out of your mouth." She does pull back then, with a roll of those gorgeous eyes.

"I want to remind you that I offered to use my mouth for a far better purpose. It's your fault I'm talking right now."

"Fuck me, you're annoying."

"Stop whining and show me how you do this," I say, setting the glass cup of trail mix back onto my chest and digging out a raisin expectantly.

Elena inhales and exhales loudly, making a show of calming herself. I ignore that as I take the raisin and try to figure out where the hell I'm going to balance it in order to get it to launch. I haven't done shit like this since I was bored in high school, but if I'm going to learn how to do something, I'm going to do it right. I watch as the little raisin bends in my grip and I wonder if I'm holding it too hard. I'm hardly even touching the damn thing!

Elena's tiny hand closes over mine and her soft skin slides along my fingers, which lets me know that this game is actually an excellent idea. I want her to get used to touching me.

"I don't know that you're ready for the big leagues yet, Mr. Maddox. Why don't you start with an M&M?" She tugs the raisin out of my palm and digs around in the trail mix, bringing a green M&M out and handing it to me.

"What?"

"We're taking baby steps here. Raisins are all different. They're like a level three on the flicking scale. You need to get a basic technique before you go tackling them."

"There's a flicking scale? How did I not know this? My life's been incomplete."

She snorts out the most adorable little laugh before stating seriously, "It has been."

"In more ways than one," I add.

Silence meets that declaration but I don't back down. This might be a night of uncomfortable truths for Elena but she needs to face them. Fast. The shifter world doesn't leave room for slow; the weak are picked off, eradicated.

I won't let anything happen to her.

But I'm going to keep pushing because my mate needs to acknowledge what I am to her, what I'm willing to face for her.

She doesn't say anything, but she doesn't come up with a smart-ass retort either, so I decide it's progress.

After a moment, Elena clears her throat and finds her own M&M, choosing to ignore my previous statement. "Take your weapon in your left hand, like this." She holds her M&M by the edges using her index finger and thumb. "Oh, wait. Are you right-handed?"

I turn to look at her, unable to let a chance to make her blush slide by, even though I know I just made her uncomfortable seconds ago. But the alpha in me does what he wants. Always has. By now it's second nature. I let my eyes linger on her until she turns to look at me, a puzzled expression on her features as she wonders why I haven't answered.

"You should know the answer to that question already."

"I should?" Her brow furrows. It takes her a minute before that blush I was hoping for arrives. It blooms like a flower, and I have to resist the urge to lean forward and drink in the scent that accompanies that sweet red shade. When I raise the fingers that were inside of her and make a quick come-hither motion, curling them just like I did for her, her eyelashes sweep gently across her cheeks—she can't hold my gaze.

I relent, deciding I need to have mercy on her. And on myself, because thinking about what she let me do to her body is going to leave me with a raging hard-on. I get back to business, raise my right hand and try flicking the M&M. While it's easier than the raisin, it's also heavier and I don't flick hard enough. It doesn't make it past the bed. "Dammit."

Elena flicks her candy and I watch the little orange circle sail right into the red power light on the corner of the tv. "Bullseye."

"There's no way you were aiming for that," I retort, though I've seen first hand how good she is. My hand automatically digs into the bowl and fishes out another M&M because I'll be damned if her skill doesn't make the competitive beast inside lift his head. I balance the M&M with one hand again and move my other hand up into position.

Elena's fingers slide over to my flicking hand. "First trick, use your middle finger."

I turn to meet her gray eyes. "Really?"

"Try it. It will make it fly straighter."

I squint skeptically at her but then flatten back out and focus, staring at that little power light on the television, lining up my blue candy, and then using my middle finger to flick it. It does fly straighter, and goes just to the edge of the bed before tumbling to the mattress and then sliding off the side.

"Not bad," Elena sits up and digs through the trail mix. "Ready for more?"

"With you? That answer's always going to be yes."

Twin raisins pelt me in the face but all I can do is grin.

I'm going to flick this girl's defenses down one at a time.

THREE HOURS AND NEARLY THREE HUNDRED M&Ms later, I've got the basic technique down. Elena stopped flicking herself after the first half-hour and just began retrieving my ammo from wherever it dropped around the room, which gave me incredible views of her ass but also allowed her to mock every single one of my misfires. She's got quite the spanking tally now. About ten minutes ago, the little spitfire crawled up onto the mattress beside me. Five minutes ago, her breathing grew slow, her constant stream of advice and insults thinning, then evaporating. Three minutes ago, I looked over to find her asleep, hands tucked underneath her cheek, looking the picture of innocence.

I stared for a minute, eyes drawn to the soft lines of her lips, unsure of whether she was out for the night or just taking a catnap. She'd admitted she never drinks though—after her fourth shot—so it was quite possible she was down for the count. I'd finished off the twelve M&Ms left on my chest, even managing to get one to hit the television control panel. But since Elena wasn't awake to see my success, it felt hollow.

Now, I sigh and stare up at the ceiling before I get rid of the rest of the bowl of trail mix, putting it onto the nightstand, and then roll onto my side so that I can just stare at her. My injuries are gone, and though there are little grumbling aches, the screaming pain is now just a memory.

My mate's soft skin beckons me and I can't resist the urge to tuck her dark hair back behind her ear and smooth over that cheek. After her cheek, my fingers skim down her neck of their own accord. I tell myself I should pull away but her draw is too strong and I find myself inching closer, tracing her jaw.

Just one kiss.

One isn't enough. Those lips are too soft and I drag my mouth over hers, desperate for another. The third goes down on her chin. Then I kiss the column of her neck, inhaling her beautiful scent all the while. Combined with alcohol, her scent makes me light-headed. And hard. So fucking hard. Some guys get whiskey dick and it makes it impossible for them to get hard. When I get drunk, I can get hard, but it makes coming that much harder.

Mate, my wolf's mind is just as muddled as my own, but his mental image is clear. *Mark her.*

I slide down the collar of my t-shirt and kiss the soft planes of her chest as it rises and falls in her sleep. But I can't pull the collar low enough, and the need to touch her starts to burn uncomfortably hot, an aching pulse. I drape a leg over hers so that I can press closer, cocoon her, mingle our scents together. For a minute, that feels like enough, mingling our scents and breath and spirits. But the dizzy fire starts back up, flames driving me. She's right here.

Right here.

So peaceful and compliant. No sass or sharp words to stop me. Just gorgeous skin and ebony eyelashes, soft breasts—my hand palms one and she moans in her sleep. I drag a finger across her nipple through the t-shirt, eyes glued to the little nub as it responds to my touch. Her body knows she's mine. Her mind just needs to catch up.

Elena moans in her sleep softly.

She's enjoying it.

I pinch that nipple and then gently flick my wrist, tugging lightly at her tender bud, trying to draw out the sensation for her.

A tiny "Mmmm," escapes her closed lips.

I wonder if she's dreaming about me.

"Elena," I whisper her name reverently, releasing her nipple and dragging my hand over her taut belly.

I ruck up the hem of the t-shirt, baring her skin inch by inch, teasing myself tracing soft circles on that stomach, dipping a finger into her naval, then letting my fingers crawl back up to those soft breasts.

I push her shirt up above them so I can marvel at her nipples and dip down to tongue the one I haven't played with yet. I lap at it for a second, smiling when my sweet mate stretches beneath me but still doesn't wake. I let my lips wrap around it gently and slowly increase my suction and pace until I notice her breathing quicken.

I slide my body down her stomach and tug at the sweatpants she's tied tightly. They won't come down with a quick tug, I have to reach inside the waistband and torture myself as the backs of my knuckles brush against the softness I want to taste while my fingers ply apart the knot.

Elena murmurs something in her sleep, but I'm not certain what, because the strings unlace and my prize becomes accessible, my focus drops down below her naval as I tug at her pants.

I'm going to give my mate the best wake-up orgasm in history.

16

ELENA

I'M DREAMING ABOUT JONAH. I know I'm dreaming because I've had this particular dream before—and it's one of my favorites.

It's a memory, or a rose-colored version of one anyway. I'd snuck into Jonah's room last Thanksgiving, while his entire house was abuzz with family. Chattering aunts, screaming wildling younger cousins, uncles standing in the backyard despite the cold, trying to escape the chores their wives would no doubt assign.

I'd crept along the high hedge that Jonah's dad kept meticulously trimmed, and had darted across the thin gap of grass in their suburban neighborhood. Jonah's window was on the first floor, so it wasn't an entirely badass feat, but my heart had felt the rush then, just like it does now. My skin prickles with awareness and my nipples tighten in anticipation, just like they did that day.

God, I love this dream.

Jonah's window is unlocked, just like I'd ordered, so that I can come in and "come" as I please. The dull afternoon autumn sunlight is weak and cold, and I'm not dressed to combat it in the black leather skirt and white t-shirt I wear. Even my thin leather jacket is more for show than warmth.

I shove up his window quickly and toss my leg up over the ledge, pulling myself inside before his gaggle of uncles notices—they're too preoccupied with their conversation about a broken lawn mower to realize their nephew is about to be defiled.

I drop to the floor, concerned when the thigh-high leather boots I wear make too loud a *thunk*. But no one knocks, no one shouts in the hall to see if Jonah dropped something. I take a relieved breath as I slowly stand to see perfection facing me.

Door locked, Jonah stands naked in the middle of his room, cupping himself modestly, waiting, just like I'd told him to. His perfect biceps are on display and even though his thick forearms block part of the view of his perfect abs, I can still see the light brown happy trail beneath his naval.

Like a magnet, I'm drawn toward him, toward those sculpted muscles in his thighs, those hands that can be just as gentle or rough as I command. Those sky-blue eyes take me in and I notice Jonah's got a little scruff today. That's going to feel amazing on my thighs. I lick my lips and let the anticipation build between us for a second. It's so delicious I can almost feel it like a tweak to a nipple.

I force myself to turn around and shut the window, carefully closing the curtains so that no one can see in.

Jonah clears his throat before saying softly, "I'm not sure this is a good—"

"Quiet. Get a pillow and get on your knees." I order.

Jonah chews on his soft pink lip, but when I tug off my jacket and he sees that I only wore a thin white t-shirt with no bra underneath, he hurries over to his queen bed and shucks the blue plaid comforter so he can grab a pillow. I march over to the middle of the room so he has space and then I spread my legs as far as they can go within the confines of the skirt. I'm not wearing panties, but I don't tell Jonah that. I'm saving that tidbit as a surprise for later.

I simply make him kneel on his pillow, controlling this delicate strand of gossamer that extends between us as he submits. He settles on the floor a foot in front of me and I give him a smile as I slowly drag up the hem of my shirt and then toss it aside. My breasts aren't big, but Jonah's always loved to touch them. Every time I deny him access to them he ends up begging. I reach for him, his head near my waist, and shove my fingers into his mouth, letting him get them nice and wet, his tongue showcasing how well he can stroke before I retreat and trace the wet digits along my nipples, reveling in the way Jonah's stare becomes as mesmerized as if I were a hypnotist.

Tiny sparks of pleasure shoot from my nipples to my mid-back, but they aren't big enough to make me wild yet.

"Jonah," I whisper just as enraptured by the sight of him kneeling as he is by the sight of me.

"Yeah?" He hauls his eyes slowly up from my breasts.

"Use your tongue and make me come. I want you to make me come so loud that someone walks by the door and checks on you."

His entire face brightens. He loves when I give him orders. And I love it too, that sweet eagerness to please. He tugs my skirt up, his palms skimming over my thighs.

"These boots are awesome. Fuck. You came all the way here without panties?"

"Yes. And can you see how wet I am for you? Thinking about you. Wanting you. Waiting for your mouth."

Jonah moans, the sound deep and low, before he dives down, licking a line on either side of my slit before blowing on it and then slowly lapping it.

Oh my.

His tongue teases and spreads me, hitting on my sensitive spots and then darting quickly away. Jonah knows my body so well, and works it gently, letting the heat rise under my skin, gradually changing the tide so that lust sweeps in and covers me with swirling wet want.

He uses his fingers to open me up and his tongue starts to plunge into me while his other hand travels slowly up to tease all around my clit. Need builds and grows brick by brick until it's a skyscraper piercing my mind, I'm clinging to the tip of the steeple.

"Jonah!" his mother calls out from somewhere down the hall. "It's time to eat! Turkey's ready!"

"Don't stop," I grit out, reaching down to cling to his hair. There's never much to cling to because he keeps it cut short. But tonight, in this dream, it's long. It falls down past his cheeks and there's so much of it.

I don't analyze, I'm too close to that peak, too close to release. I just arch myself into him and scream.

"Jonah!" his mom calls. "You alright?"

I hold his head to my pussy, grip it hard, a dark thrill racing down my spine as I hear footsteps approach but I make Jonah draw out my pleasure. "More," I tell him. I'm not ready to be done. "More."

I buck up into his tongue, as sensation turns me into a tangled mess of need. A finger slides into me.

My eyes fly open and I wake up, startled—gasping.

Jonah never fingers me until I order him to. He knows better.

I look down to find my hands tangled in long dark hair, a different mouth devouring me, my pants drooping off one ankle, thighs shaking as Black's tongue and fingers work my body to a peak so high it might eclipse Mount Everest. I'm gasping, light-headed, and I moan as he thrusts a second finger into me.

"Black?" I can't finish the question forming in my mind because one of Black's hands comes up and twists my nipple. It's as if someone set off a charge of dynamite in the heart of a mountain. My insides explode, my mind crumbles, I shake and break in ways that are irreparable.

If possible, that orgasm is even better than the one he gave me earlier.

He slowly slides his fingers out while my pussy is still clenching.

"No," I moan, hardly aware of anything but the red sparkles framing my vision.

But his fingers are quickly replaced with something bigger, hotter, thicker. Black's dick presses against me, stretching me, readying me, teasing me by sliding in the tiniest bit but not plunging inside. My hands are still wrapped in his hair as he glides his body up, caressing my torso with his before settling those huge arms on either side of me. He's so tall that he has to arch his back in order to kiss me. He does just that as he leans down and captures my mouth with his. He shoves his tongue in, forcing me to taste myself—at the very same time that he thrusts his dick home. He fucks me both places at once, his tongue with a faster rhythm than his dick, which is far thicker than I'm used to, a bigger stretch and deeper sensation. I end up breaking the kiss to gasp when he bottoms out, his cock tapping my cervix and sending out a bolt of pain-edged pleasure.

"Ohhh fuck," I breathe. It's wild and more intense than I've ever experienced because I'd never let Jonah fuck me like this. But Black works my body like an expert, drawing back and doing a few shallow thrusts to let me recover and I marvel at how he knows to do that. "You can take it, don't worry, baby."

I shake my head. "I can't."

One hand slides over and Black's forearm bears down a little on my chest as he pinches my nipple between his thumb and middle finger gently. "You can. And you will. Now be a good girl for me and take it." He thrusts deep again and pulls that nipple hard. The painful sensations from above and below connect, like a circuit has been completed, and somehow, when those two pulses join inside, they turn into a bright, blinding light and rapture washes over me … the very edge of an orgasm. I mewl a little.

"Told you. Just wait, princess. It'll get even better," he tells me as he drops my breast and lifts himself into a push-up and his pecs become level with my face, the pure muscle of them gleaming in the room light he never bothered to turn off. He fucks me missionary, his hips move faster and faster, treating me to little glimpses of those hard abs when I stare down the length of him. My hands bob overhead, still stuck in his hair as he fucks me so hard I scoot across the soft comforter toward the wooden headboard, feeling helpless, feeling wanton, feeling dominated … and to my utter shock, liking it.

One of Black's arms catches under my knee, thrusting my leg up toward my chest and changing the sensation, letting his hip bones slam harder into my ass and his dick pounds my cervix. I'm boneless as he rasps, "You'll go into heat ... and then I've got something special for you. You're not only gonna get this big cock..." His hand reaches up and gently untwines mine from his hair then drags it down between us, over my clit, causing my limbs to jerk a little in response. I'm his puppet. He can do anything he wants to me right now. He's pulling the strings. And it's pure fucking magic.

He presses my palm to the base of his cock, which is impossibly swollen and thick, thicker than any human male's cock can get, than any beta male can get, the swollen knot that only alphas can get.

"You're gonna take something I've never given a woman before, Elena. My knot. I've never tied myself in before, never wanted to. It's gonna feel so fucking good when I slide it into your cunt. But you're gonna have to be a good girl to get it."

My mind is dazed and that phrase "good girl," one I've always hated, is suddenly so fucking hot that I find myself trying to buck up into Black gently, to feel more of that knot rub against my opening.

"Not yet, baby doll. Go into heat for me and make slick until you're so damn wet not even towels will soak it up. When that happens, I'm gonna slide this knot right into you and lock in place." He drags my hand over the knot again, pressing it against me so that it rubs deliciously up and down my swollen pussy lips, gliding up over the hood of my clit, before he keeps talking.

"When you're in heat I'll fuck you again and again. For days. Little omegas are supposed to come more than ten times a day in a heat, you know. I can't wait to make you come that much."

Damn. Part of my mind is caught up in the spell of his dirty words and wants to do anything and everything he's saying. I shake my head as my fingers travel along the surface of that knot, but it doesn't seem to end. There's no way. It's too wide. And … I don't want to be tied to him or even think about that right now, I just want a fucking orgasm. "That's not going to happen."

Black growls, leaning down so that his face is just above mine and a flash of gold in his eyes tells me he's on edge too, his wolf right there with him as he takes me. "It's not only going to happen, baby. You're going to beg for it."

His dick skims over my g-spot and argument becomes impossible. I can only breathe quickly, chest heaving, as Black ruts me harder and deeper, that press inside keeping me on edge but not sending me over.

"Goddammit, touch me!" I almost yell in frustration.

He chuckles and refuses. "No baby. Not yet."

My eyes grow wide and I want to lash him with my tongue. I try to grab his hand and force it to my clit but he pulls away. Not just away. Out.

Asshole.

He wakes me up and starts this whole thing but he's not even going to get me there? I push up off my back onto my elbows, ready to rage.

Black just smiles when he sees my expression. "On your knees," he orders.

I'm the one who always gives the orders during sex, and so I'm startled for a moment … apparently too long of a moment, because Black grabs me and flips me over himself, driving back into me before I've even gotten my balance. I barely manage to get a hand underneath me before a loud smack and a burst of pain on my ass sends me careening shoulders first into the pillows.

I'm both pissed and turned on at the same damn time because that smack made fire course all the way through my pelvis. "Fucking—"

"Yeah, we're fucking, baby. And you better watch that mouth. I owe you a lot more spankings, little wolf."

Black grabs my hips and pumps faster, dirty words spilling from his mouth. "God this ass. So hot. You're so damned tight. God, yes, do you feel that? Do you feel how perfectly we fit? You were made for my cock. Fuck, you need to come again. Do you hear me? I want your cunt to pulse around me. I want to hear you scream. Get that hand on your clit right now." One of his hands reaches out and closes over mine on the pillow. He drags it down toward my swollen, sensitive clit. "You play there and I'll play up here." His fingers reach up and he tugs at my nipple.

I want to yell at him for ordering me around but his touch… My touch… My eyelashes flutter and my spine turns to butter. I start slowly circling around my over-stimulated clit as he fucks harder. When he realizes that I'm not doing exactly as he told me, Black growls into my ear. "I told you to *touch that clit*."

He picks me up, dick still inside me, and leans back onto his heels, pulling my back up against his chest so that I'm kneeling on the bed, legs spread on either side of him, like some penitent at an altar. But my arms aren't spread in supplication, my legs are, and I'm not begging for forgiveness, I'm begging for release.

Black brings his hand back to my nipple and pinches hard as he tilts his head forward over my shoulder. Watching me. Ensuring I do what he says. "Now, play with that clit. Not around it. With it."

He fucks into me slowly; he can't get as deep at this angle but the head of his cock drags deliciously over my g-spot with every stroke. My hand goes to my clit and I touch it lightly while his hands maul my breasts without mercy. The contrast of sensations … the sparks caused by his dick, the gentle rub of my fingers, the wild play of his hands … they blend together to create the perfect fusion.

I gasp, not even able to scream as my insides tighten.

So.

Damn.

Good.

My entire body goes limp and Black shoves me forward, face-first onto the pillows, grabbing my hips and ramming hard again as my pussy contracts around him. He comes silently before collapsing on top of me.

His heat and his scent surround me and for a second my mind drifts off like a sailboat caught by a breeze and driven toward a destination by a power it can't see, only feel. But as I come down from the high of sex, worry cracks the helm, creating a leak, and that peaceful feeling takes on water.

I just had sex with Black Maddox.

Alpha of the Lobos.

Head of my pack.

The man who claims that I'm an omega and he's got the right to own me for the rest of my life.

Suddenly, his touch and scent are too much. I elbow him until he rolls off of me and I move to scoot off the bed, but his hand captures me and holds me in place. He turns me onto my side and then spoons me, one arm over my waist like a seatbelt, strapping me in place.

His nose nuzzles my hair and he gives a satisfied and drowsy, "Mmmm."

I lie there tense, waiting, counting his breaths as they even out and eventually slow, trying to ignore the stickiness collecting between my thighs.

Meanwhile, my mind races in circles, in figure eights, in wild twisting scribbles that have no destination. *I had sex with an alpha. I swore to myself I'd never have sex with an alpha.* Of all the alphas ... him? One I have almost zero chance of escaping? And worse ... what does it mean that the sex was good? Great even? Oh god. I press my lips together hard in order to stay silent as I wait.

When Black's finally asleep, I carefully lift his bulky arm off of me and slide out of bed, padding silently into the bathroom. I close the door gently, so slow that even I barely register the click of the latch. Then I use the restroom before turning on the shower. When it's warm, I climb inside, determined to wash him and this indiscretion off my skin. It's only then that I allow myself to burst into tears.

What the fuck just happened?

17

BLACK

I WAKE up feeling drunk and, at first, I think I might have downed more whiskey last night than I thought I did. But the glass bottle is perched on the nightstand still two-thirds full, so it's not the culprit.

I inhale, still lightheaded and I look over, realizing the source of my pervasive sense of giddy dizziness. Elena.

I gaze down at the girl curled up next to me on top of the covers, huddled on her side, her face turned so that it's buried in the pillow and completely hidden. The underside of her hair is free of the white streaks I don't love and glows a natural luminous black in the dim light drifting in from the rec room.

I don't remember turning off the light in here. I gaze down and realize that Elena must have gotten out of bed after I fell asleep. Gotten out and returned.

Well, I didn't send her into heat like I'd hoped to, not if she's able to sleep for hours on end without waking up to beg for my cock—omegas in heat are supposed to be insatiable—but she got up and chose to come back and lay down next to me. That's still progress, given that she'd wanted to hightail it earlier.

I think she's finally beginning to accept that she's an omega. Besides, I'm not really upset she didn't go right into a frenzy. I don't mind if we have to practice a few times to get her to go into a mindless, deliciously wanton state to bring on her first heat. I'll make that sacrifice.

I'm still naked, while she slept clothed, a situation that I'm going to have to talk to her about. That's not happening again.

I run a hand through my hair, my teeth gently grinding against one another as I wonder about just what I need to do with this little gem I've discovered. Always rare and special, most omegas were slaughtered during the pack wars that established the current territories—killing their omega is a good way to drive an alpha to madness.

Finding an omega now is like finding a four-leaf clover.

But keeping her, that's gonna be a bitch. I scrub a hand down over my face, feeling stubble on the top part of my cheeks that's grown while I slept. I'm a mess. And I'm *in* a mess.

I can only imagine how much Stone's blown up my phone and the phones of any of our mutual contacts.

Technically, based on the treaty created by Stone and my predecessor, any omega born into the Lobos is supposed to go to the Dark Nights and vice versa. Good fucking will and other such bullshit.

Stone isn't the only one who's pissed at me either. Some of my elites want me to give her up because they don't want to face off against the pack that's constantly a thorn in my side.

I glance back down at Elena, knowing all the trouble I'm going to be in over a girl. Is it worth it? My chest gives an unplanned purr and I watch as Elena's hands tighten on her pillow as she sleeps.

A tiny sigh escapes from her.

We're connected in a way neither of us can really explain. Our bodies just call to each other.

"Don't start a war over some goddamned pussy!" Trevor had said last night.

Fucker has no clue.

The most fertile of all the shifters, omegas are also the only ones who can fully slake an alpha's lust. Betas ...

betas are nice. But sometimes, they aren't enough. And their scent sure as fuck doesn't drive me wild and make me hard as steel.

I've sacrificed my entire damn life to get where I am. To turn this pack around and make it safe. I've never asked for anything in return until now. But the moon goddess didn't have me find Elena by accident. The goddess knew she'd need me. She fucking *gave* Elena to me.

Mine, my wolf growls as he stretches inside my mind, rolling out the kinks in his shoulders, shaking out his paws, waking up.

I debate rolling Elena over and waking her up for another round, claiming her again, trying to start up that heat—but I've got shit to take care of, especially if I'm going to have her tight little body in my bed every night. If I've learned anything over the years it's that the moon goddess might give you a sign, but you still had to work to make things go your way.

This *will* happen. Elena will be my omega and satisfy my cock every night. I'm gonna breed her until she's got my baby inside her. And even then, I'm not gonna stop.

I take a deep breath to try to get a hold of myself as images of Elena's body swollen up and her tits round and full come into my head. I make myself focus on the other aspects of omegas. Beyond the physical satisfaction, what I've read about omegas is that they finally make alphas feel complete. They're our perfect counterparts. Soft and gentle...well, Elena's soft, I don't know about gentle. She's got some sass. But she's an omega, and the fact that I'd had to protect her in the woods, the fact that I had, even the fucking fight with Pluto last night ... I fill up with this deep sense of satisfaction about defending her.

Alphas are built to be protectors. To dominate. To control. Omegas are our opposites. They're built to submit. I can't wait until Elena stops fighting what she is, accepts it, until the day she looks up into my eyes with worship in her gaze.

Damn.

My dick is harder than a lead pipe. That didn't work.

I tell it to calm the fuck down because I've got too much to do, but I can't help turning and looking back down at her one last time before I leave. She's shifted slightly, her knees tucked up toward her chest, and there's a blue M&M stuck in her hair. Adorable. I grin as I reach over and carefully remove it.

Then I try to sit up slowly and climb out of bed without disturbing her. Mattresses always bounce up when I climb out of the divot my huge body makes. Normally, I don't care, but this morning, I press my hands down into the covers to slow the rise and try and prevent Elena from getting jostled.

She looks so tiny and thin, swallowed up by my sweats. It's hard to believe she could take my cock. But she can. And will again soon, once I've battened down the hatches.

I finally push up off the bed and stride to the bathroom, closing the door gently behind me, determined to let my little vixen sleep as long as she needs. It's probably only been four hours—I never typically sleep longer than that.

And if she's not used to drinking, or shifting, Elena's body might need a bit to recover. Meanwhile, I've got a shit-ton to do to prevent Stone from stealing her from me. Namely, I need to get a guard set up and I need to find out how to force an omega to go into heat.

I take a hot shower, reveling in the way Elena's scent still lingers in this room, fisting my dick to thoughts of her, to remembering how deep I got, thinking about how much deeper I'll go when my knot shoves inside and stretches her. One hand circles my knot as the other works my tip, gliding up and spreading my precum around, squeezing the head. *Mmmm.*

I bet Elena's throat is so warm and tight. One day, she's going to kneel there and hold still like a good little omega while I fuck her throat until tears come to her pretty eyes. I spurt against the tile wall as little silver stars flicker across my line of sight.

I carefully wash all traces of her scent off of me—I don't need any more drama today. When I step out of the shower and grab a fresh towel, I notice Matthew's already put a folded set of clean clothes on the counter. He's really earning that raise.

I dress and slip out of the bathroom. Elena's still out cold, so I move quickly to the rec room, shutting the door quietly behind me.

When I turn around, Matthew's there in his penguin suit with a coffee in his hand. It's got just the right amount of milk and I can smell the raspberry flavoring from here. Delicious.

I glance over at the basement window, but it's still dark out, so I ask, "Time?"

"It's four in the morning, your usual wake up, sir."

I grin at him and take the mug, lifting it to my lips as I ask, "Checked on our prisoner?"

"Which one, Alpha Maddox? You seem to have quite the collection right now."

I ignore the old man's jab and stride across the rec room to the basement storage room. I smack my fist sideways into the silver shield and then wait, patiently drinking my coffee while Matthew pulls his keyring out of his pocket and unlocks the door.

Pluto stumbles out of the room, his brown hair disheveled, stubble on his chin—the man hates stubble with a passion. He's naked after his monster shift last night. He shoots a furious glare in my direction before he bolts for the stairs. "Dick! As soon as I pee, I'm kicking your ass!"

Matthew's gray brows raise but he doesn't say anything.

I just chuckle and take another sip of my coffee, then I follow my butler upstairs to the third floor in comfortable silence, fighting against a grin that keeps threatening to crop up on my lips and make me look like a stupid teenager.

I've had great sex before … maybe not quite as hot as that. No, no one's tried to resist me before, or tell me what to do … definitely not as hot as that … But great sex is no reason to go around grinning like a fool. Especially since it's not locked down yet.

I unlock our patient's door but Cody's still asleep.

"Should I wake him up and yell at him for being an asshole or save it for after breakfast?"

"Personally, I like a good yell first thing in the morning before the sun's up. It's a great way to wake up. Especially when you're wounded. That startle reflex feels amazing on broken ribs." Matthew's sarcasm game is on point.

"He should be mostly healed at this point," I counter.

"By all means, then, yell away." Matthew makes a welcoming gesture toward Cody's bed.

I decide against waking the other alpha up to yell at him. I can fix other problems in the meantime. And he's not a current problem. He just needs a fitting punishment for wandering around my house uninvited.

I sigh. "Fine. Lock him back up, old man."

"Who are you calling old man, toddler?"

I chuckle as Matthew drags out his keys and locks the bedroom door.

When Pluto discovers us walking back down the grand staircase he bolts up to us and dead arms me hard. "You did that shit on purpose!"

"Of course, I did," I respond calmly switching my coffee mug out of the now-aching limb and into my good hand. I don't retaliate, because Pluto does deserve to get in at least one good shot. "She didn't believe she was an omega."

“I could have hurt her or you, you dumb fuck.” Pluto runs a hand through his hair, distress clear on his face.

“Her, maybe.” I grin as I see Pluto’s teeth grind together. As an alpha, he hates when I dismiss him as a threat.

“If she’s your mate, you shouldn’t put her at risk.”

I let out a breath because that was a blow to the gut. That statement's true. I shouldn’t have. But Elena didn't believe me. And I learned a long time ago in this world that you can't hold punches because if you do, the fight just gets worse, drags on longer than it should, and both people end up a hell of a lot more bruised and broken. A quick punch to the face, a jab of reality, is always better.

"Before you called me down there, Stone's second blew up my phone. The Dark Nights are pissed." Pluto tells me what I already know. He's got a real talent for stating the obvious.

"What do we have on them?" I ask calmly. I knew it was coming. We make our way back downstairs shoulder to shoulder, last night's fight already forgotten. The front windows show the gray hints of pre-morning light when the sun is still beneath the horizon. The moon goddess has tucked herself away. I’ll have to fight today’s battle myself. Like always.

Matthew goes on ahead of us with a quick declaration. "I'll bring omelets to your office. And some clothes for Pluto."

My stomach gives a growl of approval.

Pluto scratches the stubble on his face as he answers my question about the Dark Nights, unconcerned about the clothes. Alphas end up naked around each other too often to be able to give a shit about modesty. "We know they've pissed off some bear shifters who live in Oregon. So they're having trouble out there. Our plant in their ranks told me there's a bit of dissension. Stone's wife might be against him keeping an omega, edging her out. Her family's pretty extensive, so she might have some pull in the pack."

"Good. Maybe I should have a little chat with her."

"I'll set it up."

We stride into my office, business taking over our heads as we both consider strings we can pull. "I think we need the inner perimeter guarding Elena to consist of betas."

Pluto sucks in a breath between his teeth as he takes a seat in a leather chair at the small circular meeting table off to the left of my office door, the table where I take most of my meals. "That will leave her vulnerable if any alphas penetrate. A couple growls, orders, most betas will fold."

I press my lips together. "I know. But based on last night, I don't think we can use alphas. You and Cody were both pretty damn affected by her scent."

He sighs, nodding, drumming his fingers on the table before a grin spreads slowly across his face. "What about humans?"

"What about them?"

"We could hire some private security—glimmers."

I grab my phone before I pull out the seat across from Pluto and sink into it. "They'd have to be fucking good to keep Stone out."

"It'll cost you a pretty penny for good."

I roll my shoulders. It isn't money that's the issue. It's having a million other people in my space, people I don't know sniffing around. But this is what it'll take to keep Elena out of Stone's grasp. "Do it." I don't have a shortage of cash, between the accounting firm my mom owned and passed onto me, the three biker bars my father had, and the shifter-specific clothing stores I established, I'm sitting pretty flush.

"How soon?"

I start scrolling through the texts and missed calls from Stone. Pluto's right. He's pissed.

You fuck. You better hand that omega over untouched tomorrow night or I will gut your entire elite.

"Stone's got stones, making that kind of a threat," I say aloud, showing the text to Pluto, who rolls his eyes and shakes his head.

"He'll have a hell of a time trying," Pluto's response is just what I want to hear. We share a bloodthirsty grin.

I decide to ruffle Stone's feathers a bit, make him squawk.

Was untouched written in the treaty terms? I didn't see it there. I shoot the text back, certain the fucker will see it even though it's before dawn. He's probably hopped on a flight out here already.

Sure enough, a second later my phone rings. I swipe to answer.

"You piece of shit," Stone snarls.

"Good morning to you."

"I'm gonna stick you like a pig, boy."

"Like I did her?"

The silence from his end is a beautifully glorious thing. I sip my coffee as Stone debates whether or not I'm telling the truth or trying to get his goat. I glance over at Pluto, to let him share my amusement but he's giving me a scolding look instead, one that asks why the hell I'm pushing this.

Why?

Because I'm going to keep Elena.

And I know that's going to cost me, but she's worth the price.

Besides, if I get to pay in blood, Stone's blood, it'll be even better. Then I'll get two things I've always wanted: an omega, and the entire fucking southeast. Fifteen hundred miles of shifter territory with a lot of fucking oil to boot. It's a move I've considered for years, dwelt on, debated. But this little wolf has been my catalyst. It's now or never.

"You want a deathmatch, son? You've got it. But I don't show mercy. Your death is gonna be a slow, embarrasin'ly painful thing."

"Can't wait."

The line goes dead, just like Stone will soon. The sick, twisted alpha in me is thrilled by the prospect of violence, the idea I might get to flex my power in front of Elena as I square off against Cooper Stone.

Last night with Pluto, I'd been holding back. It's been a long time since I've had to give a fight my all. That rush of a real fight, one where death is just an inch away and you can feel the reaper's scythe sliding down your spine, just waiting for an opportunity to hook you … there's nothing like it. I don't know if it makes my soul scream or sing, but I fucking love the sound.

The logical side of me knows how big the risk is. The logical side of me is also aware that Stone's as slippery and deadly as mercury. If he can get Elena some other way, he'll do it. I can't give him an inch.

I glance up at Pluto and say, "Get those guards here as fast as you can get 'em."

He nods in confirmation. "More elites and some betas should be here in an hour. I had Tango pull a bunch of numbers for younger beta guys, those who might not crumple as easily, ones not as used to our orders."

I tap the table with my palm. "Good. Sounds perfect. After you do that, get the arena set up for tonight. Stone and I have a little appointment to keep."

Pluto's face grows pale. "You didn't."

"He challenged me."

Pluto grinds his teeth, eyes flashing before he drags a hand down over his face. "Dammit."

"Afraid I'll lose?"

"No. Afraid you'll win and be so cocky I won't be able to stand being around you for months."

I let out a harsh laugh and bang on the table. Fucker always knows just what to say.

"You've also created a security nightmare for me though. Thanks for that."

"I'll give you one of Stone's oil refineries when it's over."

His eyes widen in disbelief. "Do you know how much those things make?"

I just give a grin. "Better earn it, then. Hurry. You have just enough time to line out private security before the betas get here. And I have to do some more research."

I shove out of my seat and grab a laptop and the book on omegas before returning to the table. I've flipped open the computer and opened up a few different search tabs when Matthew brings in my omelet and clothes for Pluto. My second changes while I begin to eat.

I take a bite, the cheese inside is hot and gooey, the salty ham a perfect contrast to the eggs. Then I flip open the book, deciding it will be easier to read one-handed than type one-handed while I eat. It automatically opens to the illustration I always seek out; the binding has worn down over the years. I flip backward to find a different chapter, hoping that there's something in here that will help with Elena's wolf. It's odd that her wolf won't reappear at will.

Most shifters have the opposite problem after they come into their wolf; their animal wants out so often that they have to fight to contain it. I know I was that way.

My wolf chuffs as my mind brings up a memory of shifting in my grandmother's kitchen just before a birthday dinner for my mom. The smell of turkey had been too much, and I'd shifted and knocked the bird down from the oven where it had been cooling—still in the pan. I'd devoured the entire thing steaming hot, burning my tongue on the way down, and earned myself several whacks from her wooden spoon.

But a reticent wolf? That's unusual. And I wonder if that's part of the issue with Elena's heat. I flip to the Table of Contents, hoping it might help me.

I find a chapter title that seems useful: Omega Wolves and Their Unique Traits. I flip to the starting page and burrow into the dry text, scouring it for something that resonates.

I find this passage.

Omega wolves typically won't go into their first heat until they feel safe and secure. The environment has to be conducive; most omegas prefer to have a nest—typically a cozy, dimly lit space with a mattress, lots of pillows, a fridge, and a number of female stimulation devices. Once their heat has begun, females typically need at least twelve orgasms per day and the typical heat lasts five days. That can be quite taxing for an alpha, so nests should be prepared to help—

I have trouble not stroking my dick over my pants just reading that. The image of Elena panting up at me, chest heaving, tears streaming from her eyes as she begs me for more orgasms, is like a match to tinder and all my lust alights. I've always had a strong sex drive; most of the women I've been with couldn't keep up after round two. It's just another sign that Elena's supposed to be mine, that those tight thighs were made to clench onto me and that soft pussy was meant for this dick.

But a nest is something I never thought about. I needed to give my omega a nest. I quickly scan over all the ideal traits the book lists out for a nest, comparing them with the various rooms in my house.

For the first time ever, I'm bemoaning high ceilings. As a guy who's nearly seven feet tall, I've always loved high ceilings. Most of my house is automatically ruled out. But then an epiphany hits. The attic. I turn and am not surprised at all to see Matthew walking in with a bottle of mineral water for me.

If I couldn't smell the fact that he's human and not a mage, I'd swear the man's a psychic.

"Keys to the attic?" I ask, not bothering to explain.

Matthew's eyes widen. "Um ... yes sir." He digs through his pocket and pulls out his key ring as I grab the last giant bite and then stand. I chew quickly and swallow fast.

"Follow me." I stride from my office to the stairs, and he follows me quickly to the end of the hallway on the third floor. I only stop once we are staring at the white door that leads to the attic.

Matthew unlocks the door for me and pushes it open, revealing a steep set of stairs and the musty scent of boxes. He flicks on the light switch and then waits to allow me to go up the stairs first, though he follows behind.

When I reach the top, I see a long low room made entirely of wooden beams extending in front of me. The ceiling slants down on either side so that I can really only stand comfortably in the very middle of the room.

There are tiny round windows at either end of the rectangular space, but otherwise, it's dim and dingy. Cardboard boxes and old trunks are everywhere. The shit isn't even mine, some of it belongs to the previous owners. Some of the boxes hold records from the prior alpha, stuff I've had digitized.

I try to ignore the clutter and imagine the floor with a giant oversized mattress, bean bag chairs, low bookshelves filled with all kinds of toys ... the image of me pulling a set of anal beads slowly from Elena's ass has me gripping the top of the railing hard. Maybe a sex swing could be drilled into the rafters so that I can stand in the middle and...

"Clean this place up. I want the thickest carpet imaginable. A huge mattress going wall to wall. A fridge. Shelves. Girly shit."

I'll let Matthew order all the other things. I'll order the sex toys myself.

I turn to see Matthew's eyebrows high and surprised but he gives a stiff nod, just like he always does to my requests. "Yes sir, not a problem."

I tromp down the stairs past him. "Oh, and I want it done by tomorrow night."

"That might be a bit of a problem."

"Make sure it's not."

"Yes, Alpha Maddox."

I grin. Once Elena sees the nest I'm going to give her, she'll be saying, 'yes Alpha Maddox' too. I can't wait.

18

JONAH

I ARRIVE at Alpha Maddox's mansion early in the morning, nerves giving me goosebumps. *Is she here? Am I gonna have to see her make doe-eyes at him?*

The hollow pit in my chest expands and it feels like my ribs might break. My tongue turns sour.

I try to tell myself to grow the fuck up, but it's Elena, so that argument doesn't really work. She's not something I can sweep under the rug.

Best I can do is tell myself I'm not a pussy-whipped idiot.

It's a lie.

But it's the best I can do.

I have to somehow give back her phone and her bag. I wonder if that's why I was summoned here in the first place. I hope not. I can only imagine having to hand everything over in front of Black.

God, am I still gonna have to see her in class? Fuck. Maybe I need a semester off. I can't imagine her coming to class, wearing his sweatshirts, trying to joke with me.

Nope.

I'm definitely unenrolling. Don't need a degree anyway to be a mechanic. I just wanted some business classes so I can set up my own shop, but I'll just wing it.

I walk up the steps to Maddox's big brick house, this fancy-ass place that makes me self-conscious of the black grease beneath my fingernails and the fact that I ate a Hot Pocket for breakfast. I pick at my wrinkled Pearl Jam t-shirt and wonder if I was supposed to dress up. The elite who texted me just said to show up and "no sandals." That was literally my only guideline. No sandals.

The door's opened for me by one of the shifters my age who looks just as lost as I feel.

"Hey. Know what this is about?" I ask with a friendly grin.

"No clue. Hopefully not hazing."

"Yeah. Hope not," I respond as I enter a fancy entry room, nodding to a couple other beta guys around my age that I know from the howls. I don't remember their names, they live on the other side of town. One wears a collared shirt and slacks and I can't tell if he's the dumbest or the smartest of us.

My hand goes into my jeans pocket and I fiddle with Elena's phone, which is still in there, literally burning a hole, waiting for me to do something with it.

I study the big staircase rising in front of me and then splitting off to the right and the left like this is a castle. On the ground floor, the room I'm in seems like some kind of hub. Hallways shoot off in different directions from it.

I sniff the air delicately, trying to scent Elena, but I can't over the giant bouquet in a vase sitting on the front table.

An older guy in a penguin suit comes out of one of those halls and for a second, I feel like I'm in a Batman movie.

"Good morning, gentlemen. I'm Matthew."

Thank goodness. If he'd have said Alfred, I would have given an awkward laugh and made everyone look at me like I'm stupid.

Matthew raises a wrinkled hand. "Please follow me. Alpha Black thought you'd be more comfortable in the kitchen."

He turns and leads us away just as a couple new guys stumble in the front door behind us, looking as tired as I'd normally feel. I mean, it is only like five a.m. If it weren't for this big bunch of dread sitting inside me, I'd be yawning too. But I'm not. I'm busy glancing every direction for a sign of Elena.

I haven't caught her scent yet, but the reason becomes clear when I make it into the massive kitchen. There are at least fifteen other beta dudes here already. With the new arrivals and myself, there's probably twenty. That's a lot of male scent for my wolf's nose to get past.

My wolf is curled up inside my head, napping. He blinks open one eye when I think about scents, decides it's not important and settles his head back onto his paws.

Well, that's fucking helpful, thanks, I tell him. He doesn't seem to have any of the anxiety that's flowing through my system like I just downed three espresso shots. He has no clue that we're about to face rejection from Elena and therefore isn't worried about it. He never worries that far in advance anyway. Unless a threat is in his face, he assumes an alpha will take care of it.

Fucking annoying sometimes.

There's a huge spread of food laid out on the tables, eggs and toast piled up.

"Gentlemen, go ahead and eat. The Second will be here in a moment to provide you with more instructions."

The Second? My throat dries out, wondering what's going on. If Alpha Maddox is sending his right-hand man to give us instructions, then it must be coming right from him. I wonder what it is. I wonder if it has anything to do with Elena. It can't be about her phone if there are all these guys here. But... it can't be a coincidence that I scented her on him last night and all of a sudden big things are happening, can it?

I join the line of guys near the white marble countertop. I grab a fancy plate that feels like I could snap it in two if I'm not careful. Then I scoop up some food, listening to the conversation around me until the sound of a woman's heels echoes through the kitchen. All our heads immediately swivel. My heart beats faster, though I've never known Elena to wear heels. Not unless she was feeling naughty.

It's not her.

Relief and disappointment both sweep through me as some older woman in a deep blue power suit walks in. She's got hair that looks like our local newscaster, sprayed so high it resembles a wig. She smells human, just like the butler.

"Matthew," The woman reveals a set of wrinkles that show she smiles a lot.

I turn away, more interested in food and coffee until I hear what she says next.

"It's been such a long time since I planned a wedding this size. I'm so excited!"

I almost drop my plate. I mean, I do drop it, but I catch and fumble around with it and my eggs slide up against my shirt as I make a clumsy save.

All of a sudden, my cheeks feel hot—but not from embarrassment. There's a huge fire inside my head and everything's going up in smoke. I cough, choking. Agonized.

My wolf does wake up at that, prowling back and forth, whining and worried. *Mate?* he asks, worried she's in danger, worried something's wrong with her, worried that this perfect woman is lost to us forever.

"It's not for her," I tell myself, moving to an unoccupied window seat. But I don't believe it. I've seen people get their wolves and decide their futures in a single day before. Decide the futures of everyone around them too.

Agony vibrates inside of me.

I've known people who wished they were human before. My aunt used to all the time after my uncle fucking abandoned her. But I've never actually wished it myself.

Not until now.

Now, I wish I was just a regular guy and Elena was just a regular girl.

Mathew and that woman trot off, discussing the size of the ballroom here and guest lists and shit.

I want to vomit. The smell of eggs suddenly makes me sick.

I sit down with my plate in my lap and stare at the jumbled yellow goo, eggs who've been beaten into a pulpy mess. I'm pretty sure that's what my heart looks like right now too. Fuck me.

I set the plate onto the striped cushion beside me because now I have no appetite. I stare outside at the perfectly manicured lawn. It even has a fountain. There's a fence that looks like it might hide a pool in the distance. All these luxuries slap me in the face. They shout about the things Black Maddox can give Elena that I can't.

I've got a whopping two grand in my bank account right now. And I had to scrimp every penny of that.

I squeeze my eyes shut and tell myself that I just want what's best for her.

Not fucking true.

The selfish beast inside wants her for himself. I'm not the bigger person or the better person. I don't want to be—I want to be *her person*.

I'm about two seconds away from punching through the window next to me so that Black comes stomping in here, furious at me for fucking up his house, and I can get a good swing in before he bans me for life. Maybe even exiles me. Because then I'd never have to see her...

But even that thought, never seeing her again, isn't a relief. It cuts even worse. There's no escape. So I remain seated as conversation drones on around me and time passes. I just sit, locked inside my head like a prisoner.

Who'd have thought hell would look like a sunrise? Full of pink clouds and torment.

Finally, I shift my gaze from outside to the window pane. Wouldn't it be ironic if I fucked this house up, let my wolf out to rampage through the kitchen, and then this wedding was for Alpha Maddox's second? The chances of that are like point one percent but still. I need to see her. I have to be absolutely, one hundred percent sure that Elena's chosen him. I can't give up without knowing that.

I stand up and walk my uneaten plate over to the trash, dumping the eggs in and then putting the plate in the sink with the others.

I wander back down the hall we came from, sniffing gently at every tall white door I pass. If I get stopped, I'll say that I'm looking for a restroom. That sounds realistic enough. I make it back to the front entry without spotting or smelling Elena. But a short hallway that's almost more of an alcove, with only one door at the end, catches my eye. I move toward it and catch a very faint whiff of Elena.

She's been there. Maybe not recently, but definitely there.

"Hey! What are you doing?" A loud male voice echoes through the entryway.

I jerk my gaze from the door and over to him. Dammit. It's Pluto. One of those elite assholes, the same one I talked to at the howl. His brow is down and he's eyeing me suspiciously. I hate the fact that he's an inch or two taller than me. It just makes the gap between alpha and beta that much more glaring.

He takes a step forward, getting into my space and I drop my eyes automatically, reflexively, even though I don't back away like I would if I was shifted.

"I..." My excuse dies in my throat as nerves warn me that he'll know if I lie. I was planning on lying to that human butler, not an elite. My pulse will race and my scent might change. I've never been as good at controlling my scent as other betas. My brother lies to our father all the time. But me? I've never been able to get away with things like that.

Mom's always said it's because I've got a sweet heart. Right now, I wish my heart was made of steel. I wish I wasn't a damned beta. I shove my fist into my pants so that he can't see me clench it, doesn't see it as a challenge to him, but what I'd really like to do is shove my fist into his face and make a run for that door that carries a trace of Elena's scent.

"You're supposed to be in the kitchen with Matthew." Pluto's tone is flat. But his eyes are narrowed, not nearly as emotionless as his voice. He doesn't like me, never has. But now, I think he might not trust me.

I shrug. "He left." I stick with the truth.

"And why'd you leave?" Pluto crosses his bulky arms.

"Looking for someone."

"Well, you found me."

"Yup."

"I was about to come in there anyway and give you all a run down for today. So what did you need to tell me before I address the troops?"

"Troops?" I can't help looking back up.

"Guard dog duty." Pluto gives me a cold smile full of mean teeth. "But you came out here for a reason, right, Fido? *Tell me*." His tone changes to an alpha command on those last two words.

My body automatically reacts. The hairs in my ears tickle and my knees feel like marshmallows. A dull fog enters my mind and the answer drips off my tongue thickly, like syrup. "I have a phone I need to give back."

"A phone?"

I pull Elena's phone out of my pocket and hold it up. "She left it in class yesterday."

The phone is out of my hands before I realize I forgot to say Elena's name. I don't have to, because Pluto holds it to his nose for half a second and then quickly away.

He glares down at me. "I saw you last night. Why didn't you give it to me then?"

My wolf whines in my ear, urging me to yield my neck, to step back and tuck my tail. But I don't.

I'm not an alpha, but I'm not as cowed as my wolf is. Most of the time anyway. I even fought one of my uncles who's an alpha once. He gave me a lot of tips afterward, for standing up to entitled assholes like himself. Tip one: stay calm.

I sigh, trying to relax my pulse as I try to explain what happened last night without handing over my shredded heart on a platter like it's some appetizer. "I went to give it to Alpha Maddox so he could find her because she was missing. Then I realized he already had."

Pluto gets a twitch in his cheek, like he doesn't like my answer. But he doesn't ream me about it. He just stares down at me like he can't believe he has to deal with such an idiot.

Guess what, fuckwad? We betas feel the same way about you. We aren't allowed to say it. That's the only difference.

"Stay right here," Pluto commands as he turns and walks briskly across the marble entryway to a hall with a wooden floor and a door that opens to show me the sliver of a fancy-ass office.

When he disappears from sight, I mull over our conversation and then want to kick myself.

Fuck. Pluto said he was on his way to talk to us. He's Alpha Maddox's second right now? His right-hand man? Of course he is. It's only fitting our alpha pick a total dick to back him up. Great. Should have paid more attention to the elites at the howls. But the reality is, running into any of the ego-driven, puffed-up dickheads during a howl is the perfect way for a beta to get punked.

My friends and I generally try to avoid them at all costs. Not to mention the fact that their constant fights for rank mean that the second position shifts often. I think the first year I became a Lobo I tracked it but the second shifted about six times. Since then, I haven't bothered.

Alpha Maddox comes out of the office right behind Pluto, his huge bulk filling the hall and blocking out the hanging overhead light behind him for a second. Not creepy at all.

I try to keep my shoulders straight and not look intimidated. *I didn't do anything wrong,* I remind my wolf, though he whines and immediately wants to roll over and show his belly. Fuck that.

The alpha reaches me and stares down, his crisp white shirt a huge contrast against my wrinkled tee. I search for a flaw in his wall of muscle. I find a couple gray hairs.

Elena really wants a guy that old?

Even my wolf curls his lip a bit, though he's not about to growl, even in my head where no one else can hear.

That only annoys me more and I poke at my wolf, thinking, *Look at that old man. Black's practically ancient.*

My wolf tucks his ears back and growls at me for failing to call Black by his alpha title. But fuck it. He's taken the one person that meant more than anything from me. Not like he can take much else.

I find Black's dark eyes giving me a steady once over and my skin prickles uneasily. My nerve endings don't agree with my rebellious logic. They think there's plenty more that Black can take from me in the form of skin, blood, pain.

"How do you know Elena?" he asks quietly.

I swallow and say, "We met in a class. We go to the same college." I don't add anything else, like how *well* I know her.

He gives a brief nod as if what I say makes perfect sense. Which it does. It's the truth, even if it's only a partial truth.

"And why did you have her phone?"

"She ran out of class yesterday saying she was sick."

Again, I get that thoughtful nod from him. His alpha energy radiates just underneath his skin, almost like one of those heat shimmers that happen in the summertime, where you stare into the distance and the air itself squirms in the heat. But he doesn't shove it out at me like Pluto just did. He doesn't try to manipulate me. Just studies me.

"Name?" he asks.

With a sigh, I give him my pack name. "Murky. My friends chose it. Don't hold it against me."

He chuckles and, to my shock, reaches out and pats my shoulder. "Come on. You can say hello."

"You really think that's a good—" Pluto shuts up when Alpha Maddox gives him a glare.

"He's a beta. There won't be an issue," Black retorts, already leading me toward the door I'd been eyeing.

My heart thumps a warning. Black's being too nice. Alphas aren't nice in my experience. "Is she here, sir?" I ask, though her scent's growing stronger every second. "Did she finally shift?"

I think I already know the answer. But hearing the words from Black's lips confirms. "Oh, she shifted."

The way he says it, with that self-congratulatory tone, has me bristling.

He pulls out a key and unlocks the door and I blink twice at that. *What the fuck?* I try not to let my heart speed up, try to force it to stay slow by taking deep, meditative breaths. But why is Elena locked in a room? Did something go wrong when she shifted? Did she actually turn into an alpha instead of a beta wolf? Or worse...did she cross paths with a human on her first run?

I swallow hard as one possibility comes to mind. "She didn't hurt anyone, did she?" I ask as Black starts down a set of stairs. This door apparently leads to a basement.

He turns back toward me and bursts into laughter as though I've said the funniest fucking thing ever. Instead of answering, he just continues down the steps.

I follow cautiously, my eyes taking in a cracked wall, a broken television, a ping pong table snapped in half. A fight clearly happened down here, a big one. I even see blood staining the carpet.

Fuck. I hope that's not hers.

The hairs rise up on my neck as I take in the scene. As a beta, my wolf hates fighting. As a guy, I've been in plenty. And this one definitely looks like two shifters battling it out. Human fights don't last that long, despite what tv producers think.

Is Elena okay? Did her wolf go wild?

Her scent fills the air as I step off the bottom step and onto the plush carpet. I inhale and take it in, noting it's mixed with a few other males', plus a nasty cologne.

She's here. But was she here during that fight? Or—

My questions cut off as Black pushes open a bedroom door and I see a figure sprawled out on a mattress.

"Wake up, princess," he says softly, in a tone I've never heard from him before. But I recognize it. It's exactly the tone my dad uses with my mom.

My throat suddenly doesn't have enough room. My shirt's gotten small, the collar too tight. I can't get enough air.

Elena stirs, mewling. Black walks over to her and I watch her bat his hand away. He just grins and climbs up to straddle her on the mattress.

I turn around and walk farther into the middle of the rec room, away from them.

But it doesn't help. The walls feel too close. They're moving in. *I can't. Fuck.* I shut my eyes, but that only makes the sounds in the other room double.

Elena gasps when she wakes up and Black laughs.

"You ass—" Her typical snark is swallowed up…by a kiss, I imagine. That silence rakes across my back and digs into my skin painfully. I don't want to watch, but I don't want this fucking silence to drag on as my imagination fills in the blanks.

God, why did I come down here? What am I doing here?

"I'll just—"

"Jonah?" Elena's voice is a rope and tugs my feet around before my head can tell them to stay put.

Black's on top of her, his mouth on her neck but her face is turned toward me. Her expression mirrors the terrified horror I feel.

I spin back around, chest heaving, cursing myself for looking.

"Get off! There are people here, you pervert."

Black chuckles and I hear bedsprings shift.

One second later, Elena has rushed over and is standing in front of me. Her entire body is draped in this massive shirt that I'm certain is Black's. She's wearing sweatpants too. She's basically swallowed up by him, consumed. Their scents mingle in my nose as I struggle to breathe.

My wolf gives a broken howl inside my head.

I try to forge a smile. I don't think I pull it off. Instead, I cough and offer, "I brought your phone."

Elena blinks up at me.

Black slides in behind her and hands it to her before wrapping his arms around her waist the way I've always dreamt of doing. She pushes him back, but not hard, it doesn't look like she's really resisting.

I glance to the side and quickly start talking, trying to disguise the vicious longing in my chest. "I have your backpack in the car too, since you ran out of class. I don't know if you care about assignments ... but I wrote those down." Fuck me. I sound like a fucking nerd.

"Ran out?" Black grins. “So eager to shift, weren’t you?”

"Black!" Pluto's yell echoes in the hall upstairs. "You coming or what? These betas are waiting."

"Be right there!" Black shouts back. "Got you some bodyguards, little wolf."

Elena furrows her brow but doesn't respond, just grips her phone so hard that her knuckles turn white.

What is she thinking right now? Is this as awful for her as it is for me? As painful? Or is she just embarrassed? Does she not want to deal with me?

"Here. I'll let Murky fill you in on classes while I go give the other betas a quick rundown." He plants a possessive kiss on her cheek. "Afterwards, I've got a surprise for you."

Black strides off with no clue that he's just ripped out my heart, stomped on it, and then left me in the middle of my worst nightmare.

19

ELENA

I'VE FALLEN into a crevice between two glaciers, down into a freezing abyss between massive sheets of ice. There's no hope of crawling out of the darkness and no way I'll escape the bite of the cold. One of the glaciers moves behind my back, sliding away. The other's blue eyes pierce me and the air inside my lungs frosts over.

I wish I was dead.

Last night comes at me in a rush that fills my cheeks with blood but does nothing to stave off the awful numbness spreading through my fingers. *Oh god. I'm that girl. Black and I ... we...*

And now Jonah's here.

I want to scream that I didn't want to. I didn't mean it. That I dreamed about him, not Black. Anything to erase that look in Jonah's eyes, which whispers friends with benefits was a lie and shouts that I'm a soul-crushing monster. I feel like one.

I want to blame Black, call him a beast. He is one.

But I can't. For some reason, I can't.

Because I could have pushed him away. He might not have listened, I don't know. But I didn't push him. I was on the brink. And I let myself go over.

Jonah deserves better than me. I can see all the hurt swimming through his eyes, though he tries to hide it and it makes me hate myself.

An awkward silence wraps us in its embrace and we just stare at one another. His blond hair is dull in the basement light as he digs his hands into the pockets of his jeans, making his muscles bulge inadvertently. I study his face, realizing that I don't have to crane my neck to look up at him like I do with Black. He's still tall, at least five inches or so taller than me. But he's not a giant. He's just right.

I've never noticed that freckle just above his right eye before. Somehow, suddenly, all the things I've never noticed about Jonah seem important.

Is it the last chance I'll ever get to see them? Is he going to turn around now and leave with Black and never come back?

My perusal continues until I hear the lock click on the basement door. We're locked in together and suddenly the space feels stifling.

Jonah breaks eye contact and looks over at the stairs his brow curving.

"Why are you locked in?" He asks the easy question, not the hard ones. But that's Jonah. A peacekeeper. The friendly guy. Thoughtful. Never one to push and shove —he's the polar opposite of Black. He asks like he's curious, without condemnation or judgment.

Even so, I have to swallow a lump in my throat before I can respond. "I'm locked in to keep other alphas out." I gesture at the television and the ping pong table, at the carnage. "Apparently, *that's* what happens when another alpha scents an omega."

"An omega?" Jonah's jaw drops and he makes eye contact. All the tension in his body seems to fade away, as does the color on his face, his shock obvious.

I give a watery-eyed grin. "You didn't expect me to become one either? That makes two of us." My voice breaks and I clear my throat, looking down at my phone, playing with it, dragging my nail around the case. I don't deserve the pitying look crossing Jonah's face right now. Not after what I did.

His arm comes to nudge mine and I glance up.

Words flow out of me in a rush. "I didn't want to. I didn't mean to. If I'd have known shit was going to happen like this, I'd have taken you with me when I shifted. I was just uncertain what was happening. And then I was so excited." I shake my head as my vision swims and my tongue flails, searching for something to keep me afloat in this tragic conversation. "Black found me in the woods. There were these other alphas. Dark Nights. And then he thought I was one and got pissed. And then—"

"Hey." His voice comes out soft and warm, like butter melting on top of a roll.

I look up and my tears spill over. His expression is so understanding, so kind. And I can't stand it. He should hate me, loathe me right now for what happened. He tries to tuck me into a hug but I pull away because I don't deserve to sink into his warmth and comfort. I throw my phone onto a recliner and start pacing, hands coming up to my rat's nest hair. As I walk, I begin to shake. Last night, the reality of being a shifter scared me. The possibility of other alphas scared me. But here and now, I'm literally staring in the face of what I've lost by becoming an omega. *Who* I've lost. And that's even scarier.

I can't be around alphas. I rank lower than betas, so who knows which of them might try to flex and show their rank. Am I going to be alone now? Is getting locked in a basement going to be my new normal? My existence from now on?

Fuck, being a glimmer sounds better than being an omega. I'd rather not have a wolf. "Can I get rid of my wolf?" I spin around and look up at Jonah.

He's startled by my question and gives me a slow shrug. "I've never heard of anyone—"

I stomp towards my phone and scoop it back up off the leather seat, unlocking it and Googling. The signal's slower than a snail in the basement and I walk toward the window on the far side of the rec room, seeking a signal as I ask, "Can you even search this shit online?"

"Elena, it's your wolf—"

"I don't want her!"

"She's part of you."

"No! She showed up one time and then disappeared. She ruined everything. How the fuck can I be a nurse now? Huh? How the fuck can I even be around you after what's happened? After I've ruined everything!" I shake my head; there's so much noise inside of it that it feels like the marching band from my high school is warming up, a cacophony of disjointed and painful sounds.

"Why aren't you screaming at me, Jonah? Why aren't you mad?" The sounds inside of me go suddenly silent, nervous anticipation taking their place. Because if Jonah feels like I do, he should want to get rid of my wolf too. He shouldn't want her here. I always kind of assumed he wanted more between us but I was too scared to give it. After seeing my parents, I never wanted to be tied to someone else. Frienefits was all I wanted.

But now that I've lost him, I suddenly want everything I always scoffed at and never wished for—everything I'll never get the chance to have.

Jonah's not perfect. He's a terrible singer and sometimes dumb shit rolls off his tongue far too easily. But he's also kind. And good with his hands. And willing to eat my cooking when I go to his place for a make-fun-of-this-movie night. And he listens.

Fuck.

"I..." Jonah trails off but that kicked-puppy expression is back on his face.

"You should hate me. *I* hate me. You're my best damned friend. My—" I choke up and can't get out words but I bring my fist over my heart. Another round of hot tears well up in my eyes but I refuse to let them spill.

"I am?"

"Of course, stupid." A broken laugh slips out of my mouth and contorts into an ugly sob.

It's not fair. Screw the moon goddess. Jonah's right to be skeptical. Why the hell would she let something like this happen? I was happy with my life. Yeah, I wanted my wolf but I didn't think it would be this life-alteringly awful. Regular alphas and betas go on with their lives all the time—Jonah's aunt being the exception. I don't want to be the damned exception, I want to be the rule.

"Jonah, I don't want to be an omega. God, that sounds fucking whiny. But it's the truth."

A sympathetic look comes into Jonah's eyes, the same kind Dad used to get whenever he introduced me to pack members. There was always this moment when their eyes would light up almost like they'd said out loud, "Oh, that's why you stay. You have a kid." Then this holier-than-thou expression would come over them like they were better than us or grateful they were better than us. I turn away, pissed all of a sudden. I hate those looks. Those looks are for victims.

"Why the hell would the daughter of one of the only female alphas in our pack be a *fucking* omega?"

"I don't know." Jonah's reply is tranquil and steady, the opposite of everything I feel.

How can he be so calm? Unless he's not ripped up inside too. Unless I misread that look from him earlier and was way too arrogant in my assumption about what I meant to him. That thought steamrolls me, pressing painfully down on my insides.

I glance down at my phone, needing something to do. It is still *uselessly* loading. Part of me wants to throw it, but that would just be a literal tantrum. Instead, I study it, and its smooth, sleek design. I drag my tongue over my teeth and feel morning fuzz. "I need a toothbrush." Suddenly, I can't handle how dirty I feel on the outside, possibly because I feel utterly filthy within. "I'll be right back."

I leave Jonah standing silent and stunned in the rec room as I walk back into a bedroom that reeks of sex, the woodsmoke edge to Black's scent filling the room like it's a cigar lounge. I cover my nose, trying to stifle the memories that automatically rise with that smell. I'll probably forever associate woodsmoke and caramel with amazing cunnilingus, whether I want to or not.

I can't even look at the bed as I make my way to the bathroom and find the toothbrush and toothpaste that Matthew brought down for me.

I also quickly get ready for the day and dress in clothes from the hospitality basket. They're still Black's, but they don't smell much like him, more like a neutral detergent. That's better. I feel more like myself, the self I know, not the one who's lived through the night as the lowest-ranked wolf in any pack. I don't feel as much like a girl whose best friend just stood there while she told him what he meant to her.

I stare into the mirror and my reflection is a falsehood. It doesn't show the haggard, stripped, broken way I feel. The girl in the mirror has fresh cheeks, not bags sunken under her eyes. She doesn't look hollow even though she's empty inside. After I brush out my hair, she doesn't even look wild. She looks tame with her bare pink lips and no eye makeup. Young. She doesn't look sullied by shame or shaped by despair.

Black's mirror is broken.

I blow out a breath when I walk back into the rec room. I'm a little surprised to find Jonah drinking a beer and sitting at the bar, but Black's house is a fucked up place and I'm not surprised he needs one. Especially today.

I cautiously make my way over to him and the short marble countertop, dragging my bare feet along the carpet as I study him and the stiff set of his shoulders. When he hears me coming, he turns in his seat.

"Elena." His eyes travel to the stairs and then back to me. When they settle on my face, I can feel him drink me in like a plant swallowing sunshine. "I suck at shit.

But you know I've always wanted more, right? Like a lot more. I just never wanted to push—"

I run toward him, everything that was shattered inside of me clumsily taped back together by those words. *He feels the same.* I reach for Jonah, but he stands, keeping the barstool between us. His face cracks and his eyes drift toward the floor like they always do when he knows he's going to disappoint me. "We can't. Black will smell it."

"Not even a hug?" I ask, though I know the answer. Bitterness percolates in my stomach and hot resentment starts to brew. But I don't have any grounds to be resentful of Jonah, who still hasn't lashed out at me the way I deserve.

No, I need to save all this negative energy for Black. And I need to remember my place. I need to remember why I don't get to touch Jonah anymore, why I don't even deserve to.

I blow out a breath and try to avoid the tumultuous feelings inside, changing the subject to something lighter, neutral. I can't handle feeling anymore. I need to think about something else. "So, you came over at the crack of dawn to bring me my phone? How'd you even know I was here?"

"Didn't," Jonah responds, taking a pull from his long neck bottle and setting it down on the bar before he adds, "Got summoned."

"What?"

"Bunch of betas got called in to guard you."

I scrub a hand down my face, frustration riddled. "That fucking asshole. He was serious about the bodyguard comment?" Motherfuck. I'm just as much a prisoner now as I was locked up in that storage room.

The broken furniture screams at me, reminding me exactly why I have to stay here. Why it's necessary for Black to take all of these precautions. But I still hate it. It makes me feel like someone's fingers are wrapped around my neck, squeezing tight.

I plop down into the seat next to Jonah's without thinking before I realize I probably should have left an empty seat between us.

He probably doesn't want my tainted omega ass anywhere near him. I tuck my legs up to my chest, putting my feet on the seat and hugging my knees. "How many?"

"Twenty or so." Jonah doesn't sit back down, but he doesn't move away either.

"Damn." That's a lot.

Jonah takes a long drink, not bothering to reply. I watch him swallow. He's drinking his fill, so I let my gaze drink mine.

"I'm sorry if you were scared yesterday when I didn't come back."

"I'm sorry you were scared by some Dark Nights. Lucky Alpha Maddox was—"

"Don't say that."

"What?"

"It's not fucking lucky."

He peels the label on the beer, picking at the corner, not answering me. He knows I both mean it and don't. I'd be dead otherwise. But I feel dead inside right now, so I'm not certain Black really did me any favors.

"How bad are the Dark Nights?" I ask, staring at the wall.

He shrugs. "Depends on who you ask. They think they're pretty awesome."

I chuckle because that answer is so undeniably Jonah. "Always such a people person. No. Give me the dirt. Are they worse? Black acts like they are."

Jonah presses his lips together a few times, contorting his expression until he settles on an answer. "I know a couple of betas over there got punished for stealing by getting their hands cut off."

"Okay, so how's that compare? What's Black do?"

Jonah laughs. "Some might say Black's worse. Puts silver in their cuffs so they can't get out and ships them off to human jail." His eyes glitter with amusement for half a second. "My cousin's boyfriend got sent upstate that way. Personally, I was in favor of it at the time."

"Okay, so human jail. That's not too bad. What about other stuff?"

"Depends, he's a big 'punishments fit the crime' guy. Alpha Stone over in the Dark Nights is more of a physical punishment kind of guy. Supposedly he strings up all the bones he collects from pack violations for Halloween."

My throat grows dry. "So, another alpha isn't necessarily nicer than Black."

"They're all assholes, you want my opinion. Some worse than others. You think Stone's bad, you should be glad his son isn't in charge. Thomas Stone's pure crazy based on the stories I hear."

I nod, staring down at my hands, my solitary hope withering. "So none of them would just let me live my life?"

Jonah sets down his beer and turns to look at me. This time his eyes fill with tears. None fall, he shoves them back. But that, right there, is my answer. No alpha would ever let an omega roam free.

I'm going to spend the rest of my life a prisoner.

I look up at the ceiling and flip it off.

"Um, Elena? What are you doing?"

"Telling the moon goddess she can shove this shit up her ass. Telling my dad he's a dick for leaving me here. I don't fucking know. I'm doing the only thing I can."

Jonah plops his elbow onto the bar top and tosses up a middle finger to match mine.

We flip the universe off together.

I've never wanted to kiss him more but if I do, it'll be a death sentence.

There's a long moment of silence before I find the tiny, microscopic silver lining. "I guess there's one upside to all this bullshit."

"One?"

"You can finally order me around. Apparently, anyone can. If my wolf ever shows up again that is." I laugh bitterly.

Jonah sits back down and swivels his barstool so he can look directly at me. His lazy posture contrasts the look on his face as he studies me carefully. "What do you mean?"

"She's gone. I mean, I still want to get rid of her permanently. But I can't get her to show back up on command. Pisses Black off. He wants me to go into he…" I trail off and stare at the bar glasses, chastising myself for the fact that I almost said "heat" in front of Jonah. "He thinks he fucking owns me."

I change the subject and am a little shocked by how angry my tone comes out. I am angry, but when Black's in front of me, he just swallows that anger like it's nothing, soaks it in like it energizes him. But without his alpha presence to warp it, the fury is blazing hot.

Jonah crooks a brow and tilts his head, just listening, like he does whenever I need to rage about Mom. "He just fucking claimed me, Jonah. Like he's got the right to do that. Like I'm just *a body* and not a person."

"You know he wants more than that," Jonah shakes his head. "There's a wedding planner upstairs."

I leap out of my chair, knocking it backward and nearly nicking a tooth on the back of Jonah's stool as I fall to the carpet. I ignore how humiliating the entire fall is as I whip around and stand, a hand on either side of my head, clutching at my face. "WHAT?"

All of a sudden, I can't breathe. I can't think. I just see a veil and a dress and then shackles…myself chained to a wall in a wedding dress. Guards are one thing. Marriage…is worse.

My lungs don't work, while my stomach works overtime, churning so quickly I think I might puke. I stumble toward Jonah and latch onto his pant leg as a tear escapes and any pride I have is left shredded on the floor. Desperation is the only thing I know as I beg, "Jonah…run away with me. Help me escape. Please."

20

JONAH

BLACK'S MANSION grounds are abuzz with activity as I stroll around the yard on the afternoon patrol. The perfectly manicured grass doesn't have a single weed and the lawn slopes for almost half a mile before Black's own personal forest is visible. *Fuckwad.*

The place is big enough that guys drive around in golf carts doing rich people shit like "restocking the koi pond", whatever the fuck that is.

I stand in the heat of the sun and pretend to stare at something in the distant trees. But I'm actually thinking about Elena's proposal. She wants to run away with me.

She threw out the suggestion so calmly at first that I'd thought she was being sarcastic. But then she'd leaned forward from her barstool in the basement, the look on her face stealing my breath. Her gray eyes had sought out mine, dark hair falling forward over her shoulders.

"Jonah, find somewhere we can go. Somewhere only humans live. Where we can be together. Please."

The sun heats my face, but it's not the reason I'm sweating. Elena wants me to abandon my pack. My family. My stomach churns. Every step I take through the grass feels like my last.

The strangest part of all is that my wolf wants to do it. My wolf, who loves pack, wants to leave.

Mate, he whispers in my ear, as if that word is all he needs to know.

She wouldn't have said this a week ago, I argue. *A week ago, fuck buddies was good enough. Is she just using me?*

Mate, he replies simply.

God, I want to yank on my hair or throw something. But I have to walk casually, act bored.

If I leave, I can never come back. I'll never see my family again. My brother and my little sisters will become strangers. I don't think Black would punish my family. He's an asshole, but not that big of one. He's never punished family members for the crimes of their kin, which is better than I hear they get in the Dead Rabbits pack. Fuck though.

Leave forever?

I won't be able to shift, because a beta shifting without a pack is just asking for trouble. Beta wolves need a leader for direction and guidance. They aren't good with decisions or confrontation.

What about that? I ask my wolf. *You'd be stuck inside my head.*

Mate, he responds for a third goddamn time.

That's not an answer! I tell him. *Mate isn't the answer for everything.*

This time, his answer comes in the form of an image—a memory of a topless Elena, from the first night she'd seduced me during a study session. I'd been making flashcards at a table in the library, trying not to sneeze at the smell of dusty old books. Then I'd glanced over to find her black button-up shirt open. No bra. Those small nipples pointed right at me and begging for my mouth.

"Dare you," she'd whispered.

Best fucking moment of my life to that point.

My wolf grins as though he's made his point. Then he trots leisurely through my field of vision and appears to lie down in the grass in front of me. He doesn't seem to care about losing his ability to manifest and take control of my body, losing his shot at freedom. But then, he's an animal. Sometimes I can't even tell if he knows what tomorrow means.

He's an animal, I remind myself. Part of me, but an animal. And he doesn't look out for us long term. I have to do that.

What's best?

The idea of living without my family tastes like swallowing filthy broken glass.

But living without Elena…

"Watch it!" Two alphas shoulder me out of the way as they carry a huge chain link fence from a shed. That's the fifth length of fence that's gotten dragged out on my shift.

"Sorry," I apologize as I take a step back. "You guys need any help?"

"Betas stay by the house. Alpha Maddox's orders." One of the alphas responds, huffing as he adjusts his grip on the length of fence stretched over metal poles.

"Okay, yeah. Sure." I agree quickly, which is the best policy when it comes to alphas. "It's just that the shed is pretty close, so maybe I could bring some of that fence part way. Help you out a little." Physical activity sounds good right about now. Working my muscles so that I don't have to think. Releasing some of this tension.

The alphas both have beads of sweat rolling down their foreheads. One of them gives a brief grunt. "Whatever." Then they move off with their load.

That's as much of a yes as I need. I walk over to the shed and grab a piece of fence. It's got to be at least ten feet high and five wide, so it's a beast to handle on my own. But I wrangle it out of the tall metal shed and start sliding it through the grass, saving them a couple hundred yards of carrying. It nearly tips a time or two, causing me to curse up a storm. But it's good because it takes all of my concentration to balance that shit, all my muscles to move it where I want, to master it. I drop my section on the lawn once I feel like I've gotten a little too far from the house. My spine is sticky with sweat, shirt soaked.

I repeat the process. On the second round, the alphas are back just as I lug the huge piece of fence toward my drop point.

"Thanks, man." One of them, I think his pack name might be Warcraft, tells me as he wipes his brow and then shoves back his dark brown hair.

"No problem. I'm dying of boredom standing around."

The guys chuckle as they pick up that piece of fence. "Well, you won't be for long," Warcraft says as he heaves part of the fence up to balance on his shoulders. "No?" I ask conversationally.

"We're using this fence to build a fighting pit. Alpha Maddox is going up against the Dark Night's alpha."

My brows shoot up and my heart starts thumping faster. I have to work to keep fear off my face. "Oh yeah. When's that?"

"Tonight."

My stomach falls out of my body and I almost step on it when I stumble. "What?"

"Yeah, apparently Cooper Stone thinks he's entitled to some omega ass—"

"I think *I'm* entitled to some omega ass," Warcraft's friend quips.

Warcraft stops walking and glances over at me. "You've been inside, right?"

I nod.

"You seen her yet? This omega piece that's got the alpha's all riled up? Is she hot?"

What the fuck? Is he seriously going to talk about Elena like that? Black's going to marry her! That's his future luna! Or … is this how Black talks about her too? "I—I—Betas don't have the same kind of…"

"Yeah, yeah. You're eunuchs."

"Wouldn't it suck if she's got a grade-A pussy but a pug face?" The other alpha laughs.

"Nah. You could just go doggie all day. Or shift and fuck as wolves."

"Think she can take a knot all the way?"

The pair walk off and I'm left with a dread in my stomach that's even worse than before. Is this what Elena's future is like? No wonder she wants to run. Suddenly, all my reasons for staying seem distant. Small.

How can I leave her here with Black, knowing that she'll only ever be seen as a thing, not a person?

Even if she doesn't really love me, how could I leave someone to that fate, least of all ... her?

I swallow hard as I walk back to that shed to drag out another piece of fence. A memory of my grandfather flickers through my head as I sweat and grunt and work.

When I was four, I'd stolen a toy police car from my brother. Then I'd lied to grandpa and said it was mine.

He hadn't punished me. He'd sat me on his knee and told me this. "Once in a while, we can choose to do the right thing. As betas, it might never be a *great* thing. Nothing major. But the right thing warms your chest on cold nights. It keeps you marching on the straight and narrow. The wrong thing will haunt your dreams. It will make you toss and turn. Regret will follow you wherever you run. You won't be able to escape it. Today, you chose the wrong thing. Don't let it happen again."

I'd stolen my brother's candy bar the following week and gotten the same lecture. Every time I did something wrong while I was at his house, grandpa drilled the message into my head.

Now I finally understand what he meant.

I send a silent thank you up to him, wherever he is.

A peace settles into my chest as I make my choice.

I'm going to do the right thing.

Tonight, two alphas are going to fight.

Blood will race.

Adrenaline will be running high.

It'll be the perfect time to escape.

If we can get away with it.

21

BLACK

I RUN down the steps to the basement, hurrying because the clock hasn't been on my side all day. I had plans to fuck Elena up against the wall down here, to hold her up by her wrists, cuffing them with one of my hands and letting her marvel at my strength as my cock pummeled her. If something like that doesn't send a she-wolf into heat, I don't know what will. But my plans have been thrown off course because Stone landed early and wants to fight tonight.

He doesn't want to give me any more opportunities to defile his little omega. Or impregnate her.

He's not a complete idiot, that alpha.

Between Stone's goons, briefing the human guards, betas, and alphas, and setting up the fight … there just hasn't been time to get back to my little mate and enjoy her. I had to send Matthew to bring her meals. I ate on my feet while I was approving caterers, that's how insane the day has been. It's almost dinner and I haven't had a moment to breathe.

The awful scent of the catering drifts down through the vents even though I locked the basement door behind me. I ordered a shit ton of Indian food because, while I love it, I know Stone hates it. But I also chose it because the smell of strong spices tends to burn wolf noses.

Let Stone and his little crew try to sniff Elena out through that mess, I think smugly as I reach the bottom step and go looking for my little wolf.

I find her curled up on her side on the bed, napping in the same place she slept in last night. I can't help but smile. She's already getting comfortable here, already finding her spot. I can't wait until I show her nest to her. I'm sure she'll love that even more.

Everything's settling into place. After tonight's fight, it will be perfect. I'll gain territory and my little vixen all in one fell swoop.

I reach into my pants pocket and pull out the ring that Matthew had delivered this afternoon. It's got a diamond in the middle with two little moonstones on either side. I gently scoop her tiny left hand up into mine and slide the ring on while she's still sleeping. It fits perfectly and, for some reason, seeing her wear my ring makes my dick hard. It's physical proof that Elena belongs to me.

Mine, my wolf says.

I agree. *Mine.*

I climb over her, straddling her like I did this morning to wake her up, grinning when her soft feathery eyelashes flutter open.

"Black?" I love the way she says my name, her tone still sultry with sleep. I don't know if she's a singer, but that voice right there could charm the devil.

I just walked in here for a kiss for luck. I don't have time for much else.

But suddenly, I don't just want to see her wearing my ring. I want to see her wearing my cum. The need to claim her rises fast and quick, like a tsunami, a force that barrels through anything that resists it. The clock suddenly doesn't matter. Stone's deadline doesn't matter. Nothing but this.

I unbutton my pants and slide them and my boxers down. My dick springs out at half-mast just as my mate comes fully awake.

Her gray eyes fly from my dick to the ring on her finger and grow wide.

She's surprised and overwhelmed. Good. Proposals are supposed to be that way, aren't they? I wouldn't know. I never planned on one. But I'm claiming this omega in every way possible.

"Elena." I grab that little hand of hers, wrapping my own around it, but ensuring I can still see that huge fucking rock that marks her as taken. She tries to pull back, probably wanting another second to admire her ring. But she'll have all the time in the world for that later. I have needs now.

I strengthen my grip on her and place both of her hands on my thickening shaft and I start to stroke, showing her just how I like it, guiding her. "I needed to see you, baby."

"No. Black. Stop. We need to talk."

"We can talk in a minute. After I watch you make me come with that ring on your finger. Doesn't it look good?"

Her eyes are on that diamond ring as it glides up and down my dick, her breath coming fast and hard, her chest heaving underneath me, and I wonder if the sight of it turns her the fuck on too. Probably.

I use my left hand to dig under the covers and ruck up the t-shirt she's wearing. I bunch it up around her neck so that I can see those pretty tits.

I feel my balls tighten up and anticipation builds in my lower spine.

I'm gonna come all over my omega.

My future wife.

My luna.

My wolf howls inside my head. He's already amped for the fight but this, *this* drives him over the edge. I reach forward and latch onto Elena's hair, yanking her face up.

"Suck me, princess," I command before pressing my dick between those plush lips of hers even as I speak.

Her mouth is fucking heaven. It's tight and wet and warm. She gasps, then her tongue slithers across the underside of my cock deliciously. Even the gentle scrape of her teeth gets me hot because it feels like she's just as feral as I am right now. I hold her head in place and adjust my angle so I can thrust deeper. I enjoy the feel of her for a minute before need builds again and I push more. She gags and I let up for a second so she can snag a breath before I thrust again. My little wolf is going to have to practice her deep-throating skills.

But the fact that she's so raw and untrained in that area just makes her mine to claim. To teach.

"Breathe through your nose, baby girl. I'm about to go deep."

I slide down her throat, which clenches around me, this time not backing off when she struggles because my balls are blazing and there are flames behind my eyes.

My cock starts to ache and this sensation akin to insatiable hunger fills my stomach. A primal rush fills me, and I rut harder and faster.

A few more deep thrusts and I start to spurt, quickly yanking my dick out and fisting it so I can spray Elena's face and neck, sliding down her body as my dick pulses so that I can get the last couple drops on those perky breasts. I wipe the tip of my dick on her right breast, then drag it across one of her stiff nipples as I stare down into her tear-streaked face.

She's still breathing hard, and I'm tempted to reach down and touch that pussy that I'll bet is soaked. But I'm out of time.

"Don't touch yourself," I order with a warning wag of my index finger. "Save it for after I win. Stone's challenged me to a fight to the death for you."

Her eyes widen in fear for me.

I'm torn between amusement and the desire to spank her for even getting nervous. But my watch buzzes so I do neither as I check the time. "And I've got to go. It starts ... pretty much now. At least warm-up does. They'll bring you out at the end of the match, so Matthew will bring you a dress to change into." I run a hand over her cheek but stop because I really did do a number on her face. It's covered in cum. But I can't say I'm sorry because she looks fucking hot. Owned. Desperate.

Damn. I need to leave before I get hard again. I climb off of her petite body and fix my pants. Then I lean forward and grab her left hand. I kiss my girl's ring before I turn away.

I found her.

But the shifter world doesn't operate on finder's keepers.

To keep her, I'm going to have to rip Stone's head from his shoulders.

22

ELENA

I CLEAN myself up with shaking hands, trying not to fall apart but failing miserably. Once I'm clean I yank that awful ring from my finger and hurl it across the bedroom so hard that it chips the paint on the wall before dropping harmlessly onto the carpet.

I can't believe that just happened. Black just face-fucked me like he owns me already. My stomach cramps at the memory and I refuse to acknowledge how wet I got at being dominated because he just took. Didn't ask. Just took. But I can't even focus on that violation because what he did, awful as it was, doesn't even compare to what's coming. I can't believe what's about to happen.

I pace in the basement, frenzy whipping up a dust storm inside my ribs after Black leaves. Black and Cooper Stone are going to fight to the death. Over me.

Tears streak my vision and I have to bend forward, gripping my knees for a second as the world spins out of place.

Fuck.

Fuck.

Fuck.

My future is about to be decided and I'm going to be handed over to a killer. Whichever shifter is the most deadly gets me as his prize.

I dry heave and fall to my knees on the carpet. The luxurious pile is soft against my skin, an irony because this house is nothing more than a beautiful prison.

As if I'm dying, my life flashes before my eyes, and memories take over.

I see my parents taking me hiking when I was six, standing arm in arm and smiling at each other, their hiking vests open as the sun shines down on them and they breathe in the calm, pine-scented air. My dad's salt and pepper hair is ruffled by the breeze and Mom has her pitch-black locks pulled back in a ponytail. Mom turns to Dad and says, "I should bring you here more often. You glow, Michael."

He leans down for a kiss but pauses just before he reaches her lips, letting her come the rest of the way, letting her control the moment.

I remember screeching, "Ewww!" and holding a hand over my eyes but peeking surreptitiously as they laugh and peck one another with soft kisses.

Another recollection flicks on, replacing the hiking trip. I'm in my bedroom, staring up at the ceiling. My dad sits on the edge of my hot pink comforter. The lights are off but I see the bruise on my dad's eye as he tucks me in and sings me a lullaby. My little hand goes up to stroke his injured cheek and he hisses. "Daddy, what happened? Did you fall off the monkey bars?"

"Shh, sugarplum. Yes. Dad had a little accident, but I'm fine. Just fine. Go to sleep." He hums the rest of the lullaby.

I sink down further, closer to the floor as sobs rock through me so hard that my entire chest aches.

My future is going to be just like his … no wonder he wanted to escape it. No wonder he left me.

The image of him dead in the bathtub, the way I found him when I was eleven, fully clothed, soiled, eyes open but unseeing…

He swallowed an entire bottle of pills to escape my mother.

To escape a controlling alpha.

I promised myself I'd *never* let an alpha have me.

And now?

I wonder if my father and I are going to share the same fate.

I'm startled when my phone buzzes in my pocket. I have to swipe at my eyes in order to even see the screen. I use Black's shirt to mop up my tears, though nothing can soak up the ocean of despair inside.

Then I glance down at the text. It's from Jonah and my heart jumps as I read.

Pretend you're about to puke when we walk outside.

In a single millisecond, all that despair evaporates.

It's replaced by a thin, tense hope.

23

BLACK

THE MOON GODDESS gazes down on us from a lapis sky while all around, the drunken cheers of shifters shred the air.

I stand outside the impromptu fighting cage assembled like a baseball backstop shaped into an octagon.

My elites form a circle standing shoulder to shoulder with me, and just like a baseball team, we're discussing strategies, secret signals, the like. But unlike any game, the stakes here are life and death for all of us.

Warcraft stands next to me since Pluto is escorting a referee onto the property for the fight. The elite's entire body is tense and his eyes dart all around, ensuring that no Dark Nights are near us.

The rest of my elites stand at attention like soldiers, ready and alert but not concerned. They trust me because they know that no matter what happens I'll take care of the Lobos. I swore an oath to do that when I entered this same arena to challenge their prior alpha. I'd stood in a steaming puddle of his blood as I'd vowed to do everything to secure the future of my people.

My elites had raged when they'd first heard Stone had challenged me to a fight, that our pack was at risk over an omega. But once I'd told them my plan to ensure they were protected…their boil had turned to a simmer. Now, most of them were placidly awaiting their next instructions.

Warcraft is on edge because he likes his spot as third—less responsibility with most of the same perks. Stepping into the second's shoes makes him nervous because he's more of a planner and less of an in-the-moment type of guy. Earlier today, he'd been full of calm and confidence. But now, knowing that he's my personal bodyguard until Pluto returns, he's as jittery as a flea.

I ignore him as I glance over at the cinder block locker room where Stone was preparing for the fight. The low gray building is silent, and the high windows glow a gentle yellow in the darkening night. Stone's in there with his own elites, planning all the ways they want to kill me and then desecrate my body.

I have to suppress a shiver that rolls down my spine because fighting Prime, the former alpha, and fighting

Stone...those are two completely different kinds of fights. Stone is crafty and aware. He's manipulative. The rest of his pack might not be...but he and his son are threats.

For a second, I envision myself in the dirt, underneath Stone's foot, throat ripped apart but my brain still a few seconds from shutting down. Fear takes an axe to my spine and I breathe deep, close my eyes, and shove that thought away. Negative visualization can be just as powerful as positive, and I refuse to let the negative take me over. Instead, I turn Stone's elites into cartoon henchmen inside my head. I turn him into Dr. Evil.

They're ridiculous if they think they can win. On my territory. Against me. I work myself up.

Their tiny brains probably can't think up any means of desecration more creative than skull fucking. Meanwhile, I've tried to figure out ways to make them miserable for years if I go.

Stone's elites are known for brawn not intelligence. And while my elites are all good fighters, I've had all of them assessed like humans for their mental strengths, then pushed them to hone those strengths in service of the pack.

So, while Warcraft might not be the greatest second, and might be a little tense in the moment, he is a rather gifted strategist and accountant. And together, we designed a few fail safes to protect the Lobos. Stone's elites are going to find themselves in some deep audits. Get some tax fraud accusations. Headaches that can ruin them from the inside out.

But I don't only think long term. While I like slow, I know my elites would prefer a guillotine. So, we have a plan for that too.

I lick my lips, hoping that the fuckers in that locker room take the bait we literally set out for them.

"Water?" I turn and look over at Gilly, a shifter who's missing a tooth but has the soul of the devil in him. He gives me a solid nod.

"Good."

Shifter law dictates that I can't tamper with the fight or it's outcome in any way. A shifter caught tampering with it will be set in a silver box to starve slowly, in a constant state of burning and healing from contact with the evil material. But…there are no rules about tampering with the water bottles we provide his elites. Or the food we set out.

Gilly's afternoon has been spent injecting liquefied ricin into the water bottles so that they look untouched. He sprinkled it onto the catering, which in the tiny locker room is subs and not Indian food, trying to tempt the soulless demons into eating.

I don't know if Stone's elite will be smart enough to avoid it, but I'm betting they won't. I plan to leave Stone without any damned alphas at his back. The only ones strong enough will be my elite. So even if he does win...fat chance of that...he'll be an island surrounded by an ocean of angry Lobos.

I glance around at all my elites and give them a grin. "Spread out among the crowd and keep things under control. Wouldn't want a riot when I win."

Every single one of them gives a wolfish grin back at me.

Pluto approaches and stands behind me off to my right. He quietly says, "It's time."

I crack my neck and then follow him across the grass toward the dirt ring. Behind the stands, huge lights on poles turn the space into a bubble of afternoon amidst the darkness. My pack members make up two-thirds of the crowd, but a good number of Dark Nights who live just across the disputed border have driven in to watch the fight. There are a couple banners.

All the Lobos wear grey and the Dark Nights are in black, like this is a sporting event and they want to cheer on their favorite team. I can almost imagine an announcer over the loudspeaker leading them in a seventh inning stretch at some point. It looks so innocent and peaceful.

Then again, murder scenes always do before the fact.

STONE AND I STAND IN THE MIDDLE OF AN IMPROMPTU arena on a gated off part of my property. I've got the space surrounded by armed human glimmer guards so that if any of Stone's wolves try to pull anything, they'll have to figure out how to do it without touching humans. Otherwise, the high council will see red.

The smell of beer, Indian food, and sweaty shifters in the metal bleachers mix into a pungent aroma. My monster's going to hate that. But then again, so will Stone's. And since I spent the last hour acclimating, I should have the advantage.

A human referee comes forward, an old glimmer that Matthew knows—the man knows everyone. The ref wears a striped shirt and carries a whistle like this is some kind of civilized sport instead of a long-overdue deathmatch.

I grin over at Stone lazily as an announcer spouts off the rules through a wheeled speaker one of my elites dug up, though really, only one rule matters. We don't stop until someone's dead.

The leader of the Dark Nights is tall and broad, like most alphas. Unlike me, he's dressed in a full suit. I just wear a collared shirt and charcoal slacks. *He's all dolled up with nowhere to go but in the ground.*

My wolf chuffs a laugh at that thought as he sniffs his competition. Stone has a strong walnut scent, different from the scents we get around here. There's almost an undertone of brown sugar I think, but it's hard to be certain with the soup of scents mixing in the sky tonight.

I study him further, examining his face. His jawline isn't quite as firm as it once was, though he still clearly has muscle tone. His hairline is receding a little on either side, already turned gray, but that doesn't seem to stop him. I note the wrinkles in his square forehead, they make him look old, but the fire in his eyes still burns hot and young. His nose is slightly crooked, maybe from a fight or maybe because the moon goddess doesn't love him quite as much as she does me.

I'm betting on the latter.

"Any last words?" I ask softly, as the announcer finishes up and my bare feet dig into the thick grass.

"I'm gonna jizz on your grave." Stone replies.

"I'll make sure that gets put in your eulogy," I retort as my blood amps up, dancing through my veins exuberantly. "Here lies Stone who wanted to jizz on my grave and forsake his wife for another—"

"Not just her. You know what my boys and I are gonna do to every female in your pack after I win?" Stone's easy-going Southern tone belies the cruelty implied by those words, which saws my stomach in half. I'm utterly disgusted.

I glance up at the moon goddess wondering if she sees what a monster he is.

Stone leans in close. "Moon ain't gonna save you, boy. You're dead already."

I'm both electrified and agitated by those words. The need to fight becomes as visceral and all-encompassing as the need to come. I clench my fingers and feel a drizzle of sweat rolling down my spine as my body amps itself up into high gear, brimming with anticipation.

The ref walks over then but my ears hardly hear as the man tells me and Stone to get into position to shift into our monster forms. He spaces us out five feet apart, facing one another, then backs rapidly away to the side of the cage.

My elites line the edges of the cage, standing sentinel. Behind them, the onlookers are wild. But back in the trees, I know glimmers with guns are ready to keep everything secure.

The sounds of the crowd fade as the blood pumping through my ears becomes a booming bass beat that blocks out anything else. My eyes travel over Stone, noting his stance, the way his left arm falls a little more stiffly than his right. An old injury perhaps? I note he has his right foot forward. So he's probably right side dominant. I catalog any little detail that might help me beat him, any potential weaknesses he might have.

My heart bounces feverishly and my wolf is in my line of vision, on all fours, hackles raised, growling at Stone. He sends me a mental image of ripping out Stone's throat.

Yes, I tell him, unable to respond in more than single syllables because I'm tied up so tightly by bloodthirsty excitement.

An air horn blasts, signaling the start of the fight, and suddenly I can hear again.

With a roar, I start to transform, and I watch Stone do the same. My clothing, which I picked for effect, rips away in tattered pieces as my arms grow and become matted with white fur, as my ears turn into wolf ears, and my entire face becomes an animal's, my nose elongating into a wolf muzzle full of snarling, sharp teeth.

The crowd goes wild, my shifters standing and cheering, stomping their feet on the metal bleachers.

Stone's fiends do the same.

I'm gratified to see that my monster stands a bit taller than Stone's brown beast. But I don't get more than a second to gloat before he charges, making the first move.

A grizzled claw hurtles towards my face and I can see it coming with perfect clarity, those curved nails as sharp as any blade. I grin in my monstrous form and instead of leaning away, lean in toward the threat. I put my face into the path of that claw and use my teeth to snap at Stone's arm. He retreats. But not fast enough. My mouth closes down over a pinkie finger as his hand pulls back and I apply pressure until I hear a crunch.

Fuck yes.

First blood.

Satisfaction unfurls like a ribbon inside my head, a ribbon painted blood red.

My instinct is to howl, my wolf wants to toss my head up, but as I begin to celebrate, I realize that Stone expected that. Shifters gloat. Horror floods me as I register the fact that Stone probably let me get that hit in so that I would howl and expose my throat.

I jerk backward but his claws slice across my neck and blood jets out along with onyx-colored panic … and I wonder if I didn't just make a deadly mistake.

24

ELENA

I LOOK like the high-end hooker that these alphas think an omega is supposed to be. I absolutely hate the dress Black picked for me. I'm wearing a fire-engine red A-Line dress with a deep v neck and tight full-length sleeves. The sleeves are the only part of the thing that fully covers the appropriate body part because the neckline is so low that I feel like I'm about to fall out of it. The skirt has multiple slits so that it falls in what Matthew had called panels and I'd called fucking ribbons.

He'd laughed.

I hadn't.

But I put on the stupid thing along with the matching four-inch heels because this dress and stupid "victory presentation" idea of Black's is my key to escape. It's the only way I'm going to get out of this basement and even stand a chance.

Anxiety floods my system as I lean forward over the bathroom countertop, the harsh light making my mascara obvious. My mind races with possibilities. Jonah didn't text me again except for once.

Delete all my contact information on your phone and this text.

It had taken me nearly two hours to remove every email, every text, every photo. Each deletion had tugged at my heartstrings. But it had given me something to focus on instead of the pit of despair that my mind was digging. And it had proven that Jonah's serious. He has a plan. I just have to trust it.

How the tables are reversed. I used to come up with all our plans. Now, I'll be walking into this blind.

I hate giving up control. But this is Jonah—so I will.

I blow out a breath and purse my lips close to the mirror. I smear on some red lipstick, the only part of this entire getup that actually feels like me. And then I turn to Matthew, who's waiting patiently in the doorway.

"Lovely," he tells me. "Are you ready to go?"

I nod and stop for a moment, staring at the older gentleman, one who had actually given to me instead of taken from me. Matthew's a good guy. It's too bad he's tangled up with Black and all of this. Before I can think the better of them, words slip out from between my lips. "It was nice knowing you."

He raises a brow. "So certain Alpha Maddox will lose the match?"

I give a shrug, letting him draw his own conclusions. But my heart gives an uncomfortable little twinge when I do that. Do I want Black to actually die? I've never wished death upon someone before. After all he's done, maybe I'd be justified.

But some piece of me rebels against that.

Maybe that's just not the type of person that I want to be. Yes, that's it.

My chest spirals strangely.

The odd feeling persists and I stop fighting it, deciding that nerves have done a number on my entire system because I'm arguing with myself.

I follow Matthew out of the basement bathroom and carefully up the stairs because heels aren't my go-to footwear. I sigh, wishing I could bring a change of clothes with me, but nothing says, "I'm planning to escape" like an unnecessary secondary outfit.

I try not to glance down at the ring weighing down my left hand.

I'm wearing it for the charade, but that little circle of metal feels like a noose. I can't wait to pull it off even more than I want to lose the heels, because this ring is a death sentence. It's a harsh goodbye to everything I've ever wanted. Wearing it feels like I'm seconds from leaving my life and living the one someone else has chosen for me.

Just a few more minutes, I promise myself.

As soon as we reach the front hallway, I'm bombarded by scents in a way that I haven't been before. I get almost dizzy. "Whoa."

Matthew takes my arm and steadies me, helping me cross to the front door. "Are you alright, Luna Elena?"

His use of that term, the term of the female shifter mated to a pack's alpha, nearly makes me retch for real. I swallow back the bile because I can't ruin Jonah's plan. "The scents are a bit much," I respond shakily.

He nods. "I'll get some air purifiers out for when you return."

Gah. He's fucking thoughtful.

I nod gratefully despite the fact that I'm not going to return. And then Matthew opens the door and shows me to a group of six beta men, all brawny, who stand with their arms clasped behind their backs like this is some kind of military exercise. One of the men is

Jonah, his blond hair lit a soft blue in the moonlight, his eyes steady. He gives me a tiny, imperceptible nod.

"Gentlemen, can you please escort your luna—"

I clutch my stomach with one hand and reach for Matthew's arm with the other. "Oh, my god! I think I'm going to be sick!"

25

BLACK

MY NECK BURNS and red specks mar the bottom edge of my vision. Am I passing out or is it blood flying from my throat and coloring the very air in front of me?

I bring my elongated, clawed hand up to my throat and press my rough palm hard against the wound. The red specks remain, so my vision is what's affected.

The gash is smaller than I would have thought. And as I press into the white hair coating my throat, I realize it's not nearly as deep as I've been cut before in other fights.

I can survive this.

The knowledge fills me as surely as my own blood fills my palm and paints my fur with gore. It's followed by a thread of giddiness that pulls tight, making my spine snap to attention.

I can survive this...but only if I'm smart. I can't afford another mistake. I have to focus.

Everything narrows ... my field of vision, my sense of smell, my purpose in life—they all become centered on one thing: killing Stone.

I need to do it fast, and soon. There's a warmth and a soft pulse at my neck that tells me I have to hurry.

Luckily, his claws didn't hit my trachea, so I can breathe ... for how long is the question. Every heart-beat feels precious right now. A moment of regret slips through my mind that I didn't give Elena that last kiss. But it's a brief, solitary flash as my mind also sorts through a million steps I could take.

Stone thinks he has the upper hand right now. If I cater to that, then maybe I can pull out ahead. But I'll only get one shot at deceiving him, and I'll have to make it good. He'll expect me to go for the neck. That's where shifters always go. But the gut is just as delicate.

And a gut wound that can't heal can cause a hell of a lot of pain too.

That's what I should do—it's what he deserves.

I let my lids down halfway as if my eyes are feeling heavy. I let one of my shoulders droop.

Stone's eyes gleam with eagerness though he keeps his distance, still studying me.

I need him to expose his liver, which hides under the ribs on the right side toward the back. A good solid hit or kick there will take him out. Men can pass out in a matter of seconds from a hit to the liver. And I don't plan to hit. I plan to stab.

In our monstrous forms, our claws are stronger than our feet, so claws it is. But that means I'll have to let the bastard in close. He'll probably get in his own hit. I have to ensure it's not a deadly one.

If I make him think he's going for a kill shot, for the neck, I can duck and get myself the access to his side I need. I just have to play this exactly right. I need him to think I'm far more hurt than I am.

I let my claw gently fall from my neck and slowly slather the blood from my palm against my white fur. I know from experience that my wounds can look much more prominent because of my coloring. The blood can turn my snow-white fur a grisly, murky red.

Gasps go up from the Lobo side of the bleachers, helping sell my injury for me. My elites step right up to the fence, their hands gripping the chain link, their tension making the air thick with worry and anticipation.

Perfect.

I let my steps turn into a shuffle. I start to let my head bob unsteadily on my neck, but pain lashes out and makes me gasp so I change tactics and allow my torso to sway instead. Every heartbeat screams in my ears, "Faster! Faster!"

I need to end this fight so that I can heal. I've survived worse, but only by knocking my opponent out with a single lucky blow. My body is begging me to change from this energy-draining monster form back into my replenishing wolf so it can mend itself.

But I can't. I need to beat Stone first. And this is a fishing expedition. I'm luring Stone into complacency so I can hook him. I can't go faster.

I absolutely need Stone to believe that I'm vulnerable. I move toward him, scuffing the dirt, putting a hand up halfway as if I'm going to protect my neck, but then I clench my fist and let it fall half an inch as if it hurts too much to raise.

His shifters rise to their feet, screaming for my head. Their yells pound through my ears in time with my pulse. My breathing starts to rattle. That isn't something I fake. It's my body's warning. I'm not putting pressure on my wound, which means the sand in my hourglass is steadily drifting down.

Come on, Cooper Stone. Come and get me.

I need to amp it up. I'm not doing enough. My next move comes to me as memories start to fly before my eyes. I start to blink too much, something I saw an alpha do during a fight in my twenties, just before he blacked out.

That's when Stone grins. And I know I've caught him.

Thank fuck.

I step quickly toward Stone's right and feint a clumsy hit. Stone goes for it, thinking I'm so out of it that I can't possibly be deceptive any longer.

He goes for the jugular, just like I expected.

His muzzle opens, teeth gleaming, and I duck down so quickly that it makes me lightheaded. There, underneath the mat of his fur are his ribs.

My vision is blurred by more red at the edges—by either blood loss or glee, I'm not certain which—as I take my left claw and dig in under his ribs, deep and hard. I feel my long fingers slide beneath his skin and into something soft and slimy even as his claws rake my back. I crush my hands together, obliterating whatever organ I hold.

Then I throw my shoulder into his gut and stand, even though lifting him makes me nearly pass out. A wave of nausea battles with an adrenaline high as I straighten and stare out at the crowd.

The Dark Nights are silent. Some of their mouths gape. Some of their hands are frozen mid-clap.

Meanwhile, the Lobos howl. They cheer. They're dancing on the stands. My elite shake the gates so hard that I worry the makeshift fighting cage is going to collapse on top of me.

With a roar that burns my throat, I toss Stone over my back, withdrawing my claw.

There's a *thud* as his body hits and a second dull *thunk*—like someone dropped a cantaloupe—when Stone's head hits the packed dirt. I know that thump. I've cracked enough skulls to recognize it. If crushing his liver didn't kill him, then he's certainly dead now. Or else well on his way.

My wolf gives a victory howl inside my head.

But I don't celebrate yet. I turn because I have to be sure … but Stone's chest is already still. The light is already fading from his wolfish eyes while the dirt underneath him grows dark. Death laps up his soul as he stares at me, realizing this is his final moment.

I could say something sarcastic. Or something memorable like I did when I defeated Prime all those years ago. I'd stood over him and declared that the Lobos had entered a new era, a better one. "Today I give you freedom!" I'd yelled.

Somehow, despite the rush of adrenaline pulsing through me, I can't bring myself to defame Stone the same way.

He was an arrogant asshole, but so am I, and as opponents go, he was a worthy one. If he'd gotten his claws any deeper into my neck, it could be me lying there.

I was strategic, yeah. But I was also lucky. And spitting on Stone in front of his people—who are now my people—would start me off on the wrong foot.

I literally just added a huge territory to my pack, thousands of miles, thousands of shifters.

The reality of that doesn't sink in right away, it just kind of floats on the surface of my mind as I keep staring at Stone to make absolutely certain that he's gone. I will not turn my back on him until he's gone cold.

The referee calls out, "Cooper Stone, you have five seconds to get up. Cooper Stone. Can you hear me?"

Stone doesn't even twitch in response but that does nothing to still my heart, which still sprints, ready for a surprise.

The referee trots over to Stone, holding up an arm for me to step back, which I do. He kneels in the dirt in front of the shifter and the ref's striped shirt stretches and bunches as he checks the Dark Night alpha's pulse in two places.

The ref glances back at me and shakes his head, before standing and coming over to grip my right wrist. He lifts it high into the air and it's only then that the sounds of the crowd come back to me. The lights are too blinding for me to make out any faces, but I smile.

I smile in relief, in victory, in excitement. The world literally just became my oyster. I'm now the alpha of the largest pack in North America. Fucking hell. It suddenly hits me like a punch to the head—I'm going to go down in history. Not just a brief mention as an alpha of the Lobos. I'm going to be the alpha who reshapes the shifter world as we know it.

That thought nearly makes my knees buckle.

It wasn't something I ever planned on or something I aspired to ... it's all just happened because of a tiny, spitfire omega.

I furrow my brow, looking toward the gate that allows entrance into the arena. Shouldn't she be here? Some betas were going to walk her inside the fight ring so that my little mate could share in my victory.

The gate creaks open and I grin, though with my wolfish face, it probably looks like I'm snarling.

But Elena doesn't walk in wearing the ball gown I gave her.

Instead, Pluto strides quickly across the dirt in human form, his jaw ticking angrily.

I can't speak in this form, so I simply stare and wait.

Pluto gnashes his teeth, and my stomach drops, suspicion raising goosebumps on my skin before he tells me, "Elena's gone."

DEFILED: THE FERAL PRINCESS BOOK 2 - PREORDER NOW

Preorder Book 2 on Amazon Now!

AFTERWORD

Thank you times a bazillion for reading!

I hope I made your day just a little bit naughtier and more exciting. Thank you from the bottom of my heart for supporting my dream of corrupting minds like yours with book boyfriends who are better than reality.

If you want to laugh some more, and maybe cry a little, check out Magical Academy for Delinquents #MAD. It's reverse harem, but the harem all gets together to pull off a magical heist and it's pretty much kickass fun if I do say so myself.

If you'd rather read kinky fantasy, then check out Knightfall. In this enemies to lover RH, a reluctant princess has to win back the knights she jilted in order to save her sister and the kingdom. Lots of BDSM vibes here.

I have lots of other book babies too, and they all love to be picked up and cuddle close to your heart.

Please consider reviewing this lil read before you go so that other people can come in forewarned about how evil I am. I mean, you have a duty to your fellow readers, right?

Kisses,

Ann

ACKNOWLEDGMENTS

Thanks to RK, Ivy, Lysanne, Sue, Daphne. Thank you to Dom for all the amazing teasers. Thanks to the hubs for helping me during my daily battles with technology. Thanks to Laura at Covers by Aura for the gorgeous covers that inspired this story.

Is it weird to thank your parents at the back of a book they won't read? It's not, right? I want to thank them for supporting all my artsy and awkward phases so that I eventually turned into this smut-writing gem.

ALSO BY ANN DENTON

Tangled Crowns Series
(Completed Trilogy)

A medium-burn, medieval fantasy reverse harem romance with an enemies to lovers story.

Knightfall - Book 1

MidKnight - Book 2

Knight's End - Book 3

Depths - Book 4

Surfaces - Book 5

Pinnacle Series
(Completed Duet)

A medium-burn paranormal heist reverse harem with a badass main character.

Magical Academy for Delinquents #MAD - Book 1

Delinquents Turned Fugitives #DTF - Book 2

Darkest Flame Series

A co-write series with Katie May with medium-burn reverse harem paranormal romance containing psychotic, alpha males, student/teacher relationships, strong language and steamy situations.

Demon Kissed - Book 1

Demon Loved - Book 2

Demon Sworn - Book 3

Mage Shifter War Series

(Completed Duet)

A medium-burn paranormal mafia reverse harem with shifters and fae. Kidnapping and enemy themes. Co-written with Elle Middaugh.

Fae Captive - Book 1

Fae Unchained - Book 2

The Story of a Dark Mafia Princess

(Standalone)

A romantic satire I wrote for April Fools. They both have their problems, but sex conquers all.

The Story of a Dark Mafia Princess

Hammer Time
(Standalone)

A medium-burn paranormal comedy reverse harem featuring lots of ancient deities and potty humor. Co-written with MJ Marstens.

Hammer Time

Lotto Love Series
(Completed Duet)

A medium-burn, contemporary romantic comedy reverse harem about winning the lotto and doing whatever the hell you want with it.

Lotto Men - Book 1

Lotto Trouble - Book 2

Ruby - Jewels Cafe Series
(Standalone)

A medium-burn, fated mates reverse harem with angels, demons, and Christmas miracles.

Ruby - Available Here

The Lyon Fox Mysteries

An urban fantasy / cozy mystery series with a magicless fae, a lot of laughs, and a dash of romance.

Magical Murder - Book 1

Enchanted Execution - Book 2

Supernatural Sleep - Book 3

Hexed Hit - Book 4

Timebend Series

A post-apocalyptic fantasy thriller series. Whoo that's a mouthful. Can you tell this was my first series? Haha.

ALSO BY ANN DENTON

Melt - Book 1

Burn - Book 2

CONNECT AND GET SNEAK PEEKS

Do you want to read exclusive point of views from different characters, make predictions and claim your book boyfriends with other readers, see my inspiration for these books, and hang with fellow RH lovers? Then join my Facebook Reader Group! I promise you'll love it!

Join Ann Denton's Reader Group

Facebook.com/groups/AnnDentonReaderGroup

ABOUT ME

I'm a shy lady who has always been obsessed with reading and travel and live theater. I've lived in four states and currently reside in Oklahoma, hence the nickname from my writer friends: Annie Oakie.

I have two of the world's cutest children, a crazy dog, and an amazing husband that I drive somewhat insane when I stop in the middle of the hallway, halfway through putting laundry away, picturing a scene.

Made in the USA
Monee, IL
03 December 2021

82882471R00208